Together for Christmas

The Cape Light Titles

CAPE LIGHT

HOME SONG

A GATHERING PLACE

A NEW LEAF

A CHRISTMAS PROMISE

THE CHRISTMAS ANGEL

A CHRISTMAS TO REMEMBER

A CHRISTMAS VISITOR

A CHRISTMAS STAR

A WISH FOR CHRISTMAS

ON CHRISTMAS EVE

CHRISTMAS TREASURES

A SEASON OF ANGELS

SONGS OF CHRISTMAS

ALL IS BRIGHT

TOGETHER FOR CHRISTMAS

The Angel Island Titles

THE INN AT ANGEL ISLAND

THE WEDDING PROMISE

A WANDERING HEART

THE WAY HOME

HARBOR OF THE HEART

Thomas Kinkade's Cape Light

Together for Christmas

KATHERINE SPENCER

BERKLEY BOOKS, NEW YORK

BERKLEY
An imprint of Penguin Random House LLC
375 Hudson Street, New York, New York 10014

This book is an original publication of Penguin Random House LLC.

Library of Congress Cataloging-in-Publication Data

Spencer, Katherine, (date–)
Cape light : together for Christmas / Katherine Spencer. — First edition.
pages ; cm. — (Thomas Kinkade's Cape Light ; 16)
At head of title: Thomas Kinkade's
ISBN 978-0-425-28221-2 (hardcover)
1. Cape Light (Imaginary place)—Fiction. 2. City and town life—New England—Fiction.
3. Angels—Fiction. 4. Christmas stories. 5. Domestic fiction.
I. Kinkade, Thomas, 1958–2012. Cape light. II. Title. III. Title: Thomas Kinkade's.
PS3553.A489115C37 2015
813'.54—dc23
2015017823

FIRST EDITION: November 2015

PRINTED IN THE UNITED STATES OF AMERICA

10 9 8 7 6 5 4 3 2 1

Cover art: "Heart of Christmas" by Thomas Kinkade.
Cover design by Lesley Worrell.

Penguin
Random
House

Miracles, in the sense of phenomena we cannot explain,
surround us on every hand:
life itself is the miracle of miracles.

GEORGE BERNARD SHAW

To anyone who believes in miracles—or would like to.
The evidence is all around us.

—K.S.

Dear Reader

Thanks for the letters you've sent, letting me know that you enjoy the Cape Light books and how the stories have touched your lives. Writing is a solitary business, and I appreciate your thoughtful, encouraging words. So often, readers also say how much they'd like to live in a town like Cape Light, where even the most impossible problems are solved in a positive and, often, surprising way.

The Cape Light books were inspired by the paintings of Thomas Kinkade. The town of Cape Light is a fictional place located on the eastern coast of Massachusetts, at about the same spot as the village of Ipswich, sharing much of that town's atmosphere. But it's also closely modeled on my hometown in New York, the village of Northport, which was also founded in the Colonial era, and is a picturesque harbor town where people live, work, and raise families. Like Cape Light, Northport has a diner like the Clam Box, a fancy café bakery like Willoughby's, an old stone church, and an annual Christmas tree lighting on the village green.

But Cape Light is a place you cannot find on any map. It's a perspective on life, an optimistic state of mind that rests in the belief that anything is possible. Yes, in Cape Light there are challenges that must be faced—head-on, at times. But it's a place where one goes forward with hope, courage, and faith that things will work out for the best. Even when solutions don't seem obvious at all. As Sam Morgan tells his sister Molly in this book, "Faith is to believe what you do not see; the reward of this faith is to see what you believe." Those words of Saint Augustine neatly sum up for me the Cape Light philosophy.

What I've become aware of while writing these books is that even in real life, not just in Cape Light, difficult circumstances often resolve better than anyone ever expects. And, if you take the time to really look, miracles are all around us.

Is it any wonder that Cape Light, a place that celebrates possibility—even miracles—is a perfect setting for Christmas stories? Miracles and possibilities, great and small, are the very stuff of this season.

In *Together for Christmas*, many lives are touched by that theme. Molly Willoughby Harding faces dark moments, nearly losing her beloved bakery . . . *and* her best friend, Betty Bowman. But she finds that the people who love her most won't give up on her dream. Even when she does.

Carrie Munro, a newcomer to town, doesn't believe in miracles, at Christmastime or otherwise. But her son Noah's imaginary friend, Theo—whom Noah claims is an angel—tests his mother's doubting mind and opens her heart to trust . . . and even love.

Once more, it's the perfect season and place to share surprising, joyful outcomes. I hope this visit to Cape Light will stay with you throughout the year and help you see the infinite possibilities in your life every day, wherever your journey takes you.

All best wishes,
Katherine Spencer

Chapter One

Molly Willoughby Harding rarely worked at her shop the day after Thanksgiving. She was always exhausted from the big push the day before, cooking and delivering holiday dinners all over town. Including her own home, where she had entertained over twenty at her table, happy to offer turkey and all the trimmings from Willoughby's Fine Foods and Catering.

Her three oldest daughters, who lived in all directions now, were home for the long weekend, and she loved to spend time with them doing girl things—manicures and movie nights. Even rallying enough energy to kick off their Christmas shopping.

But on the morning after the holiday, she hurried out at the usual time while all her sleeping beauties were still in dreamland.

She drove to town quickly, the streets of Cape Light empty and peaceful. A crew of town workers were already at work stringing lights and pine garlands, and wrapping the parking meters all along Main Street in red and white candy cane striping. The annual Christmas tree lighting on the green would take place that night, Molly remembered. Her seven-year-old daughter, Betty, still "believed" and wanted to meet Santa, and the rest of the family wanted to watch.

Molly saw only a few cars parked near her shop; nothing like the usual morning rush, but respectable enough, she thought.

She parked in back, next to the catering vans. Betty Bowman's white Volvo was already there. Molly hated to keep Betty waiting; she knew Betty's free time was rare these days.

Betty's husband, Nate, had fallen off a ladder in late October while cleaning the gutters. He had fractured one of the vertebrae in his lower back so badly that he needed surgery. After weeks in the hospital, he was now in a rehabilitation facility. Betty had been in the shop very little the last month or so. Not that Molly blamed her; Betty was handling such a heavy load right now.

But Molly couldn't help wishing Betty's schedule would allow for a little more hands-on work as they began the long, tough march toward Christmas. Molly wasn't sure she could do it on her own. Betty had asked to meet this morning and Molly had her fingers crossed, hoping that meant Betty was ready to jump back in.

I'm not going to pounce on her, Molly promised herself as she pulled open the shop's back door. *I definitely don't want to stress her out even more. Or make her feel guilty.*

Molly and Betty were best friends first and business partners second. It had been true from the start and was even truer now. Molly's first concern was for Betty and Nate; everything else, even everything she had been juggling on her own in the shop, came in at a very distant second.

The big commercial kitchen looked clean and empty and was uncommonly quiet. The familiar sweet, buttery scent of baked goods mingled with the comforting aroma of roast turkey. No mystery there. Molly knew it might take days to air out the place entirely.

Both of the ovens, large and small, were cold and dark, the baker's racks practically bare. Most of the staff—especially the kitchen workers—had the day off to rest and recuperate. But a few would wander in soon.

Out at the counter and café, she heard the hiss of the cappuccino machine, the hum of the bread slicer, and the voices of her cheerful staff and customers. Sonia, the shop's manager, had opened at the crack of dawn, and Molly never worried with their longtime employee in charge.

"Morning, Molly. I thought I heard you come in." Betty emerged from the small office they shared. Tried to share, actually. The space had been converted from a closet and was filled by a tiny desk, a chair, and a file cabinet. They could never comfortably fit in there together, which had become a long-standing joke between them.

"Sorry I'm late. Were you waiting long?" Molly hung up her coat and headed for the coffee urn.

"Not at all. I'm sorry to make you come out so early. You must be exhausted."

Molly shrugged and poured herself a mug of coffee, then selected a muffin from the pan that had been left on the worktable. "A little tired," she admitted. "That turkey run takes it out of me. I'm not sure if I'm getting too old for deliveries or if we just have a lot more business these days."

"More business. You're fit and fearless as ever." Betty smiled as she sat at the worktable and set down a large file and a pile of mail she was holding. Molly took a seat across from her.

"I wish I could have helped this year," Betty said.

"I know . . . I didn't mean to complain. I'm thankful for the work, honestly." Molly looked up and spoke to the ceiling, as if she didn't want to give the heavenly powers the wrong idea. "Every day, too. Not just yesterday."

Betty laughed. "How did your dinner go? I bet you had a houseful."

"The usual suspects." Molly took a bite of her muffin. "Sam and Jessica and their kids," she said, referring to her brother, "and my folks, of course. Matt's sister and her family . . ."

"Are the girls home?" Betty's smile was wistful. Molly knew Betty felt sorry about missing the gathering. She had been invited, of course, but needed to spend the day with Nate at the rehab facility in Peabody, where he was now staying.

"Everyone checked into Hotel Harding by Wednesday night. Lauren came in late Tuesday. At least I had one princess handy to help me," Molly added, talking about her oldest daughter. "Jill and Amanda came in on Wednesday. Little Betty is in her glory, having all her big sisters around." Molly's youngest daughter, who had been named for Betty, was now seven years old.

"Amanda was with Gabriel's family for Thanksgiving dinner," she went on, mentioning Amanda's boyfriend, "but they showed up later, for dessert."

"Really? Did his folks come, too?" Betty's curiosity was piqued, her romantic radar on full alert.

"His father passed away a few years ago. But his mother and younger brother came. They're very nice," Molly reported. "And they love Amanda."

"Who wouldn't?"

Molly had to agree, even if Amanda was her daughter. Her stepdaughter, actually. She and Matt were both single parents when they met—Molly divorced and Matt a widower—both raising adolescent girls alone. Molly had always felt a special bond with Amanda and loved her as her own. Amanda had lost her mother when she was only eleven years old and once told Molly she could never think of her as a "stepmother." That term made her think of someone mean from a fairy tale, and Molly was more like the fairy godmother—sweet and loving, always granting everyone's wishes.

Probably the nicest thing anyone has ever said about me, Molly reflected.

Amanda was a classical musician and had landed a seat in the Portland Symphony string section about two years ago. She had met Gabriel in Cape Light during a brief stay at home when her career had hit a real low point. She had taken a temporary job at the church, as the music director. Gabriel had been restoring the stained-glass windows there, listening to her music almost daily as he worked. He had encouraged her dream and, after a brief separation, had even relocated his business to Maine so they could stay together.

They were soul mates, Molly thought, and felt comforted each time she realized her daughter was so happily and lovingly settled.

Betty sipped her coffee, her blue eyes mischievous behind the edge of the mug. "I hear wedding bells. You'd better prepare yourself."

Molly squinted, but smiled as well. "I thought my ears were ringing from all the banging in the kitchen yesterday. But maybe you're right. I've seen enough brides to know that dreamy look."

"And we've planned enough weddings to know how to do it right. It will be so much fun to work on Amanda's."

"Yes, it will," Molly agreed. She would plan perfect weddings for her daughters, having learned by trial and error on scores of other brides. "I have loads of ideas, don't worry. But let's not rush it. They aren't even engaged."

"A small hurdle for true love," Betty countered. "Santa never minds putting diamond rings under the Christmas tree."

Molly couldn't argue with that either. But as much as she loved talking about her daughters—and could go on all morning—she did want to catch up on Betty's news and find out if she planned to come back to work anytime soon.

"Enough about the lovebirds. How was your Thanksgiving? And how's Nate doing? Any better since we saw him?"

Molly and Matt had visited Betty's husband about two weeks ago, when he first checked into the new facility. Nate was the type of person who always put on a bright face, but Molly could tell he felt discouraged that he was still confined to a wheelchair several weeks after his injury.

"He's in a lot of pain, but he's coming along," Betty replied. "Yesterday I made a turkey dinner, including an apple pie, and brought it to him. He appreciated that. Even considering the way I cook," Betty added with a self-effacing smile.

"I'm sure he did," Molly replied. Everyone knew that Betty was not at her best in the kitchen. That was Molly's forte. But Nate always said his wife cooked with love, the most important ingredient.

"I have to be honest with you, Molly; there hasn't been much improvement. Nate's working hard in therapy, and they're doing other things—special massage and electric impulses on the muscles—but walking is a struggle. The doctors say it often takes time for the muscles and nerves to respond. It looks like it's going to take much longer than we expected. It's been very frustrating for him. For both of us."

Molly didn't know what to say. Her heart went out to her dearest friends. All her own complaints and irritations seemed so trivial in comparison.

"These things do take time." Molly forced a bright note into her voice that she really didn't feel. "He hasn't been there very long."

"About two weeks. We're trying to be patient. He'll be better by Christmas. That's what I think." Betty's tone was resolute. Molly could tell Betty wasn't sure, but was determined to be optimistic.

"Absolutely. That's a whole month away." Molly forced another smile. Which drained from her face as she also looked ahead to all the holiday parties they would cater, and the huge amount of food and baked goods they would sell from the storefront, too. On top of all that, they were opening a new, second shop in Newburyport, Willoughby's Too. Was she really going to have to run all of it on her own?

Betty flipped open the red folder she had carried in from the office. "Looks like you've booked a good number of parties already. The file is plumping up nicely."

"Like a Christmas goose," Molly agreed. "But I wouldn't mind a little more padding. I was thinking of making some calls, reminding everyone we're ready to make their holidays carefree and wonderful."

I was thinking you could make some calls, Molly really meant. Dealing with clients was Betty's special gift, polished by years of real estate sales before she had come to work at Willoughby's. Betty was a genius at handling customers. Her warm, smooth, soothing manner always reeled them in. Molly, on the other hand, knew that she was best in the kitchen. She tried hard to match Betty's panache but often grew impatient and ruffled privileged feathers.

"I can help with that," Betty offered, and Molly felt a minor surge of relief. "I'll beat the bushes and see who jumps out." Betty glanced over the sheets in the folder again. "But I don't see how we can handle too many more. Unless you plan to hire more help? I'd hate to overbook, Molly, and not be able to deliver."

"We took on some new people for the season," Molly reminded her, knowing they could not afford to hire anyone else. But then Betty hadn't been there last week when Molly realized she hadn't invoiced for two major parties and had to borrow a little from the renovation fund to meet the payroll. She would pay it back, though, as soon as the next check came in. She wished she could just ask Betty to write up those invoices. Betty seemed to zip through those things in no time; Molly knew it would take her hours. *I'll take care of it today. No sense adding to Betty's load. Or making Betty worry. She might think I haven't been on top of things.*

Betty hooked a strand of blond hair behind her ear. "It feels so strange to be away from the shop so much at this time of year. I can't believe the Christmas rush is almost here."

Like a giant wave peaking overhead, about to crash down on us, Molly thought. She could almost hear a fizzling sound, her high hopes that Betty would return evaporating like drops of water on a hot grill.

But she quickly put on a brave face. "We always say we can't do it, and then we always pull it off. At the very least, we need to hang on to our big, long-standing clients. That new outfit, Silver Spoon, is moving in on us," she added. Silver Spoon was their latest rival in town.

"Really? They've been poaching our territory?"

"Like a fox in the henhouse. They stole the Essex County Garden Club right out from under my nose," Molly confessed. "I don't know how. I met with Patsy Tolland personally and offered a very nice package. I was cutting our profit to the bone, just to keep the account," Molly explained. "I thought I'd totally nailed it. But she sent me an email last week and said they were going with another caterer. So . . . guess who?"

Molly delivered the news with a tone of apology. She had done her best, but she really believed that Betty would have done much better. Betty would have hung on to those garden club ladies; it was a plum account.

"Patsy sent you an email? After all these years? That's so rude." Betty was annoyed on Molly's behalf, and all sympathy. "She could have at least called." Betty reached over and patted Molly's hand. "Don't fret, there are plenty more holiday galas in the sea. I love their annual show, but those ladies can be a bit of a pain. Remember when Patsy threw a hissy fit over the cheese puffs? They didn't poof up to her standards."

"That was classic. You would think she was judging a rosebush competition." Molly had to smile now, too. They did deal with a lot of fussy personalities, that was for sure.

"I hope Silver Spoon's cheese puffs are droopy, dry, and flat. The garden club will be sorry they dumped us," Molly said. "Meanwhile, we can't let that silver vacuum cleaner suck up any more of our clients."

Besides, we need the profits, Molly wanted to add. But she didn't want to alarm Betty with all she had to worry about now.

It's mostly my own anxiety, Molly told herself, *and being such a scatterbrain with the bookkeeping.* Another job that Betty had handled so smoothly but was left to Molly now. *We aren't in any real trouble. I just have to get more organized.*

"Agreed. I'll get to work on it as soon as I have a few minutes to spare at home. Oh dear . . . look at the time. I've got to run. I have to get over to Peabody for a meeting with Nate's doctor and the physical therapist." Betty stood up and pulled on her jacket. "I have the client list at home on my laptop. But what about all this mail? Maybe I should go through some of this?"

Molly felt herself flush. "I can do it. I was just so busy with the turkey rush last week."

The pile of mail was clearly more than a week's worth of procrastination, but Betty didn't comment. They both knew Molly was disorganized with paperwork and a disaster at figures. Unless the math involved a recipe.

"It's okay," Betty said. "I have time to sort it out. I can pay a few bills, too. But you'll have to post them on the accounting program here."

"That would be great. I've been meaning to catch up."

Molly was relieved that Betty was going to take the pile of mail away. She just never seemed to find the time to work on it. She wasn't very good at posting the accounts, but would force herself to muddle through.

"No problem. I'm glad to do what I can. Besides, it will be a good distraction for me." Betty stuffed the mail in her big tote and pulled out her gloves and car keys. Then she looked up at Molly, her blue eyes wide. "Oh my gosh . . . we didn't even get to talk about the new shop. How's it coming? Is the renovation on schedule?"

Once again, Molly wasn't sure how honest to be without worrying her friend. Their new shop was opening soon in elegant, upscale Newburyport, about fifteen miles north of Cape Light. But just like Nate's recovery, progress on the renovations had been frustrating.

"You know how these things are. It looks like a gigantic mess right now, but I'm sure it will shape up in time. 'If you want to make an omelet, you have to break some eggs,' right?"

Betty shook her head. "Uh-oh. You only say that when things really are a mess and you're trying to put a good spin on it."

Molly felt herself blush. Betty knew her too well. "I always say that because it's true. There are bound to be a few . . . eggshells to deal with."

Betty laughed, heading for the door. "Good thing you got Sam to oversee the job. He'll get it done, one way or another. A Morgan family trait, I'd say."

Sam was Molly's older brother, and though they still fought like teenagers sometimes, Molly had come to see that they were more alike than she had ever guessed.

"There are pluses and minuses to 'managing' your older brother, believe me. I hope all goes well with Nate today. Keep me posted." Molly followed Betty to the door, reluctant to see her go. Apart from the actual grunt labor they both put into this shop, she missed Betty's company, her companionship and conversation, savoring their victories and talking over their problems. It seemed to all be on her shoulders now, and had been for a while.

But she wouldn't complain or give Betty the slightest hint that it had been hard for her. It was Betty who needed her help right now, her understanding and support. Betty needed every ounce of her own energy to help Nate get out of that wheelchair, and Molly knew the best thing she could do right now was to keep Betty's spirits up and not distract her with business stress.

Molly leaned over and gave her friend a big hug. "I know Nate is going to get well. Sooner than you think," she said. "I love you guys. If there's anything I can do to help—anything at all—just let me know, okay?"

"Oh, Molly . . . I love you, too. I am so grateful to you for stepping up like this. I hate to leave you with all this work. But maybe I can help more in a week or two? I'll check in with you soon. And I'll definitely call those clients and drum up more business. I can still work from home on a few things like that."

"That would be great. Whatever you can manage. And you don't have to thank me. It's what friends do."

"Friends like you. Who are very rare, believe me." Betty touched her shoulder a moment, then she stepped out into the chilly air and headed for her car.

As Betty drove off, Molly shut the door. Then she turned back to the worktable, the overflowing party file waiting for her. She felt deflated, like an old balloon. Or a cold, flat cheese puff. She suddenly realized how much she had been hoping Betty would jump back on board. How much she'd counted on Betty being more available in the coming weeks. Not less.

But what kind of a friend would I be if I made Betty feel bad right now? No friend at all.

Molly sat down and sighed. The steep climb to Christmas looked even steeper now. But she had to think positively. Maybe Betty would come back for the "boots on the ground" party work? Maybe she would jump in and manage a few of the events? A few hours a week? Nate could improve before the holidays and wouldn't need her as much. In a week or two things could look very different.

You have to keep the most positive possible outcome in mind, Molly reminded herself, a truth she had learned long ago. Worrying about the worst, spinning out fearful fantasies, never helped anything.

Somehow, some way, I will get through all the parties and pressure, and the renovations on the new shop, too. With or without Betty. Then I'll look back and laugh, she promised herself. *And treat myself to an extra cup of coffee and a few cookies . . . which I might as well do now,* she decided, heading for the coffee urn. *I can use a little boost to get me through the rest of the morning—that's for sure.*

"How's that cookie?" Carrie Munro asked her son, Noah. They were sitting in Willoughby's, where Noah had just started in on a double chocolate chip cookie, one of his favorites. "Is it up to your standards?"

"A lot of chips," Noah reported.

Carrie smiled. Noah was only seven, but he often answered her questions with a serious, thoughtful tone, as if he gave even her silliest questions great consideration.

Carrie often came to Willoughby's to buy bread or cake, or even some of their delicious soup and take-out foods. Her employer, Mrs. Vincent, loved the raisin loaf, with its cinnamon-sugar crust. But today was the last time Carrie would make that purchase for Mrs. Vincent. It was her last official day on the job.

"Do we have time to go to the playground?" Noah gave her a hopeful look.

"Not really, honey. But we'll go later, I promise."

Carrie rarely sat in the café, lingering over coffee, but she and Noah were early for their appointment and it seemed a good place to wait, and a good way to distract her son while she studied the newspaper. She browsed two sections today—*Help Wanted* and *Apartments for Rent,* marking both columns with a red pen.

It was hard to believe that she was suddenly both jobless and homeless, and through no fault of her own. She would have been sulking right now if not for Noah, who depended totally on her. For all his material needs, of course, but even more importantly, for a sense that he was safe and protected. Wasn't that the very reason she had taken him away from his father? She would feel like an utter failure now if she couldn't keep him both safe and happy.

They had gotten through tight spots like this before, and they would get through this one, Carrie reminded herself. She just needed to stay calm and take one step at a time. And put a cheerful spin on solving these problems.

"We'll hit the park right after we visit Mrs. Vincent's friend, I promise."

"Are you going to work for this lady, too?"

"I'm not seeing her for a job, honey. But she may have a place for us to live." Carrie ruffled his soft brown hair. "I need to find a new job, too. But it won't be hard. There are a lot of ads in the paper. I'm going to call up about a few today . . . maybe while I watch you play." She forced a smile, trying to make the changes sound easy. When she put it that way, it did sound simple.

But she wasn't surprised that Noah assumed they would live in the same place she worked. They had been living with Mrs. Vincent for over a year now while Carrie played the dual role of live-in companion and housekeeper.

Most elderly people didn't want a little boy in the house when they hired an aide, but Helen Vincent was not most people. She was exceptionally sweet and kind. Visits from her daughters and grandchildren, who lived in New York and North Carolina, were rare, and she had happily agreed to take Noah when she hired Carrie. Mrs. Vincent had never complained about him, even at his most boisterous, though Noah was a good boy generally, and very considerate. He was more mature than most children his age, his teachers always told her. Carrie was proud of him. He was, in fact, too good at times, she thought. So quiet and so much to himself. She hated to uproot him again, but there was no help for it.

"I'll miss Mrs. Vincent," Noah said. "Why do we have to leave her?" he asked, pressing his fingertip down on the last crumbs.

"I'm going to miss her, too," Carrie said honestly. "But we can always visit her. She won't be far. Her daughters decided that she needs to be in an assisted-living place now, where she'll be near doctors and nurses if she gets sick again. We've taken good care of her, but this will be safer."

Carrie watched Noah's expression, wondering if he understood. Everything had happened so quickly, she hardly understood herself.

A few days ago, Mrs. Vincent had felt heart palpitations, more than her medication could control. Carrie had finally called 911, and Mrs. Vincent had stayed in the hospital for two days while adjustments were made to her pacemaker.

It was nothing serious, but it had been a scare—one that had brought her daughters running. Very soon after their arrival, they decided it was time for their mother to give up her semi-independence. Time for her to give up her home—and Carrie and Noah's home, too.

Helen was very sorry to give Carrie the news, but her family had been pushing for this next step for a while and she couldn't put them off any longer.

"I'm so sorry, dear, but they've worn me down. I guess it is time. I hope you understand," Helen said sadly.

Carrie did understand, but she also felt the rug being pulled out from under her. Mrs. Vincent's daughters had already chosen a nursing home. They must have been working on this for a while, Carrie realized, and the hospitalization gave them the chance to put their plan in motion.

Helen had to move this weekend or lose the opening. And her daughters were eager to clean out the house and put it up for sale. To have "everything settled" they kept saying, while they were both in New England.

It wasn't that Carrie and Noah couldn't stay a few extra days after Helen left. No one was going to put their belongings on the sidewalk. But their presence was obviously an inconvenience for the family. Besides, Carrie couldn't imagine staying in the house without Helen. It wouldn't feel right. The sooner she found a new place, the better for all.

"I have a friend in Cape Light, Vera Plante. She owns a big house and rents out rooms. She's a good woman, very active in the church," Helen had told Carrie. "Why don't I call and see if she has room for you and Noah?"

Carrie had quickly agreed, appreciating the offer.

Noah's voice drew her attention as he got things clear in his mind. "So we look at this house and see if we want to live there . . . and you're going to work somewhere else?"

"That's right. If it's nice enough," Carrie added. "It's going to be different from Mrs. Vincent's. So it may look . . . different to you," she added. "But this lady is Mrs. Vincent's good friend, so we need to be polite, right?"

They were used to comfortable surroundings. Carrie feared that if Vera's house wasn't as nice as Helen's, Noah might blurt out something insulting . . . as children who are guileless and frank often do.

She also wondered about Vera's house. It might be run-down, or the furnishings shabby-looking. But it was worth a try. Maybe they would stay just a week or so until she found a job and they could rent a real apartment or a cottage. It would be hard to rent a place if she had to tell a landlord she was unemployed.

"I get it. I won't say anything . . . even if it looks really weird there," Noah promised.

"Don't worry. If it looks that weird, I won't want to live there either." Carrie smiled and handed him a napkin. "Finish up and we'll get going."

Carrie checked her watch. It wouldn't take long to get to Mrs. Plante's house from town. But she didn't want to be late and make a bad impression.

She guided Noah through the shop, which was more crowded now than when they'd come in, the counter line snaking around to the table section. They were just about to leave when she suddenly remembered Mrs. Vincent's cinnamon bread.

"I forgot something at the table, Noah. Wait right here, I'll be right back."

She positioned Noah to one side of the front door, next to a newspaper stand. Then she dashed back to the table for the bag. Luckily, it was still there, though a counter girl was just about to clear the table and take it away.

Carrie rushed back to the front of the store. Her heart jumped in her chest as she realized Noah was no longer standing by the newspapers. He wasn't anywhere in sight.

She spun around, wondering if he had followed her back to the table or decided to check out the glass case of cupcakes. Finally, she spotted him, just outside the door.

She rushed outside, nearly knocking over a customer who was coming in. "Noah, what are you doing out here? You scared me half to death."

Noah turned, and she suddenly noticed a very large dog tied to a railing in front of the store. The dog was sitting at attention, panting happily as Noah gazed at it in amazement.

"Look at this dog, Mom. She's so big. I wonder what kind she is?"

The dog was almost as big as a Saint Bernard, with the same sort of white and brown coat—but without the droopy muzzle, Carrie noticed. A friend of hers once had a Bernese mountain dog, and this one looked similar, but a bit shaggier—with a little bit of pony mixed in, too?

"Hopefully she's the friendly kind." Carrie loved dogs, but gently took

Noah's hand and drew him back. "You know you're not supposed to pet strange dogs, honey. She seems nice, but what if she wasn't?"

"I'm just talking to her. I think she's lonely. Her owner went inside."

Carrie had to smile. Noah wanted to be a veterinarian—the kind who talked to animals, no doubt.

"I'm sure they'll be right out. Say good-bye. We have to go."

"Good-bye, dog. Don't be scared," Noah said solemnly. He glanced up at Carrie with an expectant look.

"Good-bye, dog," Carrie echoed. But before they could step away the big dog jumped up, put her paws on Carrie's shoulders, and licked her face.

Carrie leaned back. "Oh my gosh!"

Noah laughed hysterically. And a man came flying out of the bakery, calling out in alarm, "Elsie! Bad dog! Get down right now!"

The dog jumped down again, staring up at Carrie with an apologetic expression. Her owner grabbed her collar. "I'm so sorry. Did she hurt you?"

Carrie wiped her face with a tissue, then dabbed at the muddy paw prints on her down jacket. "No, not at all. She was just being friendly."

"Let me pay to have your coat cleaned. I insist."

She looked up at him finally and was surprised by his warm, disarming expression. He met Carrie's gaze with startling blue eyes that crinkled at the corners. Eyes that matched the blue sweater under his gray down vest, which was marked with a few paw prints identical to the ones on her jacket. He was about her age, maybe a bit older, with thick sandy brown hair and an athletic build.

Carrie felt her breath catch as she hesitantly smiled back. "Don't be silly. I'll just throw it in the washer. She's very sweet. Besides, I think we encouraged her."

"It doesn't take much," he replied ruefully. "Elsie's very friendly, but not well trained. I shouldn't have left her out here."

"She was worried. She didn't know when you were coming back," Noah finally explained.

Carrie and the dog's owner looked down at him, then glanced at each other and shared a smile.

"That was it," Carrie agreed graciously. She petted the dog again, making her pant happily. "No harm done. Have a nice day."

"Same to you both. Thanks again."

Carrie smiled and met his glance, then took Noah's hand and walked to her car, feeling a certain lightness in her heart.

The silly dog and her handsome owner had been a bright spot in her morning and gave her and Noah something to laugh about as they headed for Vera Plante's house.

Chapter Two

It was a short drive from the village to Meadowlark Lane, a narrow street lined with tall trees and Victorian houses set back on large plots of property. The street looked quiet and safe. Carrie knew she wouldn't worry if Noah played outside here, and if she found a job in town, this house would be convenient.

"There it is . . . thirty-three." Noah pointed out the window on his side of the car. Carrie spotted a large dark blue Victorian with peaks, chimneys, and even a turret tower. The faded old house would have looked a bit ominous if not for the bright pink shutters and yellow door.

Carrie worked on the paw prints again with a wet wipe she had in the car. Fortunately, her jacket was dark green and the marks quickly blended in. She added a dab of lipstick and checked her hair, which was gathered in a clip. It was some relief to know that Mrs. Vincent had smoothed the way. She was sure her employer had said only good things about her and Noah. Mrs. Vincent had also written her an excellent letter of reference to give to prospective employers. She wondered if Mrs. Plante would need to see that, too.

As they headed up the walk, she took Noah's hand, to help settle her own nerves as well as his. Vera Plante was waiting for them. She must have been watching for the car, Carrie realized. The door opened before they even found the bell.

"Come in, come in . . . you must be Carrie and Noah," Vera Plante greeted them cheerfully. Carrie and Noah stepped into a large, shadowy entryway while Vera shut the heavy door.

A wide, curving staircase faced them, leading to the second floor. Straight ahead, a long hallway extended from the entryway to the back of the house, where Carrie could see a brightly lit kitchen. She also noticed large rooms on either side: a dining room and a parlor with old-fashioned pocket doors and old-fashioned furniture and lamps to match.

"Thanks for making time to see us this morning," Carrie said. "We'll try not to take up much of your time, Mrs. Plante."

"Please, call me Vera. No trouble at all. Would you like a cup of tea? Some hot cocoa? Vera glanced down at Noah, who did look interested in the offer, despite his very recent snack.

"We're fine. Thank you." Carrie appreciated Vera trying to make them feel welcome. That meant a lot.

The place had seemed a little worn down at the heels from the outside, but it was very well kept within. Freshly painted walls, the wood floors and furnishings bright and polished. It was certainly better than she had expected.

"Let's look at the rooms, then. I have two bedrooms adjoining, with a private bath in between. I thought that would suit you and your son. All the rooms on the first floor are open to guests. There's use of the washer and dryer in the basement and use of the kitchen anytime—as long as you don't make noise late at night and clean up after yourself. I don't serve dinner, but breakfast is included," she added.

"That sounds very generous." Carrie and Noah followed Vera up the long staircase. She wondered about the monthly rent, but Helen had said it would be reasonable.

Vera was a small woman, at least a head shorter than Carrie, and quite thin. A large baggy sweater and long wool skirt were covered by a ruffled kitchen apron and hung from her birdlike figure. She had small bright eyes and a quick, abrupt way of speaking, which Carrie thought birdlike, too. She certainly seemed nice enough so far.

Vera led them down a wide hallway and opened one of the varnished wooden doors with an old brass skeleton key. "This is the smaller bedroom. I thought it might suit your son."

Carrie walked into the room and Noah followed. She could tell he was pleased as he gazed around at the blue walls and a large soft area rug and then ran over to a set of bunk beds.

"Look, Mom . . . bunk beds!"

"Yes, I noticed," Carrie said with a smile.

Despite being an only child, Noah had always wanted bunk beds. Carrie saw a bookcase and a small student desk on the wall opposite the window. Everything Noah needed, and just as nice as his room at Helen's house.

Vera opened a door next to the desk, and Carrie saw another bedroom through a shared bathroom. It was larger, with yellow walls and a four-poster bed covered by a flowery quilt. Carrie followed her into the room while Noah tested out the bunk beds.

"This is the larger bedroom. Just had it painted last summer. I hope you don't think the color is too bright."

"Not at all. I love yellow. It's perfect." Carrie imagined how cheerful the room would look on a sunny morning.

"There's an extra little sitting area, too, if you want to read or write letters and such."

Carrie noticed a comfortable armchair and small antique desk near the window. She didn't know anyone who wrote letters anymore. Everyone sent emails or text messages. Except people Vera's age, she realized with a small smile.

"I like to read," she told Vera. "I read every night before I go to sleep. It helps me relax."

"Me, too." Vera nodded with approval. "Nothing like a good book."

Vera showed Carrie the bathroom, which was clean and updated, despite the claw-foot bathtub. Then she brought them down a back staircase, which Noah found very mysterious and exciting. They soon found themselves in the kitchen, which was large and bright, with rows of white cabinets and old white appliances. There was a long oak table with ladder-back chairs, and a black-and-white tile floor circa 1950.

"I'll give you a space in the fridge and your own cabinets, for groceries. Like I said before, there are no other boarders right now, so there's plenty of room. Still, it's good to label things. I don't like arguments when people find their favorite snacks missing."

"That sounds fine," Carrie said. She had shared a house when she was in college and recalled the ground rules.

As Vera closed a cupboard door, a large cat appeared, taking cautious steps down the stairs. It sat on the very bottom step and observed them with big yellow eyes. It was mostly black, with a big white chest and belly, white legs and paws, and a large pink nose.

"That's Chester. He's a big fellow, but very gentle. I hope you don't mind cats? No allergies or anything like that?" Vera glanced at Noah, who was eager to interact with any furred creature.

"Nothing like that. Noah loves animals." He was longing for a pet, even more than bunk beds, but they had not been in one place long enough lately to take on that responsibility.

"Can I pet him, Mom?" he asked quietly.

Vera answered before Carrie could. "Sure you can. He's a big mush. Give him one of those treats from the jar on the counter. He'll be your friend for life."

Noah found the treats and held one out to his new friend. Chester came running, gobbled it down, and twined himself around Noah's legs, begging for more.

Vera watched them a moment, then looked back at Carrie. "So, what do you think?"

"It's very nice, just what we need. I think Noah is sold, too, but . . . Helen didn't mention what you charge for rent."

"Oh, right. Nearly forgot that part . . . Senior moment." Vera laughed at herself, then quoted a reasonable rate. "A few weeks' notice is helpful if you decide to leave, but I don't fuss about that either. People come and go here. I'm used to that."

Carrie nodded, glad to hear that Vera was so easygoing. No lease or security deposits to sign. Luckily, Helen had given her an extra two weeks' salary as a thank-you gift, and Carrie felt she could afford the rooms even though she didn't have a job yet.

"I think that will be fine," Carrie said. "I'm assuming Helen told you I'm unemployed right now. But I saw a lot of ads in the paper today. I'm going to look online, too. With the holidays coming, a lot of stores are hiring. I'm sure I'll have something soon."

"Don't worry. Helen told me the whole situation. Those daughters of hers . . ." Vera shook her head. Carrie guessed she wanted to say more but didn't want to gossip. "I know you're in a tight spot now, dear. But you seem bright and able. Helen thinks the world of you. I think you'll find something soon if you call around and you aren't too particular."

"I think so, too," Carrie replied. "And I'm not fussy, as long as the pay is decent," she added, hoping to reassure Vera again. She glanced over at Noah, glad to see he was still playing with the cat and not listening in on the adult conversation.

"I know of a job you might be interested in. It's only temporary, but it's something."

"Really?" Could she actually find a new place to live and a new job in one day? Especially considering that it was the day after Thanksgiving, when many people were taking a holiday. Carrie didn't think that was possible, but she was curious. "What sort of job—as a housekeeper again?"

Vera shook her head. "Nothing like that. It's office work. The secretary at our church has to leave town for a few weeks. Her daughter is sick or pregnant or something. She's not sure when she'll be back, though definitely not until after the holidays. I was at church just this morning when she got the news," Vera explained. "Worst time of the year for our pastor, with Christmas coming. That's his big busy season." Vera's bright eyes searched Carrie's. "Can you do that sort of work?"

"I've worked in offices. I was an executive assistant at an insurance company for several years."

Carrie had to leave college just one year short of her degree. She always meant to go back if she could come up with the money or the time, but so far hadn't been able to. She had worked in a busy insurance company before Noah was born and had a lot to keep track of there, a lot of correspondence and record keeping. She was sure she could handle the demands of a church office in this tiny village, even if the pastor did think it was his busy season.

"That sounds good to me. Here's the number if you want to call. I know Mrs. Honeyfield was putting the word out to the congregation,"

Vera added as she scribbled the number on a notepad. "It won't take long for them to find somebody."

"I'll call right away," Carrie promised, slipping the paper into her pocket. The job might be a long shot. Maybe the minister wanted a church member to fill it, someone who knew the congregation and how the church worked. But it was nice of Vera to offer the tip.

The women quickly settled the rest of their business as Vera walked Carrie and Noah to the front door. Carrie asked if they could move in the next day, and Vera seemed pleased. Maybe she got lonely in this big house by herself.

"Like I said, I don't usually cook dinner. But you'll be tired from moving and unpacking, and I'd like you to feel welcome here. We can all have dinner together tomorrow night. Anything special you like to eat?"

Carrie was surprised by the kind gesture. "We're not fussy about food. Please don't go to any trouble. We already feel welcome," she added sincerely.

Then Carrie noticed a square of cross-stitching hanging near the front door. BE NOT FORGETFUL TO ENTERTAIN STRANGERS: FOR THEREBY, SOME HAVE ENTERTAINED ANGELS UNAWARES. HEBREWS 13:2. Carrie wondered if this was Vera's personal philosophy and maybe the reason that Vera opened her home and welcomed them so easily.

"I'll make a nice roast chicken and potatoes. Everybody likes that," Vera decided aloud. "We're all set. See you around noon. Bye for now." Vera held the cat in her arms to keep him from running out. Then she took one of his big paws in her hand and made him wave good-bye, making Noah laugh.

Carrie laughed, too, realizing at least one of the day's huge problems had been easily solved.

Carrie and Noah were back in the car, both buckling up their seat belts, when she turned to him. "Looks like we found a new place to live, Noah. What do you think?"

"The bunk beds are cool, and I like Chester. I bet I can teach him tricks."

"I bet you can," Carrie agreed, relieved by Noah's cheerful answer. She hated to make him move again. Even though Essex was just a short distance from Cape Light, Noah would have to enroll in a new elementary school once they moved here. She had already looked into that. She would have to register him on Monday morning, first thing.

A new class, a new teacher . . . and being forced to make all new friends. Again. Her heart went out to him.

"I like my room, too, and Vera is very friendly," she added, taking out her phone.

"Yeah, she's nice. Can we go to the playground now?"

Carrie had forgotten her promise. But Noah hadn't, of course. "Maybe. I just have to make one tiny phone call first."

She ignored his dramatic sigh and dialed the number Vera had given her. The church secretary, Mrs. Honeyfield, answered, and Carrie quickly told her she had heard about the job through Vera and that she had some office experience.

"I haven't worked in an office lately, but I did work at a large insurance agency in Worcester for several years, Webster Insurance. I was an administrative assistant to the owner, Mr. Webster. I have a reference from him. And one from an employer in Essex, too, Helen Vincent. I think she's a member of your church?"

Mrs. Honeyfield asked Carrie to hold and came back on the line a few moments later, sounding a bit breathless.

"Reverend Lewis can see you now if you're available. He has to leave the church for an appointment at one thirty, but any time before that."

Carrie checked her watch. It was already half past twelve. She had hoped for an appointment tomorrow, so she would have a chance to dress up and look professional. But she did have a copy of her résumé and references in the car, she recalled. She had been planning to bring them to the print shop today to make copies.

She recalled what Vera had said, about the word going out in the congregation. She would just have to take her chances . . . jeans, sneakers, and all.

"Great. I'd be happy to come now," Carrie replied. "If you don't mind my son coming along, too. He can read a book. I'm sure he won't be any trouble." Did Noah have a book in the car? She could always give him her cell phone; he loved to play video games on it.

"That will be fine," Mrs. Honeyfield said. "Park at the back of the church and enter through the glass doors. The office is on your right."

Carrie thanked her and ended the call. She turned to Noah, who had been watching her curiously. "Looks like we have to delay the playground a little while longer, pal. But we're getting closer. There's a job at the church. They want me to come right now and talk to the minister about it."

Noah looked puzzled. "What will you do at a church? Clean up the place?"

"They need a secretary in the office. To type letters and answer the phone. That sort of thing."

"That doesn't sound too bad."

"Not bad at all." Carrie took out her lipstick and comb again. "Better than cleaning up," she added with a grin.

"Way better," Noah agreed. "Don't worry, Mom. They'll hire you in a minute."

Carrie started the car again and headed back to the village. She did hope this worked out, but didn't want to get their hopes up. "Thanks, honey. I'll do my best," she promised him. *I will for you,* she wanted to add.

Carrie had driven by the church many times but had rarely taken a long look at it. Or a close look, she realized as they headed up the path to the glass doors Mrs. Honeyfield had described.

It was a pretty church, made of gray stones, with a slate roof and arched stained-glass windows in the sanctuary. The parking lot was empty except for a few cars. The grounds around the church building melted seamlessly into the village green, with the harbor in view. A very pretty setting, Carrie thought, and a far cry from Webster Insurance or even working in Mrs. Vincent's house. She would like working here, she thought.

"We can walk right over to the playground when you're done," Noah said, pointing to his goal.

"Yes, we can. But I thought you might want lunch first?"

"I can wait. Let's go to the playground, then have lunch. Then maybe we can go back again, after," he added.

Carrie squeezed his hand, amused at his planning. He had been so good today, she would definitely do a double shift if he really wanted to.

They were inside the church now, and she felt suddenly nervous. She saw the sign for the church office, squared her shoulders, took a breath, and headed for the door. Noah trotted quickly to keep up with her.

Mrs. Honeyfield was as chatty and kind as she had sounded on the phone. She sat Noah at a desk with a glass of milk and a few books and puzzles she had borrowed from the church school downstairs.

The minister, Reverend Lewis, came out of his office quickly and introduced himself with a welcoming smile and outstretched hand. He wasn't dressed like the ministers Carrie had known growing up, who only wore black suits and clerical collars. He wore a brown tweed sports coat, a pale yellow sweater-vest, and a reddish-brown tie that matched his reddish-brown hair and beard perfectly. Blue-gray eyes sparkled behind his gold-rimmed glasses, which gave him a scholarly air.

It was hard to guess his age. Silver strands in his hair and the crinkles around his eyes suggested a number somewhere over sixty. But he looked energetic and fit, nowhere near retirement.

"Thank you for coming on such short notice, Ms. Munro," he said.

"Thanks for meeting with me. I didn't have time to dress for an interview," Carrie replied, glancing down at her jacket and jeans. "But I have a résumé and some letters of reference."

Reverend Lewis took the pages in hand, looking pleased. "Serendipity," he said, with a smile.

"Yes . . . maybe," Carrie agreed. He seemed like a nice man, not stuffy or formal, like some of the ministers she had met.

They stepped into his office to talk about the job and Carrie's work experience. He asked Carrie a few questions, about her résumé and about herself, how she came to live in Cape Light.

"I grew up near Worcester and lived there after I was married, too. I wasn't able to finish college, but I did complete three years," she added. "The summer after my husband and I separated, Noah and I came to Essex to stay with a college friend. I wasn't having much luck finding a job in Worcester at that time, but I did find the job working for Helen Vincent, so we decided to stay here."

"I see. So you've had some changes over the last few years," he said gently. "May I ask how long you were married?"

"Nine years. I met Kevin when I was working at the insurance company. He's living in Florida now, I think," she said. "We're not in touch very often."

Florida was the last she had heard, but Kevin could be anywhere. He would get very excited about some new idea or plan and then quickly go cold on it. Which was essentially the story of their relationship.

Reverend Ben met her glance. "Forgive me for asking these personal questions. I don't mean to pry or make you uncomfortable."

"It's all right. I don't feel uncomfortable," Carrie said truthfully. She was normally more private, but for some reason, she found Reverend Ben very easy to open up to.

"It sounds as if you're raising Noah on your own, and I know that's not an easy situation."

"It's not," she admitted. "But we're managing all right so far. Leaving my husband was not an easy choice, but I felt it was best for Noah. Our home life was . . . well, very difficult and unstable. Kevin never hurt Noah or me. But it seemed only a matter of time. And he made no effort to change. It was getting worse. I had to do what I thought was best."

"I'm sure you did," Reverend Ben said. "It's very important for children to feel safe. How old is Noah?"

"He's seven. He's a good kid," she added, trying not to brag.

"I'm sure he is." Reverend Ben met her glance and smiled with warmth and understanding that was hard to describe. Then the conversation turned from personal matters to computer skills, and Reverend Ben described the duties of the job.

The meeting passed much faster than Carrie had expected. Or perhaps it had been so easy and pleasant talking to the minister, she hadn't noticed the time pass. The salary was more than she would have thought, and the hours were easy—nine to four—which would help with the issue of child care after school.

"We don't expect Mrs. Honeyfield back until mid-January at the earliest," Reverend Ben explained. "I guess that's about six weeks or so. How does that sound to you?"

"It sounds great. I would be happy to work here," Carrie said honestly.

"Good, then. We'd be happy to have you," he replied.

Carrie couldn't hide her surprise. "Don't you want to check my references or something?"

He glanced down at her résumé and the letters she had presented. "I think this vote of confidence from Helen is plenty. The stationery is positively glowing."

Carrie laughed at the image. "I enjoyed working for her."

"I'm sure you did. She's a lovely woman. And I hope you enjoy working here, too."

Carrie smiled in answer; she already thought she would.

They agreed that she could come in a little late on Monday, since she had to register Noah at his new school. Then Carrie brought up the one minor glitch in the plan, hoping it wouldn't change the reverend's mind.

"There's just one thing more. I don't have anyone to watch Noah after school right now. I'm sure I can find someone soon—or sign him up for an after-school program. But he would need to come here around three p.m. for a few days and wait for me," she explained. "He can do his homework or something. I'll make sure he's quiet."

"That's fine. He won't disturb me," Reverend Ben assured her.

A few minutes later, Carrie was standing in the outer office again. Noah was sitting at Mrs. Honeyfield's desk, drawing pictures with the art program on her computer. Mrs. Honeyfield stood at the copy machine, watching pages fly out of the printer.

"Everything's settled. Carrie is going to start Monday," Reverend Ben announced.

Mrs. Honeyfield looked pleased. "That's perfect. I'll be here Monday to show you what you do."

Carrie was happy to hear that. "Thank you . . . and thanks for watching Noah," she added. "I hope he wasn't any trouble."

"Not at all. I didn't even know you could draw pictures on a computer. Now I have something new to do with my grandchildren."

Reverend Ben laughed. "Maybe you can teach me next week, Noah. I'd love to know how to do that, too."

Noah came out from behind Mrs. Honeyfield's desk. "Sure, it's easy." He glanced up at Carrie and tugged her hand. "Can we go to the playground now?" he whispered.

"Yes, Noah. We're going. Right now." She looked back at Mrs. Honeyfield and Reverend Lewis. "Thank you both again. I'll see you Monday."

As she left the church with Noah and crossed the village green to the playground, Carrie felt as if a great load had been lifted off her. And almost dizzy with relief. A new job and a place to live—all in one day? It didn't seem possible. But it was true. She felt light-headed and lighthearted with the surprise of it.

"Well, we figured it all out, Noah. New job, new home. Done and done, pal." She held his hand, swinging it back and forth, then glanced down at him to see what he thought.

Noah seemed happy, though not nearly as surprised. "I knew it would be okay," he told her. "I think this is going to be a lucky place for us, Mom."

"Maybe," she agreed, though she wasn't such a big believer in luck. Once upon a time she had thought that way. Now it seemed to her that you made your way in the world as best as you could. Sometimes you met nice people, like Helen or Vera or Reverend Ben. Sometimes not. Today had been a good day. A very good day. That's what she knew for sure.

As they drew closer to the playground, Noah dropped her hand and ran for an empty swing. He jumped on, and she got behind him. She gave him a few big pushes, then stood back and watched him fly.

"Swing with me," he said.

Carrie hesitated a moment, feeling silly, then said, "Okay. I think I will."

She sat on the empty swing beside him, pulled back, and launched herself toward the sky. It had been a while since she last did this. She had forgotten what it was like to fly through the air so easily and see the world through Noah's eyes, at least for a little while.

She laughed with Noah, stretching out her legs and racing him to the clear blue sky. It did seem the perfect way to celebrate how all their problems had been solved so easily today.

Chapter Three

Molly was about to head to bed on Sunday night when her cell phone buzzed with a call from Betty. "Sorry to call so late, but I have good news. I've been working my way down the client list, and I have a few leads for you."

Molly shrieked happily as Betty filled her in on the details. Nothing guaranteed, but quite a few people who wanted bids on holiday parties.

"Bless your heart," she said when Betty finished. "It just goes to show—few can resist that legendary Bowman charm."

"Don't be silly. I wish I could follow up myself, but I just can't manage it this week," Betty said regretfully.

"I know. And no need to apologize. This is plenty to get me rolling."

"Mrs. Fillmore is free on Monday morning. I told her you would call to set up a time to meet," Betty continued. "I think you should jump on that one first."

It was too late to call clients, Molly thought, but she knew Betty was right. "I'll send her an email tonight and then call her tomorrow, first thing."

"Good, because it sounds like she's pressed for time and doesn't plan to shop around."

"Just what I like to hear. Low-hanging fruit. And we're right there, first in line."

Every caterer in town knew that Alicia Fillmore chaired the Events Committee at the Cape Light Historical Society. But even Molly hadn't known the society was planning a last-minute holiday cocktail party for their donors. What a plum that would be. Molly ended the call and, seconds later, tapped out a short email, just as she had promised.

Mrs. Fillmore turned out to be a night owl and answered the message quickly, setting up an appointment at Lilac Hall for one o'clock sharp on Monday.

Which would have been perfect, giving Molly plenty of time to make notes and even gather some pictures for her sales pitch, if only she didn't need to run up to Newburyport and meet with her brother at the new shop Monday morning.

Sam had no sooner solved the last problem with a building inspector than another had popped up. One that might even be worse, she suspected, though Sam had not shared many details on the phone, calling her just a few minutes after she'd hung up with Betty. Well, they would deal with that sticky wicket tomorrow, she told herself, refusing to let Sam's call throw her off track. In the meantime, she was going to concentrate on a gorgeous cocktail party for the Historical Society. Like a hound dog on the scent of its prey.

Molly heaved a giant sigh as she drove toward Newburyport on Monday morning. She longed to see the progress at Willoughby's Too but wasn't sure she could bear the gruesome details of this latest crisis. Especially if it meant pushing off the opening date yet again. She had woken up to an early-morning email from Sam:

> Promise me you won't panic. It's not pretty, but it's not the end of the world either. We'll work it out.

That made her more nervous than ever. She hoped the delay wouldn't be too long. And she hoped something could be done to make the time lag shorter. She hadn't even told Betty yet about Sam's call, thinking it best to see for herself what needed to be done.

She also didn't want to be reminded that Betty had never wanted this location for the shop. Betty preferred another, smaller spot on a side street. One in a newer building that didn't need nearly so much work.

But despite the long renovation, Molly was sure the extra cost and effort would pay off soon. The new shop was in the perfect location, right on the waterfront, where all the foot traffic was concentrated, especially in the summer months.

The truth was, Betty had not been eager to expand the business at all, and Molly had more or less coaxed and persuaded her to take this step. This was part of the reason why Molly was now so reluctant to share the everyday, disheartening details of the renovation—and the cost of construction and all the unexpected problems that were quickly eating through their business-expansion loan.

But it's coming along, and we will open and make back all the money and then some, Molly assured herself as she parked her SUV and walked toward the new store.

Several brawny men in work clothes and boots walked in and out, with coils of electrical cable slung over their shoulders, or carrying large white slabs of drywall with dusty gloves.

She was dressed in a suit, her good wool coat, and high-heeled boots for her meeting at the Historical Society, and she cautiously stepped inside, as if walking into an active beehive. A very dusty beehive.

The sounds of electric drills, sanders, and hammers buzzed and banged all around. She tried to gauge the progress, to see the turn-of-the-century Parisian café she envisioned emerging from the morass of construction she currently saw: the walls laid bare to the studs; the ceiling disemboweled, a tangle of wires and cables hanging; the thin, shaky plywood boards where a luxurious tile floor would be laid.

The high ceilings, the original moldings, and even the antique gaslight fixtures were still visible. But her beloved caterpillar was still such a long, long way from emerging as a glorious butterfly, Molly felt she might cry.

She rotated in one spot on her dressy, high-heeled boots, like a doll in a music box, finally spotting her brother in his yellow hard hat.

"Hey, I'm here," she called out, waving to him. "I'm going to wait upstairs."

Sam waved back and nodded. He was talking to an older man, Molly noticed, both of them leaning over an old-fashioned radiator that had been pulled away from the wall. The older man—a plumber, she presumed—shook his head sadly, like a doctor giving a bad diagnosis.

She didn't need a caption to know what that conversation was about. *Well, we expected to need new plumbing. Some new plumbing,* she mentally corrected herself as she climbed up the stairs to the store's second floor—another reason the space cost more, and another reason she liked this location better. They had extra room for more customer seating, or even a private party, and the windows up here gave an even better view of the waterfront and harbor. And, luxury of luxuries, they had room for a real office.

"If you're going to do something, do it right" is what Molly had always believed. In the long run, it never paid to skimp, whether baking or doing anything else in life.

She tried to remember that philosophy once Sam came upstairs and started explaining the latest problem and the newest unexpected costs.

"We were taking a wall down in the kitchen to update the wiring. That's when we found the leak." He pointed to a wall that had once held a sink. "It was coming from up here, going on a while. Just a little drip on and off. Which is why no one noticed it during the inspection, I guess," he added, anticipating her question. "There's a lot of mold in the insulation, and it's spread everywhere. We need new Sheetrock and insulation on that wall, for sure. Maybe even the whole room down there, and up here, as well."

Sam's serious expression and businesslike tone scared her. He was usually the "Don't worry, it's not that bad" guy.

Molly's words came out in a shocked squeak. "The whole place, you mean? New walls and insulation in the whole building?"

"Maybe not that bad. But we have to check all of it. We'll never pass final inspection if we don't."

How many times had Molly heard that line lately?

"What about the building owner? Isn't he responsible for this mess?"

Sam shrugged. "I took a look at the lease and, unfortunately, it's not clear. You could have your lawyer call, I guess."

Molly knew what that meant, too. A holdup on the work until two attorneys—hers and the building owner's—negotiated what the owner might pay for. Or not. A big bill from the law firm, for sure. And even further delays with the shop opening.

She sighed, her thoughts making all the twists and turns in this tricky question. "I'm not sure it would be worth it. We might end up waiting weeks just to get a response from the owner."

"I think you're right. I'll definitely keep track of the costs if you want to approach him later," Sam added. "Right now, your priority seems to be opening up here."

"You got that right. So, what do you think? What is this going to take?"

"At least a week. Maybe more. Really can't say until we see how much needs to be replaced. I wish I could be more precise or give you better news," he said in a more sympathetic tone. "Hey, those big gilded mirrors came in," he added, trying to cheer her. "I have them in the shop for safekeeping. They're going to look great."

Molly forced a small smile. She had pictured the decor so precisely, and the mirrors were perfect, just what she'd had in mind. Though they were also a bit pricier than what the budget allowed for. Right now, the thought of the expensive fittings and the unexpected bills made her feel queasy. Was this new store turning out to be Molly's Folly?

Pride goeth before a fall. The bleak saying popped into her head, out of the blue.

She looked up to find her brother staring at her. "Are you all right? Do you want some water or something?"

She shook her head. "I'm distracted today." She pulled out her phone and checked the calendar and her list of reminders. She couldn't help noticing that the shop was originally scheduled to *open* on Friday, November 27, then was pushed back a week to the upcoming Saturday, December 5, and then was adjusted by a few more days. And now it would have to be pushed off again. She heard the clock ticking like a meter on a taxi. Every delay was costing the business money. A lot of money. It wasn't only the cost of renovations, but the lease and utilities on a totally nonproductive space. And right in the heart of the holiday shopping season, when they could be making their biggest sales of the year here.

She had been counting on this place to generate some much-needed revenue to help with the overdue bills back in Cape Light and pick up the financial slack in general. But it was turning out to be another leaky hole in their bank accounts. A big one.

She took a calming breath. "Last week you said December ninth or tenth. What are you thinking now? How about the weekend of December eighteenth?" she offered. "Hardly ideal, but we'll get a full week of pre-Christmas sales. That will be something, at least."

"Molly, I'd promise you the moon if I could. But there's just so much we can do. I have a full crew down there, starting early and working late. And it's not just the work. It's passing the inspections, too. I have no control over that. I can't make any promises or set any dates right now. I'm trying to be honest with you. It is what it is."

That was not the answer she wanted to hear. But she knew her brother was being straight with her and working very hard. He probably even regretted taking on this job. Still, so much seemed heaped on her at once, Molly couldn't help losing it a little.

"Really? Well, maybe that's not good enough, Sam. I wish you could think of something—some way to finish sooner, so we have a chance of opening by Christmas. We're going to miss the biggest shopping time of the entire year. Don't you get it?"

Sam regarded her with his level, patient gaze. "Of course I get it. But I think you need to *get* the big picture. This place will be open a long time, God willing, and people will shop here all year long."

Molly sighed. She hated when he was so logical; it drove her nuts. "Not all year long. Nobody hangs out at a bakery right after Christmas. Everyone's on a diet," she countered in a grumpy tone.

She hadn't meant to sound sarcastic or blame him for the series of unfortunate events. But when she saw his expression harden, she realized her regret was too late.

Molly knew her brother went to great lengths to hold on to his temper. She also knew she was very good at testing that control.

"We're turning ourselves inside out to finish this job. Believe me, Molly, you're not the only one who wants this to be over."

"I'm sorry. I know it's not your fault. I'm just so frustrated. Nothing about this new store is going according to plan, and it's costing a bloody fortune."

Sam met her glance, calmer now, soothed by her apology. Lucky for her, he was always quick to forgive. "I know it's rough," he said. "You just don't know what you're going to find when you start poking around these old buildings." *I told you that,* he might have added, but kindly didn't.

"Talk to your designer," he suggested. "Scale down the interior, find some cheaper material for the floor and the fixtures. Most of that stuff is returnable. And you can look at what you spent on equipment, too. Maybe go for the lower-end oven or fridge?"

They were all reasonable suggestions, but Molly balked at backtracking in that direction. Would it really save that much money? Did she have to give up her vision to make this work? Sure, she would save some money now, but there might be breakdowns later if she skimped in the kitchen.

Quality ingredients, that was her standard. Her hallmark. That's what she was known for.

"I can't skimp. It will look cheesy. It has to be good quality stuff to pull off that Belle Epoque look. I don't want it to look like some cheap catering hall in Squantum. And I don't want a lot of cheap or secondhand equipment that will keep breaking down. That's what we're stuck with back in Cape Light. I'm past that stage, Sam."

Sam sighed and practically rolled his eyes. "Top-Shelf Molly, that's what we call you."

That's what they called her *now.* Since she had wrestled and scrapped her way to the top of the heap. She wasn't about to give up the title either.

"Yup, that's me." She stood up and patted her brother on the shoulder. "I'm sorry I blew a fuse. But you must be used to that around here," she joked.

"Not since we put in the circuit breakers. But I get your meaning. I wish I had better news. Maybe you should talk to your bank and tell them what's going on. I'm sure this happens a lot. They'll probably give you an extension on the loan. And a little breathing room on the grand opening," he added.

A little breathing room for him, too, she realized. But it was a good idea. She had thought of that a few times as a fallback plan. Had it come to that point yet? *I'm just panicking,* Molly realized. *I should talk this over with Betty. She'll know what to do.*

"Thanks for the advice. Meanwhile, take care of those mirrors. I'm going to be admiring my gorgeous reflection in here very soon," she predicted.

It will be the perfect backdrop for a photo of me and Betty on our grand opening day. With a huge, vintage-looking flower arrangement on the long marble counter. White lilies, maybe? Hydrangeas and roses with some snapdragons mixed in?

Molly let her fantasies take over, not daring to glance back at the reality of the place as Sam followed her down the dusty steps into the cacophonous work area and out the door.

"Don't worry, it's going to look much better the next time you come," her brother promised.

"I'm sure it will . . . It couldn't look much worse." She gave Sam a quick buss on the cheek and a light punch on his muscular arm, then headed for her car.

Sam's right. I can't fret. It's a process. And a watched pot never boils and all that, she reminded herself. *I just have to focus on something else, something positive.*

Sitting behind the wheel of her SUV, Molly took out her appointment book. Her to-do list was instantly reassuring, with several party leads from Betty to follow up on and the appointment with Mrs. Fillmore at the Historical Society today, underlined in red.

That one's going to be a slam dunk, Molly promised herself, feeling an instant boost. Besides, Betty still had loads more clients to call. There was still plenty of time to sign up more parties. They could make up the revenue for this moldy mess easily. Maybe charge more for some of the menu items? Or ask for more payment up front? Or was that a problem now with the Silver Spoon underbidding them? *I'll talk it over with Betty when I report in on Mrs. Fillmore. At least Betty is trying to keep her hand in. That's more than I could expect right now.*

As Molly headed back to Cape Light for her appointment, she mentally reviewed her usual sales pitch, barely noticing the familiar scenery and landmarks on the Beach Road. She nearly flew right by the gated entrance to Lilac Hall and turned just in time. The big mansion that housed the society was a grand and imposing building, instantly summoning up images of the Gilded Age, the era in which it was built by the Warwick family. The Warwicks had been the wealthiest family in the area at the time, owners of two canneries, a lumber mill, and miles of property around the mansion that had since been sold off.

The mansion and a good portion of the property around it had been donated to the county about thirty years ago, when Oliver Warwick ran into legal difficulties. Molly always had mixed feelings about visiting the place, admiring the amazing architecture and well-preserved decor, but also feeling intimidated by the building's grand atmosphere and all it represented to her.

Molly had expected to be alone with the committee chairwoman, but as she approached the meeting room on the second floor, she heard several voices—including a few that elicited a flurry of nerves.

She hesitated in the hallway, wondering if she should duck into the ladies' room for a last-minute check on her hair and lipstick. Too late. One of the women seated at the big mahogany table had spotted her and pinned her with a quizzical stare.

Molly quickly slipped on her happy saleswoman face, pushed her shoulders back, and sailed forward.

"Molly, so good to see you. Thank you for coming in on such short notice." Alicia Fillmore stood to greet her and ushered her over to an empty place near the head of the table. "I think you know everyone on our committee?"

"Yes, of course. Hello, ladies. So nice to see you again," Molly said politely as she scanned the circle.

Alicia Fillmore was the youngest of the group, in her mid- to late forties, Molly guessed, a bright, slim brunette with a warm manner, but also very business minded.

The other members greeted her politely, all of them older than Alicia. Some were easy to deal with, Molly had found, and others more particular. Lillian Warwick Elliot, the most difficult, sat at the far end of the table, her chin tilted up, as if she had noticed a distasteful smell when Molly walked into the room.

"I thought Betty Bowman was coming," Lillian said bluntly. "Didn't you say we were meeting with Betty?" She stared at Alicia, ignoring Molly entirely.

"Betty couldn't make it. But she sends her best," Molly replied quickly. "How are you, Lillian? It's good to see you."

Lillian finally deigned to look her way, her gaze imperious. Molly hoped she hadn't sounded sarcastic; it was almost never nice to see Lillian, despite the fact that she and Lillian were practically family. Sam had married Lillian's younger daughter, Jessica, over fourteen years ago, and Molly had entertained Lillian at her home on countless holidays and occasions. Molly had grown to love Jessica and her older sister, Emily, who was the mayor of

Cape Light. She was even fond of Lillian's second husband, Dr. Elliot, whom Matt had bought his practice from. It was just Lillian who was impossible. Lillian still treated her like the rude, rough-around-the-edges girl she had once been, the girl who barely graduated high school, a single mom, scrambling for years to make ends meet with so many random, menial jobs, including one as Lillian's house cleaner and another extremely short stint as her cook.

As much as Molly tried to shake off those memories and the feelings they elicited, or even laugh them off, Lillian could still get under her skin with a single word of disapproval or a mere shriveling look. Molly wanted this job and hated being thrown off her game by Lillian's disapproving stare, the intimidating aura that seemed to roll off her cashmere and pearls like a heavy, sweet perfume.

"So, where should we begin?" Alicia's bright, businesslike voice broke through Molly's wandering thoughts and the icy chill that had seeped into the room.

"Start anywhere. I'm ready to jump right in," Molly replied in her best "at your service" mode.

"Oh, brother . . . here we go," she heard Lillian mutter.

Molly kept her focus on Alicia, hoping the chairwoman had missed Lillian's snide remark.

"Perhaps Betty's already told you a little about the event we'd like to hold. A private reception for our big donors," Alicia explained.

"Not too big, but very elegant," the woman seated across from Molly added. Jaqueline Phillips, Molly recalled.

"Elegant, of course," Molly echoed. She flipped open her notebook and jotted down details. This part was hard for her, listening and not talking. Betty always had to remind her not to jump ahead and talk too much. She forced her lips together and gazed at the chairwoman with an attentive look.

"Not a sit-down meal," Alicia was saying. "Perhaps we could offer passed hors d'oeuvres?"

"We can do all passed hors d'oeuvres, of course. But maybe a few stations would be a good idea?" Molly suggested. "A raw bar with oysters?"

"Good Lord. We aren't looking for the Rockport Oyster Festival. Were you about to suggest chowder and beer kegs?" Lillian pinned her with a pinched, sour look while the rest of the women struggled to keep straight faces.

Molly felt her face go red. "A seafood bar can be very elegant, Lillian. We can serve caviar and champagne . . ."

"Yes, of course. Of course that's what you were implying, Molly." Alicia quickly smoothed the moment over. "I think that sounds perfect. I love the idea of caviar."

"Nothing too messy, though," Claudia Bausch said.

"I don't think we should have too many stations. It starts to look like an all-you-can-eat buffet." Jaqueline glanced at Lillian, as if seeking her approval.

Molly knew she was losing control, and all because of Lillian, who had started them imagining worst-case scenarios instead of the wonderful event Molly knew she could deliver.

"We don't need to have any stations at all," Molly said quickly. "It can be all passed hors d'oeuvres, white-glove service, and the finest foods. We can determine the menu later. Where will the party be held, Alicia? Here in the mansion?"

"Well, we have two choices," Alicia replied. "The great room, of course. It's a very grand space and very formal. Or the second-floor gallery. It's smaller but more intimate, and this won't be a huge crowd. We plan to keep the guest list under a hundred."

"What do you think, Molly? We can't decide," Claudia admitted.

Molly hesitated, knowing that half of them would disagree with her, no matter what she said. It was worse than a trick question.

"I've staged some beautiful events in the great room," she finally said. "And it's a wonderful space, especially for weddings and concerts."

That was all true. The great room was sort of an enclosed courtyard at the far end of the mansion, with a ceiling that soared two and a half stories high, along with a stone floor and stone walls, and was adjacent to an outdoor courtyard. It was perfectly beautiful for large events but hard to decorate and harder to heat.

"But considering the time of year and the size of the party," Molly went on, "I would suggest a smaller, more intimate space. A big benefit of the great room is its views of the grounds. But at this time of year, that's not much. The gallery on the second floor is probably too small, though."

Everyone looked at her, surprised that she had rejected both choices.

"What do you suggest?" Alicia asked with interest.

"The Cape Light Fire House," Lillian muttered.

Molly stared her down. "The larger gallery on the main floor might be just right," she countered.

"That's an interesting idea," Alicia said, and Molly could see that they all—with the exception of Lillian—were considering and intrigued by the idea.

"I think it could work very well," Molly went on. "Especially with those big tapestries along the walls and the big hearth. It's already very festive. We could decorate in a simple palette, a Victorian look. White flowers and fresh greens, pine and holly—"

"Really. How original," Lillian said dryly.

"With touches of gold here and there," Molly added, her tone a bit more curt and harder edged than she intended. She had to stop letting Lillian get to her. "Just the edges of the ribbons. It will be very subtle. You need to add a few bright spots."

"I think white and green is very tasteful," Claudia agreed.

"And it will go well with the room's decor," Jaqueline said.

"Oh bother, don't tell me about the room's decor. I lived here, for goodness' sake." Lillian sat back, crossing her arms over her chest. She looked as though she wanted to leave but was determined to stick it out. Molly almost wished she would go. But that wouldn't have been good for her sales pitch either.

"Here, let me show you some pictures. I brought along my books . . . Just general examples," she added quickly, lest anyone start taking these suggestions too literally. "We can really do any variation of what you see in there."

"Oh look at this . . . that's lovely." Alicia was the first one to take a book, and to show the others a photo of a flower arrangement.

The other women eagerly leaned forward to see. All except Lillian. Molly wasn't surprised.

Lillian Warwick Elliot is a curveball I didn't expect. But I've shown her before, and I'll show her again, Molly told herself. *I'll just watch for my pitch and hit this one out of the park.*

"You did all your homework, Noah, right? Are there any more supplies you need? We can get them in the morning before I drop you off."

Noah had just climbed into bed on Monday night. Carrie walked around the room, picking up pieces of clothing and some scattered books and toys. They had moved their belongings to Vera's house on Saturday, and Noah was already very comfortable in his new room. He'd chosen the lower bunk bed and put up photos of his favorite Red Sox and Patriots players on the wall next to his bed. The wall above his desk now displayed his favorite superheroes.

"I don't need anything special." Noah pulled the covers up to his chin, then placed his favorite stuffed animal nearby, where he could see it. He still slept with Whiskers, a floppy, worn-out stuffed rabbit.

Carrie sat on the edge of his bed and smiled down at him. He was such a good sport, dealing with so many changes right now. "I know it's hard for you to switch schools, honey. I hope you like your new class."

"Mrs. Fischer is nice. She's nicer than Mrs. Barton so far."

"That's good. I'm glad you like her."

"Do you like your new job, Mom?"

"I do. I didn't get to do too much today. Mrs. Honeyfield showed me where everything is in the office and how the copy machine works. Things like that. But I think I'm going to like it. It doesn't seem too hard."

Her routine and duties were not very complicated, though there was enough to keep her busy. It was definitely an easier job than she'd had at the insurance company.

"Reverend Ben said I could play basketball with some kids who come to church tomorrow. Can I?"

"Sure, I'll look into it," Carrie promised.

It would be good to get Noah involved in activities with boys his own age. But she would have to find out if she had to be a church member, or Noah had to be a Cub Scout, or something like that.

"We'll definitely find something fun for you to do in the afternoons. Most days anyway," she promised. "For now, you need to take the same bus after school that you took today, and get off at the village green. I'll be there to meet you, okay?"

"Don't worry, I won't forget. Everything's working out fine," he added in a grown-up tone. "My angel said it would."

Carrie sat back, wondering if she had heard correctly. "Your angel? I didn't know you had an angel, Noah."

He shrugged under the covers. "Of course I do. Everyone does."

"I didn't know that either." Carrie wondered where he had gotten this idea. Maybe at church while he was waiting for her? But Noah had been alone in the conference room next to her office doing homework most of the time. Maybe he found a book there. Or maybe Reverend Ben told him about angels?

"Did you hear about angels at church today?"

Noah shook his head. "Nope. Reverend Ben talked to me about basketball," he reminded her. "Theo told me."

"You mean, a friend at school?" He hadn't mentioned making friends with anyone on his first day. But it was encouraging.

"Theo is my angel," Noah explained patiently. "His real name is . . . it's sort of long. I can't remember exactly. But he likes 'Theo' for short."

Carrie nodded, feeling more confused. "He told you this? His name and all that?"

Noah shrugged again. "We talk all the time. He's always hanging around, watching what's going on. He likes to help us. That's his job. He helped us find Mrs. Plante's house. And he helped you find your new job."

Carrie nodded. Noah had an imaginary friend. He had never mentioned one when he was younger, but she knew it was very common. He was probably lonely. Though she did wonder how the friend had turned out to be an angel. She never talked about anything like that.

"That's very sweet, honey. Please thank Theo for being such a big help."

"I do, Mom," he said with a touch of irritation, as if she had just reminded him to remember his manners at a birthday party.

Carrie wanted to let it drop, but couldn't help her own curiosity. "So where did you meet Theo—at school today?"

"Theo's been visiting me for a while. It didn't just start today."

"Oh, I didn't realize. You never mentioned him. How long do you think it's been?"

Noah shrugged. "I don't know. While we lived at Mrs. Vincent's. Maybe since last summer?"

"Okay." Carrie nodded. "When does he visit? Any special time?"

"Mostly at night," Noah replied.

"I see. Maybe you're having a dream?" Carrie offered in a comforting way. "A very nice dream."

"It's not a dream, Mom," Noah replied, sounding very sure.

"All right, whatever you say. But it's nice to have happy dreams, Noah. I hope all your dreams are sweet and happy." Carrie stood, then leaned over and kissed Noah's forehead. "Good night, honey. I'm going to leave that little light on in my room, okay?" She glanced over at the partially open door between their bedrooms. "If you wake up and you need me, just call. I'll hear you perfectly," she promised.

"I won't need you. Don't worry." He didn't add, *Theo will help me.* But Carrie almost expected him to.

She didn't ask any more questions and slipped quietly from the room. Noah had an imaginary friend or maybe was dreaming of angels. That made sense to her. He often had nightmares, which had started even before the divorce. She had hoped that once they were living far from her ex-husband, the bad dreams would stop. But the night terrors did come and go.

She was actually glad to know that Noah had a recurrent "nice" dream. Even if the fantasy had evolved into some sort of imaginary friend.

Once he made some friends at his new school, Carrie was certain that Theo would stop visiting. It wasn't anything to worry about, she decided as she grabbed a book from her room and headed downstairs to sit with Vera. Though she did hope that Noah didn't tell too many people about his angel.

Chapter Four

By Thursday afternoon, Carrie was feeling very comfortable in her new job, and when the phone rang, she answered it in a professional tone. She was surprised, however, when the caller asked to speak to her and not Reverend Lewis.

"This is Ms. Munro speaking."

"This is Mrs. Fischer, at Harbor Elementary." Carrie was on instant alert, recognizing the voice of Noah's new teacher.

"Is anything wrong? Is Noah all right?"

"Noah's fine. But I did want to speak with you about something that came up this morning in class. Is this a good time to talk?"

"Yes, it's fine." Reverend Ben had gone out to lunch, and even if he were in his office, Carrie would have wanted to know what was going on.

"Noah didn't have his math homework this morning. He told me he lost it," Mrs. Fischer explained.

Carrie was surprised. "I know he did it. I looked it over with him.

He must have left it around the house somewhere. We can look for it when we get home."

"That's what he thought, too. But he didn't say you would help him find it. He told me that his angel would help him. In fact, he said, 'I'm sure Theo will find it for me.' He's mentioned the angel once or twice before, so I already knew who he was talking about. Is this something Noah talks about frequently at home?"

"The first I heard of it was Monday night," Carrie admitted. "Right before bed. He hasn't mentioned it since. I think it's an imaginary friend. Or a dream he's been having, and he thinks it's real."

"I don't think you should worry, Ms. Munro. It does seem as though Noah has created an imaginary friend. He's a bright boy and seems very well adjusted otherwise. Noah's had a big change, moving to a new town and a new school."

"Yes . . . It's not the first time either. Ever since my divorce, we've had to move a lot. Noah was having nightmares for a while, but that seems to have stopped. I'll talk to him about the angel."

Mrs. Fischer was silent for a moment, then said, "Noah doesn't think he's lying. He really believes this Theo character exists."

"Yes, I know." That part did concern her. "Do you think he's having trouble telling the difference between what's real and what isn't?"

"I don't think that's what's going on," the teacher assured her. "But there's a child psychologist on our staff, Dr. Carlson. He works with all the elementary schools in the district and has an office in his home. I can give you the number if you'd like to call him. Noah's created this friend for a reason, and considering what you've just told me, it might be a good idea to have Dr. Carlson help Noah sort it out."

"That does sound like a good idea." Carrie took down the information. "Thanks for your help."

"Not at all. Noah's very bright, and he gets along well with the other children in the class . . . though he is a bit quiet. But I expect that once he makes a few friends, that will change. And he might find he doesn't need his imaginary friend as much either."

"I was thinking the same thing myself. But I will call Dr. Carlson," she added. "If anything else comes up, please let me know."

Carrie hung up, feeling surprised by the call. Noah's teachers had rarely gotten in touch with her, and never once for bad behavior.

But it wasn't bad behavior. Noah wasn't willfully lying. Not like his father, Kevin, did constantly. Noah really believed that something—*someone*—named Theo visited and talked to him. And helped him with his problems. That wasn't hard to understand. After all, he was a little boy with a vivid imagination, and this was a way of working out his worries. It was probably nothing, but it would be a good idea to have Noah talk to this school psychologist all the same.

She was about to call Dr. Carlson when Reverend Ben came in. She handed him his message slips and a letter he had asked her to type.

"Thank you, Carrie." He looked over the letter, signed it, and handed it back to her to be sent in the mail. "Anything wrong?" he asked, studying her expression.

Carrie shook her head and glanced at her computer. "Not really. I had a call from Noah's teacher, Mrs. Fischer. He's having a little trouble adjusting to the new class. Nothing serious."

"These changes can be hard on children. It's just his first week there," Reverend Ben replied. "Anything I can do to help?"

Carrie thought it was nice of him to offer, but she couldn't think of anything. For one thing, she would feel a bit awkward telling Reverend Ben about Noah's angel. She didn't want to get into a debate, or seem disrespectful. Reverend Ben probably believed in angels and might not even see any problem with Noah's story. And the reverend might not appreciate Carrie's view that it was all a fantasy.

"His teacher gave me the name of a child psychologist," Carrie said. "She thinks it would be a good idea to have Noah visit."

"I think that's a good idea, too," Reverend Ben agreed. "He probably just needs time to adjust to the new school and all that. But it might help you worry less."

"Maybe," she agreed with a smile.

"Don't worry about fitting in the appointment around your hours," Reverend Ben added. "You take care of Noah. That's the most important thing right now."

Carrie thanked him. She had been wondering what sort of hours the psychologist had and how she would manage the visit. But Reverend Ben had anticipated that concern without her even asking. Carrie had never worked for such a kind, considerate employer. She already knew that after only three days at the church.

THE WOODEN PLAQUE HANGING OVER MOLLY'S DESK READ, *I'd Rather Be Baking!* in bright red letters, next to a yellow smiley face wearing a chef's hat. A gift from her older daughters, over ten years ago, when they were much younger and she had just opened the shop. The sign rarely failed to cheer her, but as she worked on the accounts today, sorting bills and making out checks for her employees, it made her feel even more drained, stretched thinner than a crêpe suzette.

I would rather be baking . . . than working on all this bookkeeping. Betty had taken home a wad of mail—including several bills—last Friday, and Molly wasn't sure yet if she had done anything with it. Molly had texted her earlier, but Betty hadn't answered. She was probably too busy with Nate. But the delay had saved Molly from spending *all* day on invoices. She was hoping that Betty had already paid those bills.

Still, the minutes passed like hours for Molly when it came to this part of the business. *How did I ever end up on the other end of a calculator instead of an egg beater? Pounds and ounces, tablespoons and cups, that's the only sort of math I'm good at.* These pages of numbers—invoices and deposits, cutting payroll checks and balancing accounts—they made her eyes cross. How did Betty do it and manage to make it all look so easy? It was one of those great mysteries.

Molly squinted at the balance she had scrawled at the bottom of the page. If she was going to cover the bills in the "to be paid" pile, she was going to have to dip into the loan for the new shop's renovations. Again. Much as she hated to do it, it seemed to be the only solution. Their account looked so low, despite the ton of business they had done on Thanksgiving. Molly just couldn't figure it out.

The scary part was, those renovations were evaporating the loan all by themselves. She considered Sam's advice about asking the bank for a larger loan. The bank would understand about the unexpected repairs, she thought, and an expanded loan would take some pressure off.

But she knew she had to talk to Betty first. She couldn't borrow more without asking her. For one thing, the bank would require both of their signatures on the new agreement. For another, Betty needed to know what was going on.

Betty was rarely an "I told you so" type, but she wouldn't even have to say it. Molly already felt responsible for the extra expenses and the extra debt, since she had insisted on the larger, grander location. No help for that now, she decided. She put aside the bills, stacked up the paychecks, and shoved the rest into a file folder.

Maybe it isn't such a desperate situation yet, she told herself. *If we sign up more parties and there are no more surprises with the new shop, we might squeak this one out.*

Her cell phone rang and she quickly checked the caller ID: Alicia Fillmore. Finally. This call could solve their problems—or at least a few of them. Mrs. Fillmore had been in touch throughout the week, asking a million questions about the menu and all the special touches Molly had proposed for the society's cocktail party. Molly cleared her throat and smiled. She had this one. She felt it in her bones.

"Alicia, hello. How's everything?" Molly said cheerfully.

"Meetings, meetings, meetings," her client replied. "I've just emerged from one with the Event Committee." Molly crossed her fingers and squeezed her eyes shut. "You've been so helpful, and we loved so many of your ideas . . . but we've decided to go with another caterer. The decision was really out of my hands," she added, in a way that sounded as if she wanted Willoughby's but someone else had swayed the group in another direction.

"Was it the price I quoted? That was just an estimate," Molly said quickly, trying to sound cheerful and calm. "Let me pull the paperwork. I'm sure we can do better for a long-standing client like the society."

"That's very generous of you . . . but I'm afraid it won't help. They've voted on this and, as I said, one or two committee members felt very strongly about trying someone new."

"I see," Molly said quietly.

"Your food is wonderful, and I know you would do a wonderful job with the rest of it. I will be sure to get in touch next time," she added.

"Yes, please do. And if anything changes, please keep us in mind," Molly said smoothly.

Who scooped this job right out from under my nose? Was it that Silver Spoon? I bet it was, Molly's inner voice whined silently. But, of course, she couldn't say that.

"Always happy to hear from you, Alicia," Molly said finally.

"I enjoy doing business with you, too, Molly," Alicia Fillmore said. "Enjoy your holidays."

Molly echoed the sentiments and said good-bye. She felt so frustrated and angry. And so sorry for herself, slapped in the face by that stupid committee. She knew who had curdled this pot of cream: Lillian Warwick Elliot. Not exactly a cheerleader for Willoughby's Fine Foods. And Lillian had at least one or two allies in that circle.

A gut feeling told her Silver Spoon had stolen this plum from her Christmas pudding. Betty knew everyone in town and could find out easily. Still, Molly hated to tell Betty that they had lost the job, even though she knew her pal would be sympathetic.

Betty would have reeled them in, Molly thought as she got up from her desk. She tried to shake it off, telling herself that she would find another major party. Even Silver Spoon couldn't steal *all* her business.

It was nearly evening. Her jacket and tote bag in hand, along with the bills to be put in the mail, Molly shut off her computer and the light above her desk.

When she looked up, Sonia was standing in the doorway. "Molly, you're still here. Thank goodness."

Molly didn't like her alarmed expression. "What's up?"

"The big oven broke down. It shoots right up to five hundred degrees. Look at this." Sonia held out something for Molly to see. It looked like a charcoal briquette in a charred silver wrapper. "I just lost four dozen chocolate cupcakes. I walked away for one minute, honest."

Molly could see that Sonia felt bad. Molly felt bad, too. But not for the same reason.

"Don't worry, it's not your fault," Molly said quickly. "That darned oven is over the hill. It's having a senior moment."

Molly sounded much lighter than she felt, quickly falling into fearless-leader mode as she walked into the kitchen with Sonia.

The oven had been acting up lately. She knew they needed a new one; repairs could go just so far. But the shop certainly couldn't afford a big-ticket item like that right now. She had barely paid for the appliances at the new store.

"Should I call that guy who came last time? He left a sticker." Sonia peered at the colorful sticker on the oven door.

"I'm not sure." Molly eyed the information, too. Had she paid this guy for his last visit? Or was the bill among the pile she had set aside? Or one that Betty had taken home with her last Friday? She checked her watch. It was after five. Whoever came tonight would charge double for an emergency call.

"I'm not sure what to do," she said honestly. "It might have to wait until tomorrow."

Sonia seemed surprised. "But what about the order? The night baker can't do all this with the small oven."

Sonia was only responsible for a few dozen cupcakes. If the oven hadn't failed, she would have been on her way home. The night baker, Eddie, made most of their wares. He didn't come in until ten o'clock.

Molly eyed the baking order for Friday, a long list that sat on the metal table. Eddie could never get through this with the small oven. There would be too little to sell tomorrow if she didn't do something.

She took off her coat, hung it up again, and took an apron down from the same rack. "I'm going to bake with the small oven, see where I get. I should be able to make a dent by the time Eddie comes in," Molly mused aloud. "Can you stay and help—for a little while?"

Sonia had a family and small children in day care. Her hours weren't that flexible. Molly had been there herself and had the T-shirt and totally understood. She felt bad even asking.

"Sure, for a little while," Sonia agreed. "I just need to make a phone call."

Molly smiled with relief. "I'd better call home, too. Let's hope that's the Little Oven That Could tonight . . . instead of one that's going to explode."

She tied on her apron and pulled out the shop's recipe binder, almost embarrassed she didn't know these formulas by heart anymore. Then she dialed Matt and tucked the phone against her cheek as she gathered bowls and ingredients and set up the big mixer. She quickly relayed the bad news about the oven. "I'm going to stay with Sonia and bake for tomorrow. I should be home around ten. Just make sure little Betty works on her science project. She keeps putting it off."

"I will. But I hate to see you working so hard, honey. Isn't there someone you can call to pitch in—some other employee?"

It was a logical question, but it still got under her skin. There was no one she could ask to run over on such short notice. People were home with their families, or doing whatever they did away from the shop; some had second jobs in other kitchens.

"There's no one to call on such short notice. It's no big deal," she insisted. She didn't mean to sound cross but knew she was starting to. "I'm sorry . . . it's been a long day. I really didn't need this on top of everything else. But you just have to roll with the punches sometimes."

"Very true. And you always do that so well," he reminded her. "I'll let you get to it. Check in later. Let me know how you're doing."

"I will," Molly said contritely. Matt was amazing, the best husband in the world, and she knew she had been totally blessed that he'd fallen in love with her. Molly tried to remember that. But sometimes he just didn't understand that her business could be a roller-coaster ride.

She focused on the recipe binder again, the little touches she liked to add coming back to her. *Way back when, you did it all yourself, baking all night and making all the deliveries every morning, too. Remember? You'd rather be baking? Well, here's your chance.*

Sonia stayed and worked with Molly until seven that evening, making a considerable dent in the order. After she left, Molly stirred and sifted on alone, her apron spattered, her hair covered in a bandana, and the radio tuned to her favorite pop music station and turned up loud to compete with the big mixer. She barely heard the back door of the shop open and was surprised to see Betty walk in.

Betty looked surprised to see her, too. "What are you doing here? It's almost nine o'clock."

"I know. What are you doing here?" Molly echoed, though she was certainly happy to see her.

"Just dropping this mail off on my way back from Peabody. Sorry, but I barely made a dent. I didn't want to hang on to it any longer, though. Looks like a few bills in there are late already."

"Yeah . . . I know." Molly nodded, feeling embarrassed. "I was working on the accounts today. I'll get it straightened out."

"I know you will. Sorry I couldn't do more. But why are you baking? Isn't Eddie coming in tonight?"

"Yeah, he should be here—soon, I hope." Molly checked the time. She had asked Eddie to come in earlier than the start of his usual shift, but he wasn't sure he could manage it. "The big oven broke, and I'm getting a start on the order. Eddie won't be able to do it all with the small one."

"Oh rats . . . that stupid oven. It's been going for a while. Guess it's time for a new one." Betty walked over to the baker's rack and picked out a soft roll that had been set there to cool. "I'm just going to steal one of these. I haven't had dinner yet."

"Take something home, a sandwich or soup or something. There's plenty in the fridge," Molly reminded her.

She really didn't want to get into the pros and cons of buying a new oven right now. For one thing, she was exhausted, and for another, if Betty was too overloaded and stressed to even go through a few bills, Molly doubted it was a good time to review all their financial issues.

"I think I will." Betty walked over to the fridge and peered into the shelves filled with take-out items. "I have to get home for a call with

Nate's doctor. I've been trying him all day, but he's been in surgery. His PA promised he would call me tonight."

Molly had started back to work, measuring more flour. But she set the measuring cup down as something in Betty's tone caught her attention. "Has something happened with Nate?"

She heard Betty sigh but couldn't see her face. She was still gazing into the refrigerator. "Same old, same old. He's in a lot of pain and not progressing much on walking. I don't want to bore you." She finally emerged with a sandwich and a small salad and shut the chrome door. "I did want to ask you about something, though, a letter I found in those bills. It looks like you hadn't even opened it."

Molly felt a chill of dread. Had she let something really important slip? Her voice came out in a squeak. "Really . . . what?"

"Here, read it." Betty put her take-out food aside and pulled a letter from the file of bills she had put on the worktable. "You're getting an award! Why didn't you tell me?"

"I am? That's news to me." Molly quickly unfolded the letter, relieved to see it wasn't a past-due bill. It was from the Cape Light Merchants' Association.

"Molly, you're too much. Just read it," Betty said, still smiling like the Cheshire Cat.

Molly finally did, reading quickly. "'Each year the Cape Light Merchants' Association honors an outstanding member of our village, a retail business owner who has made a significant contribution to the thriving economy of our community, and who also displays a dedication to service . . .' Blah-blah-blah . . . ," Molly added, fully expecting the letter to wind up with some pitch for a donation. "'We are happy to announce that this year, you have been chosen as our distinguished honoree, Business Owner of the Year, and your award will be presented at a gala cocktail party and banquet on Friday, December eighteenth, at the Spoon Harbor Inn.'"

Molly stared at Betty. "Business Owner of the Year? Is that nutty or what?"

"It's not nutty at all. It's about time they gave you that award. I can't believe Charlie Bates got it last year."

"He did?" Charlie owned the Clam Box down the street. In fact, he had practically been born there. Molly wasn't sure how he stayed in business. She thought the food was awful, but people loved the atmosphere, so he got away with it.

"In that case, I definitely deserve it," Molly decided. She checked the letter again. "If I'm getting an award, you get one, too. We should be sharing this," she insisted.

Betty shook her head. "Not this one. You started this business from scratch and put years in building it up before I ever came on the scene. Look at you—you're still at it, willing to do whatever it takes to make this business work. You definitely deserve all the glory. I wouldn't share it even if they asked me to."

Molly still didn't think it was fair but could see that Betty was sincere. She had started the business from nothing. Just a dream that she wouldn't give up. She had been working all sorts of random jobs, supporting her two girls as a single mother before she met Matt and baking at night and on weekends for local restaurants and coffee shops. Even the Clam Box.

It had taken even more grit to go back to school for business courses and get a loan from the bank to open the shop. And, most of all, courage to take the risk. But Molly had made the leap, and the bridge had appeared. Her life had changed so much since that time.

"You've come a long way, Molly. You've done a lot for this village, too. I'm so happy you're finally getting some recognition. You should be proud of your achievements. I know I'm proud as punch for you."

"Come on, Betty, you're embarrassing me now," Molly said, though she did think the award was a sweet note of victory, a validation for all those times she thought she couldn't do it—and the perfect reply to all those people who had doubted her, the ones who had hired her to clean their houses or looked down their noses because she had barely finished high school. Some who were still looking down their snooty noses at her. The news did take some of the sting out of losing the party at the Historical Society.

"When is it again? I want to mark my calendar right now," Betty said, taking out her phone.

"December eighteenth . . . right before Christmas. That stinks. We'll probably have ten parties to do that night. I hate to take off from work. Even if it is for an award."

Betty laughed at her. "You can run in with your apron on, say a few words, and run out again. How's that sound?"

"About right to me. I'll have to buy a dress and get my hair done and all that . . ." Molly didn't mind fluffing up, as she called it, once in a while. For fun. But this award thing seemed like a major chore . . . and it was coming at a very bad time.

"Don't worry about that. You'll look great," Betty promised her. "We'll figure out how to cover any parties that night, too. I don't think I saw any booked yet for that date."

Molly put the letter aside, feeling her spirits dim. "Not yet . . . and we didn't get the Historical Society either," she reported unhappily. "Alicia Fillmore called me with the bad news this afternoon."

"We didn't?" Betty sounded shocked, making Molly feel even worse. "What happened?"

Molly shrugged. "Alicia said it wasn't the price. I even offered a discount. And she said it wasn't our food. She sounded as if she wanted us, but said others on the committee wanted to go with someone new."

"That's too bad. I felt sure we had that one."

"I did, too . . . and I think I know who persuaded them away from us—Lillian Elliot. She was giving me the stink eye the whole time I was there . . . and I have a bad feeling the job went to Silver Spoon." Molly sighed, feeling upset all over again, mostly at herself. "I'm sorry I screwed it up. That one should have been a no-brainer."

Betty's look was not the least bit recriminating, and was instead very sympathetic. "I have to admit I'm surprised. But you can't blame yourself . . . or even Lillian. Sometimes clients just want a change. And committees are very hard to sell. Take it from me, they can rarely agree. You know what they say—'A giraffe was designed by a committee.'"

Molly finally smiled again. "I never heard that one. But I like it."

"It's true. And if they booked Silver Spoon . . . well, I hope they learn their lesson. Because Willoughby's Fine Foods is definitely a cut above and always will be. And now we can boast about our award-winning baker and caterer and founder," Betty reminded her.

"Ha! Good one. I guess that award counts for something."

The timer on the oven dinged before Betty could reply. Molly dashed over to the small oven and pulled open the door to check the pans of Danish she had been working on. She looked them over with a practiced eye, then lifted the edge of one with a spatula. "Not done yet; two more minutes," she reported.

"Can I help? I'll grab an apron and pitch in until Eddie gets here."

Molly was tempted to take Betty up on her offer, then glanced at her weary face, the circles under her eyes, and her pale complexion. Betty hadn't even had dinner yet and sounded anxious about the doctor's call she was waiting for. Molly didn't want to make her miss that.

"No way. You go home. I'm going to leave right after this batch of Danish is done. Eddie can do the rest." Molly didn't know that for sure, but wanted Betty to believe it.

"Okay, if you really don't need me. I still feel bad, leaving you here. Keep me posted about this oven situation, okay?"

"Don't worry, I've got it covered. And you helped me a lot just by hanging out and talking. Especially about those hysterical Historical Society ladies."

Betty laughed. "Anytime, pal. Wait until Lillian hears about your award. I wish I could see her face."

Molly did, too, come to think of it.

They said good night and Betty left. The kitchen seemed suddenly quiet, despite the noisy radio. *I miss Betty so much, talking things out with her, sharing these little defeats and victories; it's not just the bookkeeping or managing the staff. I wish Nate would hurry up and get better so she can come back to work again.*

Yeah, I know that sounds awfully selfish, God . . . Molly added, directing her thoughts to a higher plane. *But I have to be honest with you. Do you think you could help us out, please? When you have a minute?*

Chapter Five

Carrie took Noah to visit Dr. Carlson on Friday afternoon, right after school. She had explained the night before that she was taking him to a special doctor who just wanted to talk for a while. But as they were driving over, Noah seemed to have forgotten all about it—and forgotten her carefully worded explanation.

"Why do I need to go to a doctor? I don't feel sick." He watched out the window as his beloved playground shrank from view.

"Dr. Carlson isn't that kind of doctor. He just talks to you about your feelings." She chose her words carefully; she didn't want Noah to feel odd or ashamed about this. "He's very nice. He's like a good friend, who can help you with things that are bothering you, or anything you're worried or confused about," she continued. "Like starting in a new school . . . or if you have bad dreams." She glanced over to see if he understood.

His small brow was furrowed under thick bangs. "I don't have bad dreams anymore. Theo took care of that."

Carrie nodded, staring straight ahead at the road. She had been feeling a glimmer of a doubt about going through with this appointment, wondering if it was really necessary. But Noah's last reply brushed that question aside.

"You can tell the doctor about Theo. I think he would like to hear about an angel."

Noah shrugged, staring out the window again. "Okay. But there's not that much to tell."

They found the house easily, on a heavily wooded lane off the road that led down to the beach. There were few houses, and all were far apart. Dr. Carlson's stood at the end of the road across from a large tract of woods.

It was a small house, but cozy looking, painted forest green with amber- and cream-colored trim. Carrie thought the style was called "craftsman's cottage," but she wasn't sure. It was well kept, with a neat porch; a dark, polished wood door; brown shutters; and two dark green Adirondack chairs near the front door.

Dr. Carlson had told her that the office entrance was around the side. Carrie noticed a large garden in the back, though the flowering bushes and shrubs were mostly brown now. She wondered if Vera would let her help garden if they stayed at her house through the spring and summer. But first things first. She didn't want to think that far ahead right now.

She pressed the doorbell with one hand and held fast to Noah's hand with the other. They waited a moment, and he glanced up at her.

"Maybe the doctor forgot we were coming," Noah said quietly.

Was he nervous? She hoped not. She waited another moment, then pressed the bell again. "I don't think so. I just spoke to him last night."

"Look, Mom . . . that looks like Elsie, doesn't it?" Noah tugged on her hand and pointed.

It took Carrie a moment to remember who Noah was talking about.

Then she saw the big dog that had jumped up on her outside the bakery on Friday. "It does look like Elsie," she agreed. And she also recognized Elsie's owner, who had made an equal, if not greater, impression on her.

The pair walked quickly up the drive in their direction. Elsie was almost galloping, her handsome owner trying to keep up. Elsie was on a halter and leash this time. A good thing, because she seemed even bigger when in motion, her shaggy fur, white with reddish-brown markings, fluffing out in all directions, her big tail wagging wildly.

"Calm down, Elsie. Now sit, please." The man managed to get the excited dog to halt—though not sit—then he looked up at them. "Oh . . . hello. Nice to see you again." His smile grew even wider. His leather jacket hung open despite the cold, a striped scarf trailing around his neck. His khaki pants were smeared with mud here and there, and Carrie spotted a twig in his thick brown hair. She wondered if he was a neighbor who had come to give them a message from Dr. Carlson. Maybe the doctor couldn't see them today for some reason?

"Ms. Munro . . . and Noah?" Elsie's owner said, standing only a few feet away from them, as close as he could get while holding back the dog, who gave up all pretense of obedience and strained to greet and sniff them.

"Yes, we're here to see Dr. Carlson. Has he been called away for some reason?"

"No, not at all." He shook his head emphatically, smiling self-consciously now. "I'm Dr. Carlson. Have you been waiting long? I'm sorry. Elsie got off her leash, and I had to chase her down. I didn't expect you until half past three." He glanced at his watch, apologizing. "Maybe my watch is slow."

Carrie tried to hide her surprise. She had expected someone older, and not nearly as good-looking. And much more formal or official . . . or something? She certainly had not expected the man from the bakery with the silly, wild dog. She nearly laughed, but stopped herself just in time.

"It's all right, we just got here. I didn't recognize your voice on the phone when we made the appointment."

"I didn't recognize yours either," he replied. "It's very nice to meet you both. Again." He reached out and offered his hand, first shaking hands with Carrie and then with Noah. "The door is open. Please go on in. I'll follow, with this wild beast." His tone made Noah chuckle.

Carrie and Noah walked inside to find themselves in a waiting room. There were a small couch and an armchair, a few large plants, and a table with magazines.

Dr. Carlson followed and quickly opened one of the doors. He released the dog's leash and she ran off; into the house, Carrie assumed.

Noah looked around the waiting room. "Is this where we're going to talk, Dr. Carlson?" he asked.

"Please, both of you, call me Jeff," the therapist said with a smile. "Actually, you can hang up your coats out here and come into my office anytime you're ready. I thought we could talk in there."

Carrie slipped off her parka, then helped Noah with his. Dr. Carlson opened another door and stepped aside as they walked in.

He had already told her how the session would go. He would talk to Noah awhile with Carrie close by, and then he would ask Noah if he wanted to play a game or draw. Carrie would stay in the room with them so Noah would feel comfortable. In this first session, his aim was to build trust and help Noah feel relaxed talking to him, he had explained. They would talk about the angel if Noah brought it up. Or they might not. Not this time, anyway.

Dr. Carlson would be evaluating Noah to determine whether his fantasy was a sign of a deeper issue or something that she shouldn't be worried about. He might be able to tell that with one visit, or it might take longer, he'd told her.

Carrie knew this sort of thing couldn't be rushed, but she hoped it didn't take too long for the psychologist to get a sense of what was going on with her son.

The office was large and sunny, with bookshelves covering one wall and a row of large windows on the other. A dark orange couch and two armchairs stood near the door, a desk and chair not far from that. In another corner, Carrie noticed a soft round area rug; a child-sized table and chairs, with crayons and paper ready for drawing; and several baskets overflowing with toys.

Jeff Carlson sat in an armchair and beckoned them over with another reassuring smile. As they settled side by side on the couch, he began to talk, looking mostly at Noah. "Your mom told me that you just started at a new school. Is that in Cape Light?"

"Yup. I used to go to Bridge Street School, in Essex. But now I go to Harbor Elementary."

"What grade are you in?"

"Second. Mrs. Fischer is my teacher."

The psychologist leaned back in his seat, gazing at Noah with a relaxed smile and an interested expression. "I know Mrs. Fischer. I visit with children at the school sometimes. How do you like it so far?"

"Mrs. Fischer is nicer than my old teacher, Mrs. Barton. The kids are all right. I just started on Monday, so I don't really know yet."

"Yes, of course. It's only been a few days, not even a week," Dr. Carlson agreed. "What's your favorite thing to do at school?"

"Gym class . . . or lunchtime," Noah said with a grin.

The therapist laughed, a deep, warm sound. "You like sports?" Noah nodded. "What kind do you like to play?"

"Soccer and baseball. I was in Little League back home, in Worcester. Before me and Mom moved away. And my dad moved to Florida," he added.

Carrie felt a pinch in her heart hearing Noah call Worcester "home."

And hearing Noah mention his father. Noah rarely spoke of him. Weeks and even months passed between Kevin's calls. He didn't send a penny for Noah's support, not that she was surprised. Their home had turned into such a battleground at the end, she was surprised to hear Noah speak of it so wistfully. She hadn't made a real home for him since the divorce, had she? Although she had tried very hard.

"I've been to Worcester many times. They get a lot of snow in the winter. The most in the entire state, and that's saying a lot. We don't get nearly as much here, because we're close to the ocean," Jeff explained. "When did you live there, a long time ago?"

Carrie met the psychologist's glance briefly. She had told him all of this information yesterday, when she made the appointment. But she guessed it was important to hear how Noah explained all the changes he had been through the last two years.

Noah shrugged. "I was little. In kindergarten . . . Two years ago, I guess?" He glanced at Carrie, and she nodded.

"Yes, you were much younger," Dr. Carlson agreed. He waited a moment, then said, "I have a lot of toys here. Would you like to see them? Maybe we can play a game or draw some pictures."

Noah's expression brightened, and he turned to check out the toy corner. Then he glanced at Carrie. "Can I, Mom?"

Carrie smiled at him. "I think that's a good idea. I see some cool things back there."

Carrie was surprised to see Noah so at ease with the therapist. He was usually very shy with people he didn't know well, especially adults. That was part of the reason he didn't make friends that quickly. But Jeff Carlson had a very gentle way about him, a manner that was very warm and engaging.

"Let's see if we can find something fun to do. Your mom can wait right here for you."

Noah followed him over to the little table, where they both sat down. Carrie hid a smile as she noticed that Dr. Carlson's knees nearly hit his chin as he fitted himself into the little chair. She watched them a moment, then took the first magazine in the pile and made herself stare at an article. Actually, she was trying to eavesdrop, but they were talking softly, and she really couldn't hear what they were saying.

Carrie glanced at her watch, noticing the time was winding down. Noah was drawing a picture now as Dr. Carlson looked on, admiring his work. Noah liked to draw and seemed to have some talent for it. Though all children seem like great artists at his age—especially to their parents, she suspected.

A few minutes later, Noah ran over to her, the therapist trailing him. "Noah drew a picture of his family. I think it's very fine work. A lot of detail and very nice colors," he added. "He's a good artist."

Noah held it up for her to see, and Carrie was almost afraid to look. Did he miss Kevin more than he had ever let her know? Was that it? Had she done the wrong thing, breaking up their family?

But when she looked at the picture, she was totally taken in by the colorful array of stick figures, grass, and flowers. It didn't seem to be sad or mourning the past at all.

"That's beautiful, Noah." The picture really was splendid. She easily identified herself, with her wavy brown hair, which he had drawn with spaghetti squiggles; her blue eyes; and her favorite blue dress, a big triangle on the bottom of her body. She was holding the hand of a smaller figure, which was Noah, of course, with a scribble of brown hair on his head and a blue baseball cap, with a tiny red spot that she knew was supposed to be the emblem of the Red Sox. No towering figure of Kevin in sight, which was a relief.

"There's the grass and flowers," she said, pointing to the green stripes on the bottom of the page. "And there's the sun," she added, her fingertip on a big yellow circle in the corner of the page. "And this is a bird . . . or a butterfly?"

Noah frowned, and she felt a pang of conscience. Had she hurt his feelings by not recognizing the other figure in the drawing?

"It's Theo. My angel. He's part of the family now, too, Mom," Noah said in a matter-of-fact tone.

He glanced over his shoulder at Dr. Carlson, who wore the same calm expression she was getting to know. "Noah and I were talking a little about Theo. He sounds very helpful."

Carrie didn't know what to say. She wasn't sure she liked Dr. Carlson seeming so comfortable with this angel idea.

"Theo helps me a lot," Noah agreed.

"That's good, Noah," Jeff Carlson said. "It's good to have someone watching out for you."

Noah nodded, looking back at the picture again.

"It was fun talking with you today. And drawing," the therapist told him. "Maybe you and your mom could come back sometime."

Noah shrugged. "Sure. Maybe," he said. He didn't look opposed to the idea, Carrie noticed.

Dr. Carlson turned to Carrie, who had come to her feet. "I'll be in touch, Ms. Munro. I can call you this evening or over the weekend."

"Tonight would be fine. Is nine okay?" she asked, fairly certain she could get Noah into bed by then. "I can call you."

"Not a problem. I'll speak with you then."

Carrie glanced over at Noah as they drove toward Vera's house. "So, what do you think of Dr. Carlson?" she asked.

"He said I could call him Jeff," Noah reminded her. "I think he's nice . . . Mom, can we have a hamburger tonight at the Clam Box? Please?"

Carrie hadn't expected such a short answer followed up by a question on a completely different topic. But he had missed having an after-school snack, she remembered, and had to be hungry.

"Good idea. I'm hungry, too." She waited a moment, then said, "So you wouldn't mind seeing Dr. Carlson again? I mean, you may not have to. But if he thought you should. You didn't just say that so you wouldn't hurt his feelings?" she added, knowing how sensitive Noah could be to other people.

"It was all right. I had fun . . . Do you think he would let me play with Elsie next time? I wish he hadn't put her in another room."

Carrie smiled. She should have seen that one coming. "I don't know. I guess we could ask him."

After an early dinner at the Clam Box, she took Noah back to Vera's house, gave him a bath, and let him watch a DVD. At nine o'clock he was in bed with the lights off and seemed to be asleep.

Carrie slipped downstairs anyway, to make sure she had privacy. Vera was out for the evening and the house was empty. She made herself a cup of tea, then tried the number on her cell phone.

Jeff Carlson answered on the second ring, and after a brief but friendly greeting, he began talking about the session.

"I enjoyed spending time with Noah. He's very bright and open, not afraid to express his opinion. You described him as shy."

"He can be shy . . . but he wasn't with you," Carrie explained.

"I'm glad to hear that. It's important for Noah to trust me and feel comfortable. It seems to be a good start—if you want him to continue seeing me."

"I'm not sure," she said honestly. "I'm glad that he talked about the angel with you."

"We didn't talk about Theo too much. He just showed me the picture and explained who Theo is. He has a very strong belief in this personality. This guardian. It's very real to him."

"Yes, I know." Carrie didn't mean to sound abrupt. She knew that she had to have patience. Noah was just a little boy, and this situation had to be handled with sensitivity and care. But another part of her just wanted to get it over with. As if he had gotten a bad cold, and she could take him to a pediatrician and be prescribed a pill. But even medication for a cold takes time, she reminded herself.

"So your son has very little contact with his father?"

"Little to none," Carrie told him. "Maybe someday they'll have a relationship. I don't want Kevin to be a total mystery to him, but this seems to be Kevin's choice. He rarely called or came to see Noah when he had the chance, and now he's moved to Florida." Carrie paused, trying to keep from sounding too emotional. "I suppose Noah misses him, even if he never talks about him. Is that it? Is that why he's come up with this story?"

"Possibly," Dr. Carlson said. "But it may not be the only reason."

Carrie was not surprised to hear that, though it still made her feel sad and partly to blame. "I didn't intend to separate Noah from his father entirely. But my husband had a terrible temper. He never physically hurt either of us," she added, "but he drank a lot and had angry outbursts. It seemed just a matter of time before he would lose control. Noah began to act withdrawn and frightened. He began having nightmares all the time. And there were other problems, too. I did what I thought was best," she said finally. "Though there are bound to be some consequences for Noah. I wish that wasn't so. That's the part I do regret."

"I understand. It sounds like you did need to take him out of a very hostile environment. Noah is doing well, considering what you've told me about the last two years. He doesn't seem either withdrawn or frightened."

"No," Carrie agreed. "Once we got out of that house, Noah seemed to come back to himself. He's still shy, but he stopped startling at every sound. And the nightmares eased."

"Then you did the right thing for him."

Jeff Carlson's simple words made her feel worlds better. Carrie practically sighed aloud with relief.

"I don't think you should worry about his emotional health," he went on. "Whatever the reasons are for Noah's belief in this angel, he obviously needs this belief right now. It makes him feel safe and stronger. As if he has a good friend at his side, protecting him. At this age, some children are fixated on superheroes or sports champions or battling knights in video games. A lot of children have imaginary friends. Some professionals believe it's a sign of intelligence."

"I've heard that, too. But, Dr. Carlson, I'm afraid this angel thing is . . . maybe more than that. I think I told you that Noah lost his homework this week and told his teacher his angel would help him find it?"

"Yes, I remember that situation . . . and please, call me Jeff," he reminded her. "Did he find his homework that day?"

"It was under his bed. I wasn't in his bedroom when he found it, but he said later that Theo told him to look there." Relating this story made Carrie feel anxious about the situation all over again. "The thing is, Dr. . . . Jeff," she corrected herself, "Noah's father was . . . well, a liar, to be blunt about it. A very convincing one. He lied to me . . . to both of us . . . with such a straight face and so sincerely that I could never tell whether he was telling me the truth or not. I can't tell you how many times he told Noah some story or made some grand promise that he would never keep."

"I see. And you're wondering if Noah picked up this habit?"

"Yes, I am. I'm afraid Noah got the message that it's okay to make up stories. It's okay to lie to people—and himself. But it's not okay. I know his angel story seems harmless. And maybe it's much too soon to worry. But I just don't want Noah to think it's right to be anything less than honest. I'm afraid that if this goes on too long and Noah keeps talking about the angel and believing it's real, he'll never learn that."

Carrie stopped herself from saying more. The subject of her husband's dishonesty and all the hurt it had caused her and Noah touched on wounds that were still close to the surface, making her feel and sound much more emotional than she wanted.

Jeff didn't answer right away. Finally he said, "Thank you for telling me that, Carrie. I understand better now why this situation is disturbing for you. Maybe there is some basis there for Noah's behavior. I've only seen him once, so it's impossible to say. I can say that I didn't observe him exaggerating or being vague or duplicitous in the answers he gave to my questions about his experiences."

"What about the angel?" Carrie asked.

"For now, I'd call that imaginative. Overall, Noah was a lot more factual than most children his age, who do tend to exaggerate when they tell you a story. Because of the way we perceive things at that age, very much through our emotions," he reminded her. "It's a magical time and an important one, one that helps us renew our optimism and imagination as adults."

"I never thought of it that way," Carrie admitted.

"If Noah continues to see me, I'll look at his behavior in the context of everything you've told me. I will try to find out if this fantasy is a sign of some deeper issue he needs to work through. But I can't tell you that I'll try to 'talk him out of' the idea. So far, I can't see that it's harmful to him. In fact, it seems helpful right now."

Carrie couldn't deny that. Any challenges or problems Noah had lately didn't seem to worry him, because of this angel idea.

"I understand," she replied. She had to have patience. Noah was probably fine. Whatever was going on didn't seem serious. That's what Jeff was trying to tell her. "I do want to know if it's a sign of anything . . . more serious. I think Noah should see you again. At least a few times," she added cautiously.

"Good. I'm eager to work with him," Jeff replied. They set two appointments for the following week. Then Jeff asked, "Is there anything special he likes to play with at home? He can bring his own toys or games if he wants to."

"He did like the drawing . . . but he said if he came again, he wanted to play with your dog."

Jeff laughed, a deep, warm sound that made her smile. "That can be arranged. Elsie's too excitable to ever be a certified therapy dog, but she does help me from time to time."

"Oh, Noah will be very happy to hear that."

After they ended the call, Carrie sat in the quiet kitchen and finished her tea. She climbed up the back staircase to the second floor and peeked into Noah's room. He was fast asleep, clutching his stuffed rabbit. She walked in quietly and fixed his covers, then watched him breathing peacefully, his expression totally serene.

Maybe Noah was visiting Theo in his dreams, she thought wistfully. She did feel calmer and less worried about the situation after talking with Jeff Carlson. Something about him was very warm and reassuring. She wondered if that was just his training or his natural personality. He clearly loved children and related well to them. She wondered if he had children of his own. She hadn't noticed a wedding ring, but that didn't mean anything. Many men didn't wear one. He was very attractive and intelligent; she guessed there was a romantic partner somewhere in the picture.

What in the world was she thinking about that for? What difference did it make if Jeff Carlson was single or not? She had no interest in a social life right now. Not for a long time; not until she and Noah were properly settled.

Noah had tossed his covers off, and she leaned over and pulled them up again to his chest. She saw the picture he had drawn in Jeff's office, taped to the wall at the head of his bed. She stood back, gazing at it. Was it really such a bad thing to believe that some mightier, benevolent force was watching over them, guiding and helping them? Maybe not, she mused.

Standing alone in the dark, in a strange new place, Carrie wished—for just an instant—she could believe it, too.

CHAPTER SIX

"AMANDA? WHAT ARE YOU DOING HERE? IS EVERYTHING ALL right, honey?" Molly pulled the front door open and quickly stepped aside as her daughter and her daughter's boyfriend, Gabriel, walked in from the cold, bright Sunday morning.

Molly had just rolled out of bed, beckoned by the doorbell even before her alarm clock sounded. She tugged her bathrobe closed, chilled by a blast of cold air from outdoors.

"Everything's fine, Mom. Everything is great. Sorry we woke you up." Amanda quickly kissed her cheek. She glanced at Gabriel, and Molly noticed the two share a secret look.

"We got to town early, Mrs. Harding. I hope you don't mind that we stopped by?" he said politely.

"It's all right . . . we need to be up early today, anyway. We're lighting the Advent candles this morning. We're supposed to be at church a few minutes before the service starts."

That was all certainly true, but Molly did miss the extra hour in her cozy, warm bed that these surprise visitors had just stolen.

"I thought you were going to meet us at church today," Molly added as the two took off their coats and scarves in the entryway. "You must have made good time coming down from Portland."

"We did," Amanda replied.

Molly had already headed back to the kitchen to turn on the coffeemaker. Amanda and Gabriel followed. She'd known that they were coming to Cape Light today. That part wasn't a surprise. Amanda had been invited to play a solo at this morning's service, some special music for the first Sunday of Advent. In his thoughtful way, Reverend Ben had coordinated her visit with Molly, Matt, and little Betty lighting the candles. But the plan had been that they would all meet at church, and the couple would come back to the house afterward for brunch.

As the coffeemaker sputtered and hissed, Molly pulled several mugs from the closet and set out milk and sweetener.

"Where's Daddy? Is he up yet?" Amanda asked.

"I don't think so. He'll be down soon, once he smells the coffee."

"Maybe you should wake him up. And Betty, too," she added.

Molly gave her a quizzical look as she placed a bunch of teaspoons and napkins on the counter. "I will. In a minute." She stared into the cereal and cracker cupboard. "Do you guys want anything to eat? A little oatmeal or toast?"

"We're fine," Gabriel assured her.

When she turned again, Amanda had her hand out. "I had my nails done, Mom. I thought it was a pretty color. What do you think?"

Molly took hold of her daughter's left hand, surprised to hear that Amanda had even set foot in a nail salon. While her other daughters racked up frequent manicure miles, Amanda would tease them for their vanity. Had she finally been converted?

But in addition to the pale pink polish, which was not all that remarkable, Molly spotted a sparkling round diamond in a beautiful antique setting.

She stood with her mouth hanging open a moment, then hopped up and down, screaming, "You're engaged? You're engaged! Amanda . . . I can't believe it! You little rat! Why didn't you tell me?"

Molly was laughing and hugging Amanda and Gabriel both at the same time. "I'm so happy . . ." she wailed, feeling about to cry. Her legs gave way, and she landed on a kitchen stool. "I had no idea. What a shock . . . I'm going to have a heart attack . . ."

Amanda was laughing, too, and crying a little, Molly noticed. "Mom, calm down. Take a few deep breaths or something . . ."

"Molly, are you all right?" Matt rushed into the room in full emergency mode. He had obviously jumped out of bed when he heard the noise, dressed in his pajamas, his dark hair still mussed from sleep.

Molly just nodded and smiled. She waved at Amanda. "Tell your father. Go ahead."

"Daddy . . . Gabriel asked me to marry him last night. And I accepted. We wanted you and Mom to be the first to know." Amanda stood close to her fiancé, his arm wrapped tightly around her waist.

"I hope we have your blessing, sir," Gabriel added. "I love Amanda more than anything, and I'll do everything in my power to take care of her and make her happy."

Matt stood staring at the couple for a moment, his mouth hanging open a bit. Then he glanced at Molly. He looked as stunned as she had felt, and she wondered if he did not approve of the match for some reason.

Suddenly a huge smile broke out on his face, his eyes growing wide and shining joyfully. "That's wonderful news! Congratulations! I had a feeling this was going to happen soon."

Matt pulled Amanda close in a hug. She was still his little girl, after all was said and done. Then he stepped back and pumped Gabriel's hand, slapping him on the shoulder and finally hugging the young man close, too.

"What a way to start the day," Molly said, shaking her head with amazement.

"A wonderful way to start any day," Matt insisted. "What happy, happy news."

Molly had to agree. "I can't wait to announce this in church today." She glanced at Amanda, who was somewhat shy and felt uncomfortable with too much attention. *Unlike people like me, who adore it,* Molly thought. "I hope that's okay with you?" she asked the couple.

Amanda rolled her eyes and glanced at Gabriel. "I guess we expected that."

"If you don't, my mom will," Gabriel said with a laugh. "We're going to tell her this morning, too, before the service."

"I'll just have to get Reverend Ben to pick me first, then. I'm going to sit in the front row or something, so he sees me."

Everyone laughed, even though she was perfectly serious.

With all the excitement at home, Molly, Matt, and little Betty reached church just in time. Since they were lighting the candles today, the deacons had reserved them seats in the front row. Molly had forgotten about that perk. *How convenient,* she realized. *Close enough to enjoy Amanda's playing—and to catch Reverend Ben's attention when the time comes.*

Molly looked around, scanning the pews for someone she could share the happy news with. But Betty was sitting off to the side, and she could only wave at her. Sam and his family had come in but were sitting toward the back. She saw her mom and dad, sitting near Sam. She nearly got up and walked over, but the organ sounded the opening notes of the first hymn, and she sat back down again.

The choir was singing and marched into the sanctuary, down the center aisle. Molly readied herself to walk up to the altar with her family when the hymn was over. She and Matt had been invited to light the candles once before, years ago, when their older daughters were young. It felt like a bit of an honor, being chosen, though Reverend Ben and the deacons tried to give every family a turn.

She did feel proud of her family this morning, and she did feel blessed, she realized, glancing down the row at Matt, little Betty, and Amanda and Gabriel. It was a banner day, one that eclipsed all the stresses and business woes. A day that served to remind her of what was most important in life. Not broken ovens or fussy clients or even mystery mold hidden behind old wallboards.

It's easy to focus on life's blessings, here in a candlelit sanctuary, with a choir sweetly singing a Christmas hymn, she thought. *The trick is to remember this feeling the rest of the week—when all your plans are going haywire.* Molly closed her eyes and savored the last few bars of the hymn.

I can do better. I'm sure of it, she promised silently.

AT THE BACK OF THE CHURCH, CARRIE SAT WITH NOAH AND VERA. She followed along with the music in her hymnal but did not sing. Noah, who was sharing a hymnal with Vera, was singing loud enough for both of them.

Carrie had not intended to come to church, but Vera had persuaded her. They were sitting at breakfast when Vera started fretting about the weather, saying it looked like rain and one of the tires on her car looked flat. She was worried about missing the service, saying she had things to do at church today.

Carrie had offered to drive her there and pick her up. But somehow, Vera made it seem as if it would just be more efficient if Carrie and Noah came in and stayed for the service, pointing out that it would be interesting for Carrie to see what went on at the church on Sundays.

"And you should hear at least one of Reverend Ben's sermons," she added, sounding as if it wasn't quite polite of Carrie, being the minister's secretary now, not to hear him preach.

Carrie's mother had been a very gentle, spiritual soul, who attended church regularly and often took Carrie with her. But once Carrie was older and on her own, she had fallen out of the habit and even out of feeling some faith. Her marriage had left her disillusioned, too. She didn't begrudge others their beliefs. She almost envied Vera and Reverend Ben the comfort they seemed to get from the church. But she didn't feel that church was the right place for her. She felt it was dishonest somehow to participate.

She would come this once, for Vera's sake. Vera had been so good to them the past week. And Carrie was curious to hear Reverend Ben give a sermon. He was such an intelligent, thoughtful, and kind man; she hoped his sermon would reflect his personality. Most sermons she could remember were either boring or dark and gloomy.

Reverend Ben opened the service with the weekly announcements, which Carrie had typed up and practically knew by heart. There were still a few congregants coming in, and Vera poked her with a sharp elbow as an older couple was shown to seats nearby—a silver-haired woman walking on the arm of a small, wiry man, who was neatly attired in a three-piece suit, including a bright red bow tie. Obviously husband and wife, in their late seventies, Carrie would guess. Both were quite dignified looking.

"That's Lillian Warwick Elliot and her husband, Dr. Elliot. She's very well-known in town," her landlady confided in a hushed tone. "He is, too. Retired now. Sold his practice to Dr. Harding, up front, quite a long time ago now."

Carrie nodded; she had come across the Warwick name a few times this week. She didn't like to gossip, but it was interesting to connect faces with the names she'd read on church lists.

"Any other announcements I may have missed?" Reverend Ben asked.

A ruddy-cheeked, cheerful-looking woman raised her hand and then stood up to speak. "Sophie Potter. Still lives on Potter Orchard," Vera said quickly and quietly, "though her granddaughter runs it now. She's very active on committees. You're bound to meet her, too."

Carrie nodded again, trying to hear Sophie Potter's announcement. "I just want everyone to know we're holding a meeting after church about the Christmas Fair and the Adopt-a-Family project. Claire North is running that project this year."

A tall woman, with silvery-blond hair arranged in a neat bun, raised her hand and smiled. "Any help is welcome. If you can't come to the meeting, give me a call. We'll be printing our flyer very soon, with a shopping list."

"What's Adopt-a-Family? I didn't hear about that yet," Carrie whispered to Vera.

"The church is put in touch with a family who's in need of help at Christmastime. It's often a family getting back on their feet, moving to their own home after living in a shelter. They need all sorts of things to get started. And we buy gifts for the children to find under the tree. Practical items like boots and coats. But fun things, too."

"That sounds nice," Carrie replied. She understood what it was like to have a setback and then try to get a foothold on a slippery slope. She was practically in the middle of it herself.

Though Noah and I have come a long way since we first left Worcester. I do need to count my blessings, she reflected as the choir began to sing again. *A lot of people have it much worse. I have a good job and a nice place to live, and Noah is happy and healthy . . . except for this angel thing . . . I'll make a donation to that project,* Carrie decided. *It will be a good example for Noah at Christmas.*

A family walked up to the altar to light the first candle for Advent. Carrie had typed out the bulletin, so she knew all about this ceremony, and knew the couple's names, too. Molly and Dr. Matthew Harding and their daughters, Betty and Amanda. They all said their parts of the prayers, and Dr. Harding held his youngest daughter up so she could light the candle.

Now, instead of Vera whispering to her, Noah poked her arm and said, "I know that girl. She's in my class. Her name is Betty."

"Maybe you can say hello to her later," she whispered back. "Tell her she did a good job."

Noah looked horrified at that idea. "No way," he whispered, crossing his arms over his chest.

Carrie smiled and put her arm around his shoulders. She couldn't help feeling wistful as she watched the Harding family return to their seats. They looked so happy. She had been happy with Kevin for a short time, too. She had married him believing they would stay together forever. But it hadn't worked out that way. Maybe someday she would get it right. It was touching—and inspiring—to see such an obviously happy family.

Carrie thought Noah would get restless and bored quickly once the prayers started, giving her an excuse to wait outside for Vera. But Noah was surprisingly interested. Of course, he had gotten to know Reverend Ben a little over the past few days and was now quite focused, watching him at work. He had already remarked about how different the pastor looked in his white robes, compared to his weekday appearance in an ordinary sports coat and tie.

When Reverend Ben invited all the children to come up to the front of the sanctuary, Carrie thought Noah would hang back. But he went up quickly, on his own, after glancing her way for permission. Perhaps he just wanted a chance to visit Betty Harding, Carrie thought with a smile. She saw him choose a spot by the blond-haired little girl when the children sat down on the carpet for the children's sermon.

Reverend Ben sat on a small stool, close to their level, and talked to them about the Scripture lesson in a simple and amusing way. Then the children left the sanctuary for Bible school, shepherded by their teachers.

Noah came back to their row but didn't sit down, asking instead if he could go, too. Carrie was surprised. "Sure, I guess so . . . Do you want me to walk you down to the classroom?"

Noah shrugged. "Okay. That'd be good."

Carrie got up from her seat to go with him. "I'll be right back," she whispered to Vera.

"Don't worry, I'll save your seat," Vera replied. Carrie could tell by the spark in her eyes she was teasing—and also pleased to see that Noah wanted to go to Sunday school.

See? Just what I told you, Vera might have said to her right then and there. *Church is good for a child. I knew he would like it.*

Carrie's guess was that Noah was interested by the novelty of church, but his interest wouldn't last very long. In fact, half an hour of Sunday school might change his mind.

She quickly settled him in the right room for his age group, then came upstairs again. When she returned to the sanctuary, the sermon was just starting.

". . . and as we all know, the Christmas story starts with the angel Gabriel's visit to Mary, and the message that she will give birth to a very special child. That's how we begin the season of Advent, the weeks between Thanksgiving and Christmas Day—which for many of us is a very hectic shopping and preparation marathon," he said, making many laugh.

"But for us, in this church, it's very much like the anticipation of any extended family for the birth of a new baby. It's a time of hope and expectation. And preparation.

"Did Mary and Joseph make a wish list at Babies"R"Us—including cribs, swings, jogging strollers, and maybe a special padded, infant donkey seat?" he added, making everyone laugh again. "Of course not. Though even in that day, there were probably customs and comforts for laboring mothers and newborns that Mary and her baby went without.

"I believe that this, too, is a metaphor for us, a spiritual lesson to contemplate," he added in a more serious tone. "I can't help but feel each year as Christmas approaches that I should be ever more mindful not to get caught up in the outer preparation. The shopping, decorations, food—all of which is necessary in its own way, certainly. But it can also be a hollow effort, a monthlong to-do list, performed without pleasure—or even a deeper sense of what we're celebrating. One that robs us of the sense of joy and wonder in this truly miraculous, blessed event."

He paused and took a breath. "So, where do we find the line between joyful anticipation and stressful expectation? While the weeks between Thanksgiving and Christmas are filled with hurried activity for many of us, I ask you all this year to pause and look inward. Look away from TV commercials and gift catalogues, to the spiritual message—and the questions—inspired by the angel Gabriel's visit to Mary, which we find in Luke, chapter one:

"'And the angel said unto her, Fear not, Mary: for thou hast found favour with God,'" Reverend Ben read from his Bible. "'And, behold, thou shalt conceive in thy womb, and bring forth a son, and shalt call his name JESUS. He shall be great and shall be called the Son of the Highest; and the Lord God shall give unto him the throne of his father David: And he shall reign over the house of Jacob for ever; and of his kingdom there shall be no end.'"

Reverend Ben paused and looked up again. "What does that mean? How do we, as the extended family of this radiant, expectant mother, prepare for the birth of a child such as this?" He smiled calmly, his gaze sweeping over the sanctuary. "In the coming weeks, in this season of Advent, those are the most important preparations for Christmas we can make. To contemplate with joyful, grateful hearts the imminent arrival of Mary's unborn. To ask how we can best love and serve Him."

Carrie soaked up every word, surprised at how her attention had not wandered once from Reverend Ben's sermon. He was a relaxed and down-to-earth speaker, talking to his congregation in a conversational and even humorous tone, as he might talk to a good friend.

Her mother's church had been nothing like this. That minister was severe and serious, always talking about sin and temptation in a way that made her feel frightened and even guilty. But Reverend Ben had a special talent for putting spiritual ideas in everyday language. His sermon touched her and made her see her life differently, and think about things she hadn't considered for a long time. The last two Christmases, all she could think about was that she and Noah on their own were free from Kevin. She hadn't thought much about the meaning of the season, only about giving Noah the best holiday she could. But now she felt safer, stronger, and maybe there was room in her life for a little more of the true Christmas spirit.

After the sermon, Reverend Ben announced it was time for the congregation to share any happy events of their week or any serious concerns.

Carrie saw Molly Harding waving her hand wildly in the front row. Reverend Ben was standing right in front of her and stepped back, wide eyed with mock surprise. "Yes, Molly, please. If you wave any harder, you might become airborne," he teased.

"Reverend Ben, I love you . . . and I'm going to ignore that." Molly laughed and stood up, tugging down the jacket of her red wool suit. She was a pretty woman with bright blue eyes and thick, dark hair that fell to her shoulders, curling in all directions. "I do feel like I might float away today. We have some big news. My daughter Amanda and her boyfriend, Gabriel Bailey, are engaged to be married. They just told us this morning."

"What wonderful news. Congratulations, everyone!" Reverend Ben smiled happily, and the congregation broke out in applause.

Vera leaned closer to give Carrie the inside scoop. "Amanda is actually her stepdaughter, Matt's child from his first marriage. But the girl lost her mother when she was very young, and she and Molly are quite close. The boy, Gabriel, works in stained glass. He fixed all these windows when they were ruined by that big storm a few years ago. Did an excellent job, too." Carrie gazed at the beautiful stained-glass windows that graced the sanctuary. She had noticed them before, a perfect complement to the church, which was mostly made of dark gray stone.

"I knew they'd be married soon," Vera added, as if she wasn't surprised at all.

Carrie smiled at her but didn't reply. She wished the young couple happiness and hoped it all worked out for them. A loving, close family helped. They seemed to have that on their side already.

After the sharing of Joys and Concerns, Amanda Harding played a beautiful piece by Bach on the cello. The service ended soon after that, with Reverend Ben moving to the back of the sanctuary during the last hymn to give a final blessing.

Carrie stood quietly, head bowed, listening to his closing words and feeling an uncommon sense of peace. When she lifted her head, she found Vera watching her.

"Would you like to go to coffee hour? Everyone's very friendly."

"I'm sure they are." Carrie smiled, thinking that if the church ever lacked for members, Reverend Ben ought to put Vera on the job. "But I think Noah will be a little restless after Sunday school. Maybe another time. I'll take him to the playground for a while, and we'll wait for you," she offered.

She did think Noah would be ready for some fresh air by now. Sitting through the service had been enough church for her for one day, too. But she didn't want to hurt Vera's feelings or leave her stranded.

Vera patted her arm. "Don't worry, dear. I'll catch a ride with Claire or Sophie. You ought to go find Noah. The children will be upstairs by now and eating all the cookies in Fellowship Hall. And don't forget, you and Noah are going to help trim my Christmas tree later, right?"

"Absolutely. Noah can't wait," Carrie said, grateful again for the invitation. "We'll bring home some pizza, so no one has to cook."

"That sounds perfect."

Yesterday, while Carrie had been carrying some of her empty boxes to the basement, Vera had been struggling to bring up her Christmas decorations and artificial tree. Carrie and Noah had helped her, of course, and Vera had asked if they wanted to help her put the tree up Sunday night.

"Maybe you have a few ornaments you would like to hang on it, too. And we can all put our gifts under it before Christmas," Vera suggested.

Carrie had been pleased by the invitation. It solved a problem for her. She knew Noah wanted a Christmas tree and didn't know if a small one in his room would be enough to make him happy.

Carrie had liked Vera the first time they met, but she hadn't expected to get along with her quite so well. Vera was a very kind and easygoing person and had done a lot to help Carrie and Noah feel comfortable in her home. Not like boarders at all, or at least not what Carrie had expected it would feel like to assume that title.

As Vera headed off to meet up with her committee, Carrie looked for Noah and soon found him in the hallway, near the church office, looking for her, too.

"Hi, honey. Ready to go?"

"I guess so . . . They have snacks in there," he told her, glancing at Fellowship Hall.

"Yes, I know. But I thought we would get some lunch in town and go to the playground." Maybe he would see some children from school there, she thought, or make some new friends. "How does that sound?"

Noah liked that plan just as well and quickly pulled on his coat and gloves. Carrie was already in her coat, and they headed for the glass doors. But not before Reverend Ben glanced her way. He was standing near the big doors of the sanctuary, greeting church members who waited patiently in line to speak to him. He was well liked here, that was for sure.

He caught her eye, nodded and smiled. Carrie smiled back. But as she walked away she wondered if he, too, would now be encouraging her to attend services. She didn't think so. He wasn't that type. He had stated very plainly, when he described the job, that church employees were not expected to be members of the congregation.

The service had been much nicer than she had expected, much more upbeat and relaxed. But she didn't plan on making a habit of coming to church on Sunday. This job was only temporary, and their time in Cape Light might be temporary, too.

BY THE TIME MOLLY, MATT, AND THE HAPPY COUPLE HAD ACCEPTED all the good wishes bestowed by friends and family after the service, the number of brunch guests had almost doubled. Molly swung by her shop to pick up more crumb cake, croissants, muffins, and a few quiches to pop in the oven. She already had a fridge full of ingredients—including a double batch of waffle batter—ready to go, but worried it wouldn't be enough.

It was all hands on deck when they got back to the house. Matt and Gabriel finished setting the table in the dining room as Amanda and Molly took over the kitchen. Little Betty ran between the two rooms, happy to do whatever anyone asked.

Matt shook his head in resignation, watching Molly and Amanda set out the array of baked goods and breakfast foods on large platters. "Practicing for the wedding reception already?"

Molly laughed. "Good one, but I think I have time for that."

"Actually, Mom, since you brought it up . . . we don't want to wait that long," Amanda said cautiously.

Gabriel was in the freezer, filling an ice bucket, and quickly turned to chime in. "We'd like to get married really soon."

Molly nodded, careful of her reaction. "Soon . . . like in a year or so? Next spring," she offered. Most brides she worked with took two years to plan a wedding. Even a year was cutting it close.

Amanda and Gabriel clearly had other ideas. They glanced at each other in surprise. "Next spring? We were thinking more like this spring," Amanda replied. "February or March?"

Molly could not hide her reaction. In addition to the giant wave of work planning her own daughter's wedding would involve, she saw a giant meteor of expenses hurtling toward her.

She swallowed back a lump of panic, her voice coming out in a squeak. "We can't plan a nice wedding in four months, honey. That's just not possible. A year from now, maybe, if we get right on it." She struggled to sound calm and reasonable. "But it's hard to get married in the winter, messy and difficult. Snow boots do not go well with a wedding gown," she warned, hoping to push their expectations a few months further on the calendar.

"What about this summer? Late summer," Amanda negotiated. "Like, eight months from now?"

"This summer would be good, Mrs. Harding," Gabriel agreed, putting an arm around Amanda's shoulder and looking at her with so much love that Molly felt her resistance melt. *Lovebirds, of course they want to get married soon.*

Still, she persisted, hoping to give herself some breathing space between business expenses and wedding costs. She wanted Willoughby's to be solidly in the black before she took on a new round of bills. "The fall is better, September or October. It's still hot in August. You'll melt in your formal wear. Does not look attractive in the photo album."

"The symphony starts by then, Mom," Amanda reminded her. "I'll be too busy. We won't be able to have a honeymoon."

Molly sighed, feeling cornered. She glanced at Matt for some support, but he, of course, was oblivious to her dilemma. "I like the late summer idea. Maybe Labor Day weekend?" he suggested. "That would be good for out-of-town guests, and the weather is reasonable by then. If anyone can plan a great wedding quickly, it's you, hon. I have no worries."

Molly glared at him. *Traitor,* she thought silently.

"And there are a lot more flowers in the summer," little Betty said logically. "That's important for the flower girl, and that's me." Amanda had already named her bridesmaids: all of her sisters, including Betty, and two friends from college.

Molly was relieved to hear the doorbell ring, ending the conversation. The first of their guests had arrived.

"I'll get it!" Little Betty ran to the entryway. "It's Grandma and Grandpa . . . I see their car."

"Should Gabe and I start the waffles, Mom?" Amanda was already wearing an apron, and she helped Gabriel with his.

"Absolutely, you guys take over on the waffle iron. We need to get you two into Cooking Boot Camp pronto if you're going to get married that quickly." Molly smiled at the happy couple, and they smiled back, knowing they'd gotten their way.

A SHORT TIME LATER, THE SEATS AROUND THE LARGE DINING ROOM table were filled with guests—almost as many as they had entertained on Thanksgiving: Molly's parents, Marie and Joe Morgan; Sam and his wife, Jessica; and their two younger children, Tyler and Lily. Betty showed up, too, looking tired but thrilled about the wedding announcement.

Lillian and Ezra Elliot, her brother Sam's in-laws, had been sitting next to Jessica at church, and Molly had felt obliged to extend the invitation to them. Lillian had declined, claiming they had a prior engagement. From the surprised look on Ezra's face, Molly wasn't sure that was true. She wondered if Lillian felt too guilty to be her guest after ruining the Historical Society deal.

That's not exactly fair, Molly reminded herself. She had no proof it was Lillian who turned the committee against her. And Reverend Ben's sermon had struck a chord with her. She did need to put aside these petty stresses and worries and focus on the blessings of the season.

This was a day to celebrate and savor, a true milestone for their family, she realized. She couldn't waste it being distracted by things she couldn't change or situations that truly didn't matter.

She watched Amanda and Gabriel show off her ring and answer questions about their plans, their glowing faces putting her weekday struggles into perspective. Her family was her true joy, her true treasure. She would be wise to count her blessings and remember that.

Betty had to leave early to get to the rehab center, though she had barely been at Molly's house long enough for a quick bite and some coffee. Molly walked her to the door, sorry to see her go.

"I'm so glad you came. I wish you could stay a little longer—and help me keep control of all the wedding talk," Molly told her friend. "I don't think Amanda has any concept of reality in that department."

Betty laughed. "I can see that. Eight months isn't much time. We'll need to hustle to pull this one together."

"Yeah, we will." Molly was happy to hear Betty include herself in the effort.

"They're probably not thinking of a big wedding. That should make it easier," Betty added.

"Good point. A fast wedding just can't be a big wedding. I'll find a way to mention that to the happy couple."

"You do that. I'm off to Peabody. Nate is going to love these waffles," Betty added, picking up the care package Molly had prepared.

"It's the least we can do. Give him our best." She and Betty shared a quick hug.

"I'm going to come in this week, a few hours at least," Betty promised. "I can tell things are heating up at the shop. I hate to leave you with all the work."

"Nate comes first, but any time you can spare would be a huge help," Molly said honestly. *And then I'll tell her about our finances,* Molly promised herself.

When Molly returned to her guests, the men had disappeared to the family room to watch a football game. Amanda had her laptop open on the kitchen table, and her sisters, Lauren and Jillian, were both on the screen, in separate little boxes.

"Hi, Mom!" Lauren sang out. Molly stood by the laptop and waved.

"Hi, honey. Can you see me? It always freaks me out when you girls do this Skype thing," she confessed.

All of her daughters laughed at her, on-screen and in the room. "We were just talking about the dresses," Amanda said. "I'm thinking long. They look better in the pictures."

"Not always," Molly mused. "It depends on the dress and the photographer. You may not want such a formal look for a smaller wedding," she added.

"Oh, I don't think it will be small, Mom," Amanda said quickly. "Gabriel and I both have big families. And you and Daddy have a lot of friends. And Gabriel and I have a lot we need to invite, too."

Her sister-in-law Jessica glanced at Molly, sensing her dismay. "It's hard to make a guest list for a wedding," she said diplomatically. "Don't they have a computer program or a phone app for that yet?"

Molly sat at the table and poured herself more coffee. "I don't think so, but that's a great idea."

But even such a handy tool would not help her now. Amanda was right. Both the bride's and the groom's families were large and close-knit. No way were they going to slide by with less than one hundred and fifty on the list . . . More like two hundred when all was said and done. Molly quickly calculated the cost of food, drink, gowns, flowers, music, and all the extras, and silently shuddered.

Amanda, who had ended the Skype call, now turned the laptop screen toward her mom. "I've found some gowns online I like. Want to see?" She showed Molly a beautiful, elegant ivory satin gown.

"Oh, honey, you'll look gorgeous in that," Molly said sincerely. She met Amanda's glance and smiled, feeling suddenly teary. "I can't wait to see you walk down the aisle. You're going to be the most beautiful bride in the world."

"Mom, please don't get all gloppy on me." Amanda patted her hand.

"I can't help it. I love seeing you so happy, sweetheart."

Any worries about pulling the wedding together at top speed, or even the expense, totally melted when she focused on Amanda. Why bring dark clouds on this happy day? What was money for anyway, if not to help her family? To make the ones she loved most happy? She would do anything for her daughters—even plan a big, fast, wonderful wedding, if that's what Amanda wanted.

Piece of cake, Molly told herself. Five tiers, trimmed with miniature orchids and maybe rose-colored satin ribbon? She could see it now.

VERA'S CHRISTMAS TREE WAS NOT VERY TALL. IT WAS EASY ENOUGH for the three of them to carry it into the house and set it up in a stand in the corner of the living room. Carrie worked on the lights while Vera and Noah sifted through boxes of ornaments and other decorations, some Vera's and others belonging to Carrie and Noah.

"I get tired of my Christmas decorations. You put on as many of yours as you like," Carrie heard Vera tell Noah. "I'll just work on these nutcrackers and music boxes."

Noah was very pleased to be in charge of the ornaments—a very kind gesture, Carrie thought; she suspected that Vera wasn't bored with her own selection at all. At Vera's stage of life, most people didn't even bother putting up a tree. Vera's Christmas spirit was clearly still in its prime.

She and Noah didn't have all that many ornaments, so there was still plenty of space for Vera's, and the boughs of the little tree were soon full of decorations and twinkling with lights.

"How about a tree topper? I don't think this star works anymore." Vera stared down at the ornament in her hand, a star with lights inside that she must have purchased decades ago, when her own daughter was about Noah's age. "The lightbulbs finally wore out," she decided after plugging it in a few times. "We sure got our money's worth, though." She put the ornament aside and stared up at the empty spot again. "That was my only one."

"Sorry, we don't have a tree topper." Carrie knew this without checking. "I'll look around this week and buy something for you."

"I can make one," Noah said. "The teacher showed us how today in Sunday school."

"Sounds good to me," Vera said quickly. "Is it hard to do?"

"It's easy. I just need some paper and tape and stuff. I can make it right now. You'll see."

Before Carrie or Vera could ask more, Noah ran up to his room. Vera laughed and started closing up the empty boxes. "'Ask, and it shall be given to you . . .'"

Seek, and ye shall find, Carrie finished silently. A comforting line of

Scripture, she thought, even if it didn't always turn out to be true. True enough in this case, it seemed.

Working together, Carrie and Vera quickly cleared the boxes from the room. "I think we did a nice job," Vera said, surveying her transformed living room. "Now, there's Christmas for you."

"Very pretty," Carrie agreed. "You have the perfect house for Christmas, Vera."

Vera blushed with the compliment, but Carrie was sincere. Vera's cozy, antique rooms and furnishings were the perfect match for Christmas decorations. The room looked lovely with the tree decorated and glowing with lights, the wooden mantle over the fireplace draped with pine boughs and displaying Vera's collection of nutcrackers and miniature, snow-covered houses.

There were also beautiful Christmas music boxes and snow globes scattered about. A carved wooden bear, with a red cap and scarf, stood knee-high next to the fireplace, where Noah had already hung his stocking.

"Thank you, Vera, for letting us decorate your tree. It meant a lot to Noah and to me," Carrie said. "I really didn't know what I was going to do for him . . . have a little, artificial tabletop tree in his room or something."

"Don't be silly. No need to thank me. I appreciate all the help, and it's nice to have company to do these things. It's really no fun alone," she admitted. Carrie knew that was true, but thought it was generous of Vera to be so considerate of them anyway.

The table was set and the pizza hot when Carrie finally called Noah down to dinner. She called from the back staircase in the kitchen, and he quickly came pounding down the steps.

"I finished. Here it is," he announced as he jumped into the room.

He held out a decoration made from construction paper: a white upside-down cone with a circle of paper for a head taped on top. Some yellow crayon had been drawn in for hair, along with two bright blue eyes. Two strips for arms were taped in place, then pulled forward, so that it looked like the hands were clasped in prayer. But the most striking feature on the figure consisted of two large, crescent-shaped wings that were covered in tinfoil and taped to the figure's back.

Vera spoke first, luckily, because all Carrie could do was stand there with a shocked, frozen smile on her face as Noah proudly set his creation on the kitchen table.

"My goodness, that's beautiful, Noah. I always wanted an angel on the top of my tree. Did you really make that all by yourself? Just now?" Vera was clearly delighted.

"Yup." Noah nodded, beaming with pride. "The wings were the hardest part. The foil kept wrinkling."

"Well, it looks perfect to me," Vera insisted.

"Very pretty, honey. I thought you were going to cut out a big star," Carrie said. She guessed Theo had given Noah the idea. Or at least had served as the model. "Let's have our pizza while it's hot, and you can put the angel on top after dinner, before you go up to bed," Carrie suggested.

"Good idea," Vera agreed. "All that up and down the stairs today has worked up my appetite. What a treat! I hardly ever have pizza."

"I hardly have it either, even though it's my favorite," Noah confided.

Vera laughed. "Well, here it is. Let's enjoy it. It wouldn't be special if we had it every day."

DINNER WAS CLEARED UP QUICKLY, AND JUST AS CARRIE PROMISED, Noah climbed the stepladder and placed the paper angel on top of the tree while Vera and Carrie looked on.

Vera applauded. "It couldn't look prettier if I bought one in town. Thank you, Noah. I'll treasure it always."

"It's just paper, Vera. It might not last that long. But I can always make you a new one," Noah replied.

Carrie took him up to bed and kept him focused as he washed up and changed into his pajamas. He was eager to get back to the book he was reading, *Stuart Little*, about the adventures of a brave little mouse, which sat open on the nightstand. Carrie understood; it had been one of her favorites, too.

Mrs. Fischer wanted all her students to read at least twenty minutes a day. Not a problem for Noah, who had learned to read in kindergarten and was already tackling thick chapter books. Carrie knew it was a trait to be encouraged. She had found the old saying was true: You could never be lonely with a good book at hand. During the difficult years of her marriage and afterward, she had turned to reading so many times as a wonderful escape from real life. But now she wondered if Noah's love for stories and his active imagination had created his angel friend.

As she expected, Noah returned from the bathroom and jumped into bed, grabbing the book before he was even under the covers. "I can read a little, right?" he asked her.

"Sure. Twenty minutes. Then shut out the light, okay?" She watched as he flipped through the pages to find his place. "Do you remember where you were in the story?"

He nodded. "Stuart is in a sailboat race in a pond in Central Park. That's in New York City. There's a huge storm. His boat might sink," he added, sounding very concerned.

"Yes, I remember," she replied with a smile. She glanced at his desk. A notebook and math textbook were piled neatly, a test sheet on top. Noah hadn't failed, but he hadn't done that well. She noticed he had already made corrections on the problems he had missed.

"I almost forgot," he said. "You have to sign that test."

Carrie looked the page over quickly and signed on top. "You did these all perfectly. What happened the first time? Did you forget to study?"

Noah shook his head. "Theo helped me fix them. He won't give me answers on a test, though. That's not right."

"No, that wouldn't be good," Carrie agreed. She wasn't going to comment on the angel thing either way, she had decided. Her new policy, though it was a hard one to stick to.

Noah suddenly looked up from his book. "Are we going to church again next Sunday?"

"I'm not sure." Carrie folded his sweatshirt and set it on the back of a chair. "Why do you ask?"

"Just wondering. Reverend Ben looks cool in his robe."

Not the word she would have used, but she knew what he meant and smiled again. "We can go from time to time, if you want. But we don't need to go every week. Mrs. Honeyfield will be back after the holidays, and I'll need to find a new job . . . I'm not sure it makes sense to join a church right now," she said finally.

"I know. But I hope you do find another job here. I like it better than Essex. There's more to do. I like my school better, too," he added, slipping down farther under the covers.

"I will do my best to find a new job nearby. Don't worry. We won't move again," she promised. She was determined to give Noah some real stability in his life.

"Good, Mom. Because Theo thinks this is a good place for us to stay. And he likes the church. He's been in a lot of them."

"Your angel came to church with us?" No way to avoid the subject, was there?

"Sure. He goes everywhere with me. Wouldn't an angel want to go to church? I bet he goes sometimes even without me," Noah mused.

"That does make sense," Carrie agreed quietly. She walked back and sat on the edge of his bed. "Would you like to see some of your friends in Essex after school this week? I can set up a playdate for you."

It wouldn't be easy, fitting that in around her office hours, but Carrie felt she had to make the effort. Maybe Noah just felt lonely. Maybe that's all there was to this angel thing. "I'm sorry we had to move, and you have to make all new friends."

Noah shrugged. "It's okay, Mom. I'm going to play basketball at church this week, remember? I don't need to see the kids from Essex, too."

"Right. I almost forgot." The after-school basketball practice was really for church members, but Reverend Ben had worked it out so that Noah could play, which was good for Carrie, too—keeping Noah active and having fun while she finished her work. "But if you want some playdates, just let me know. I'm sure I can figure it out. Good night, honey. Have a good sleep." Carrie leaned over and kissed his forehead.

"'Night, Mom," he murmured, his eyes returning to his book.

Carrie slipped out of the room, wondering if Noah's angel would put on sneakers and shorts this week. Wings would give him an unfair advantage at jump shots. She had to smile at the idea. Still, when it came to Noah's angel, she felt in over her head. She was hoping Noah's visits with Jeff Carlson would sort it all out.

Chapter Seven

Ever since Sunday morning, Molly had felt as if she were floating on a cloud, buoyed by the news of Amanda's engagement. She felt a new wave of happiness each time she told someone the story.

On Wednesday morning, she swept into the shop's kitchen to find the early crew busy at work. Somehow the oven was working, the kitchen clanging and humming with activity, the radio set to the younger staff's favorite station—chaotic, electronic noise with the occasional wailed lyrics thrown in. Played at full blast, of course.

She hung up her jacket and found an apron, tying it over her business outfit. "Hi, guys. How's it going?" She hated to feel like a control freak—as some employees did call her behind her back—but she could rarely resist walking around and looking over everyone's work. Especially when it came to the few new hires, who had not been completely trained in the Willoughby Way yet.

"What are you working on, Oscar?" she asked their new cook. "Potato leek?" She peered into the huge soup pot and picked up a spoon, poised for a taste test.

Oscar stepped back and shrugged. "Taste it if you want. But that recipe Sonia gave me is pathetic. Don't you have a different one?"

Molly put the spoon aside, bristling. "What's the problem? In your humble opinion," she added tartly.

Fresh out of cooking school, the kid thought he was God's gift to the culinary arts. He shrugged and rattled off a list of random, exotic, and somewhat ridiculous ingredients he would prefer, including piquillo peppers, sautéed chive flowers, and fiddlehead ferns, which weren't even in season. Molly could barely keep from laughing.

"Interesting. But definitely not our style here. If you don't like the soup, don't eat it," she suggested with a tight smile. "Stick to the script and you'll be fine."

She heard him muttering as she walked over to the worktable, where Abby and Kira were mixing fillings for quiche Lorraine and a batch of vegetable paté. Their baking assistant, Teddy, was glazing a tray of beautiful pear tarts.

"Gorgeous, Teddy. The crust is the perfect color," she praised him.

"Thanks, Mol." Teddy smiled and carried the tray out to the storefront.

"There was a mishap in the cold box and we lost a carton of eggs," Abby reported. "Sonia ran up to the food warehouse to replace them. She'll be right back."

"Thanks, Abby. Everything seems under control. Good work," Molly added, moving along.

Molly wondered about the egg accident but figured she would get the details from Sonia. A carton of eggs in their business meant about ten dozen, packed in a large cardboard box. Not a huge expense, but it must have been a mess. She hoped it was properly cleaned up.

As she headed for the office she saw Oscar taste his soup, muttering again, and smiled. He would learn. There was always some trendy ingredient around—sun-dried tomatoes one year, fiddlehead ferns the next. You had to find your cooking identity. You couldn't be swayed by every fad that came along.

She found Betty in the office, focused on a phone call. True to her word, Betty had been around the shop for a few hours each morning before she headed to Peabody to visit Nate. After they lost the Historical Society cocktail party to Silver Spoon, they were both determined to sign up more parties. Betty set that as her priority, making call after call from their little office and going out on appointments to meet clients.

Molly didn't want to disturb Betty, but just as she was about to head back to the kitchen, Betty hung up the phone. "I got it!" she said happily. "Vicky Hillsboro, a New Year's Day brunch. It's also their wedding anniversary, so she's increasing the usual guest list. She'll drop off a check for the deposit tomorrow."

For a moment, Molly thought she might topple over with relief. Even though Betty hadn't mentioned an amount, Molly knew the sum would be substantial. Vicky Hillsboro went all out for her parties. Molly instantly felt lighter, as if she had been given a miraculous reprieve. She would be able to pay some bills, and she wouldn't have to tell Betty that the wheels were falling off their business. Molly sent a quick, silent thank-you to God, and another to Vicky Hillsboro.

She gave Betty a heartfelt hug. "You are a total genius," she told her. Though Molly had started this business from scratch on her own, she knew it had only flourished and grown because of Betty's involvement.

"I wouldn't go that far. But it does take a certain knack," Betty admitted, rising from the chair. "Selling is more listening than talking, most of the time."

"Maybe that's my problem. I never know when to put a lid on it," Molly admitted.

"No comment," Betty said with a mischievous grin.

"Ouch . . . I asked for that, I suppose."

Betty laughed and brushed past her, eager to go. "You know I'm only kidding. Got to run. See you tomorrow."

"Great. Sam wants me to take a look at the progress on Willoughby's Too. Can you come?" Betty hadn't seen the renovations in weeks. Molly wasn't even sure how long it had been.

"I'd love to. Can we meet here and go up early?"

"Sure, I'll tell Sam. I know my reports haven't been glowing, but we are making progress."

"Can't wait," Betty said, checking the time on her phone before stowing it back in her handbag. "We've got a big meeting with Nate's doctors later. Wish me luck."

"Absolutely. Ten times over," Molly promised. "It will be good news, I know it."

Betty forced a smile, then waved and headed out the door just as Sonia came in, carrying the large egg carton in front of her.

"Hey, Sonia. Sorry you had to run out. I would have stopped on my way over if I had known," Molly said.

"That's all right." Sonia put the carton down on the worktable and took off her coat. "It wasn't any big deal. But something came up at the store."

"Oh, what was that?" Molly followed her back to the walk-in refrigerator and then inside, where Sonia stored the eggs safely on a shelf.

"I used the company credit card, and it was declined," Sonia explained. "I paid for the eggs, it was no big deal. But you should call the credit card company . . . and here's the receipt from the eggs."

"Oh sure . . . I'm sorry. I thought I paid that bill this month. I'd better check. And I'll give you some cash for the eggs right away."

"No problem," Sonia said lightly as they headed back into the kitchen.

Molly was so embarrassed. She didn't know what else to say.

Had she paid that bill yet? She couldn't remember. She had to take care of this right away. It was good of Sonia to cover the purchase and not make a big deal out of it, but Molly knew she would be embarrassed if the other employees had overheard. She was glad now that Betty had left just as Sonia walked in.

The Hillsboro party was a godsend, but even so, Molly knew the deposit would not wipe out the entire stack of overdue bills on her desk. If only some other big job would come through, Betty would never have to know how bad things had gotten. *But why shouldn't Betty know?* a niggling voice inside her asked. Didn't Betty have the right to know that Molly was struggling with the accounts and that they might even need a larger loan from the bank? It was Betty's business, too.

Molly took a deep breath, trying to silence her inner argument. She had told Betty about the mold in the walls of the new shop, and the broken stove in Cape Light—but only as exasperating, comic episodes. She had carefully sidestepped the real story, the hard facts of what all this meant to their finances. She had never even mentioned that they might need a larger loan to complete the renovation. Now that they had more parties signed up, maybe the bad news wouldn't sound so dire? Either way, she had to tell her.

Tomorrow morning, before they headed up to the new shop, Molly decided. She had waited too long already. That's what this box-of-broken-eggs situation was telling her.

It will be hard to admit I've let things slide and lost control of the wheel a bit, Molly thought. *But Betty will understand. She'll probably have some good ideas I haven't even thought of.*

THE NEXT MORNING, MOLLY WAS THE FIRST ONE IN THE KITCHEN AND was glad to see Betty walk in a few minutes later. The rest of the staff wasn't due for at least half an hour. She hoped to have privacy for their talk.

"Hey, Betty. I'm glad you're here early," she began in a cheery tone, though she did feel some butterflies. She watched Betty take off her coat and head toward the stove, where she turned on the teakettle. "I told Sam you were coming up today. He's excited to show off the work."

"Great. I'm excited to see it." Betty didn't sound excited, Molly noticed. Her typically bright voice sounded flat, and she barely made eye contact as she dropped a tea bag into a mug as the kettle began to boil.

"There is something I thought we should talk about before we go. About our accounts—" Molly plowed on.

"Oh, darn . . . what did I do now?" Betty jumped back as the mug of tea and scalding water crashed to the floor, the teakettle falling, too, liquid splashing in all directions.

"Are you all right? You didn't burn yourself, did you?"

Molly ran over to help, grabbing a cloth on the way. She bent down and began to mop up the mess, wiping off Betty's boots.

"I'm all right . . . It didn't hit me," Betty said in a trembling tone. "I wasn't paying attention. I'm just so . . . so upset."

She took a deep, shaky breath, her head hanging. Molly looked up at her, then stood up, so that they were face-to-face.

"Betty, what's wrong? What's the matter?"

Betty was pale, with dark rings under her eyes, as if she hadn't slept a wink. Her makeup was tear streaked; she looked as though she had been crying all morning. Molly reached out and touched her shoulder. "Did something happen to Nate? Is he all right?"

"Nothing happened, exactly. But he's not all right. I met with his doctors last night. Nate's not doing well at all. He isn't making any progress. In fact, they say he's lost some ground lately."

"How can that be? You said he was having therapy twice a day." Molly felt awful. She understood why Betty was so upset. "I thought the surgery went well. Is there something else wrong with his back? Something they didn't see before?"

Betty shook her head. "It's not that. At least, they're not saying yet that he needs to be operated on again. It's his emotional state. He's very depressed. The pain has barely let up, and he's lost his motivation—and his hope of walking again." Her voice faltered and she shut her eyes, holding back tears.

Molly squeezed her hand, her heart breaking for Betty, her very best friend in the whole world. "But he will be able to walk again . . . don't you think? I mean, after the surgery the doctors said he had a very good chance."

"We thought so, too. But it's not as simple as we expected. His doctors think that being in the rehab center has been depressing for him. Nate won't admit it, but he's doubting that he'll make a full recovery. They said that his physical condition isn't even as important now as his motivation and willpower."

"But what can you do for him—besides visiting and encouraging him?"

"Take him home," Betty said simply. "They said he might do better if he moves back, and I agree. And he wants to come home," she added. "We'll have to get some help, of course, including a physical therapist who will work with him a few times a week. And I'll have to help him exercise every day, too."

Molly was stunned. Betty would have to help Nate with everything, not just exercising. It would be very hard for her, even with help in the house. Molly's heart went out to her.

"Betty . . . I feel so bad for you. I thought the doctors were going to give you good news."

"I did, too," Betty admitted. "It seems silly now, but I was thinking he might come out for Christmas. Or they could just let him out for a day or two, so we could be together for the holidays. I even thought he might be walking with a cane by then."

Molly was silent for a moment, unsure of what to say. "Going home might be the perfect medicine for him. Just what he needs to get back in the fight," she said at last, trying her best to sound encouraging.

"I hope so, Molly. I'm praying that it helps him. If it doesn't, the outlook is pretty bleak." Betty stared down at the floor for a moment, then met Molly's eyes. "I'm so sorry this is happening right now, at our busiest time of the year. I came back for a few days and now I'm disappearing on you again, completely. But I can't see how I'll have any time or any empty space in my mind to focus on the shop right now."

"Don't even think about it. I understand. I'd feel exactly the same. You have to be there for Nate right now. What could be more important than that? Selling a few more crab cakes and Christmas cookies?" Molly rolled her eyes, trying to draw a small smile from her pal.

Molly's words were sincere. Her worries about the shop seemed insignificant compared to the crisis Betty and Nate faced right now. What did a broken oven or even an unpaid bill amount to, compared to that?

"Oh, Molly, you're the best." Betty was sniffling again and dabbed her eyes with a tissue. "Driving over here, I was so worried, wondering how to tell you. But I knew you'd understand. I'm so grateful to you, honestly."

"Don't say another word. I just wish I was able to help you in some way. How about dinners? I could send food over every day. You won't have to worry about cooking or shopping and all that. I'll take care of everything," Molly promised.

"Nate will be happy to hear that. You know what a disaster I am in the kitchen. He says even the hospital food is better than my cooking." Betty finally cracked a smile as she tugged her coat back on.

"You have other talents, believe me," Molly assured her.

Talents she would sorely miss. But Molly didn't want to think about that right now. She was just getting used to having Betty back some of the time, and now it felt as if the rug had been pulled out from under her.

Betty gave Molly a big hug as they stood at the door. "I'm not going to forget this, Molly. Ever. I'll make it up to you someday, I promise."

"Betty, please . . . you're not just my partner. You're my best friend in the world."

She watched Betty's car pull out of the parking lot, then closed the door again. She felt suddenly, utterly, and totally alone, despite the greetings of her staff as they walked in and the sounds of the customers out in the café in the midst of the morning rush.

How would she ever get through the next two weeks without Betty? The prospect looked even bleaker than before. How would she get all this work done—or put out all these financial brushfires?

She hadn't been able to tell Betty about the mess she had made of their accounts either. When could she possibly do it now?

A beep from her phone broke into her thoughts. A text message from Sam. Could she come up to the shop later than the time they had planned? He had to check on another job but could meet her at three.

Molly texted back that it was fine with her. It would give her some time to sort things out here. They were scheduled for several parties on Saturday and Sunday, December 12 and 13. Betty had planned to oversee at least two of them, but now Molly realized she had to revise the schedule. Maybe she could split herself in two? *What I'd give for a clone right now,* she mused.

She had to call the bank and ask about an increase in the loan. She had to find out if it was even possible. *I'll talk to Betty about it once I get the details and know they'll let us sign for it.*

In a way, it seemed fortuitous now that she hadn't unloaded all their business problems on Betty this morning. What if she had done that without even knowing what Betty was going through? Betty didn't need to be worrying about this stuff, too, on top of wondering if her husband would ever get out of a wheelchair.

I have to tell her sometime—and soon, Molly resolved. *I know I do. But until then I'm on my own here, the captain of the ship, sailing through some choppy seas and praying I don't sink us all.*

SAM DROVE A HARD BARGAIN, BUT MOLLY WASN'T WILLING TO GIVE in. He should know that by now, she reminded herself, as they squared off in a room still stripped down to its wall studs, a room that would someday be the kitchen of Willoughby's Too.

She suddenly wished Betty was at her side for backup. But that simply had not happened this morning, and Molly was determined to push as hard as she dared for a quick opening.

"What do you think of Saturday, December nineteenth?" Molly asked. "That's nine days from now. Your guys are pros. I'm sure they can do it by then." She had her calendar out, and all her persuading, flattering, negotiating, and begging strategies out as well. All she wanted from him was the promise of one measly little date—the date for the shop's grand opening.

Sam didn't reply, just rubbed his forehead and pushed his hard hat back over his curly black hair, which was touched with silver strands lately.

"I'd love to give you a firm date, Molly. But I just can't say. We still need inspections and certificates of occupancy, and we haven't even finished cleaning out that mold down in the basement."

The mold again. Molly wanted to scream. It was more extensive than Sam had predicted on her last visit; it had spread into walls in the basement. She could hear the men below working on it, their labor making a racket that was hard to talk over and causing the temporary flooring she was standing on to shake.

But Molly persisted. She had to. So much hung in the balance. Sam just didn't understand. And how could he? She had to be fair; he didn't know half the story.

"Hey, let's be creative here," she said, hoping she sounded calm and encouraging. "There must be some way we can work this out. I know you can't get the kitchen in by then, but what if you just finish the retail area? Not even the café, but the counters on this side"—she framed the space with her hands—"and paint it a little and get it looking good enough for us to open the doors and start selling stuff? We don't have to bake here. We'll bring up stock from Cape Light."

Molly watched his expression, hoping he would agree. *Please, God, let Sam say he can do this. It would make me feel soooo much better to know some dough was coming into this place. Instead of just going into our broken oven and mold problem.*

She had no idea how her crew would bake double with a kitchen that could be declared an appliance hospice. But she would figure that out later.

"That would be a stretch, Mol, a big stretch." Sam reached out and touched her shoulder. "I'm not sure if we can even get a certificate for just one section of this store. But I'll make some more calls. Maybe I can get someone to jump us up the list a little. The problem is, we're not even ready for an inspector to visit. December nineteenth is only six days before Christmas. Will that really make such a big difference?"

"Of course it makes a difference. Those are the biggest days of the entire year for us. This place was supposed to open December first, Sam, remember?" She didn't want to sound so cross but knew her tone was getting sharper and louder. Even worse, her eyes were filling with tears. She blinked, pretending the dust was bothering her. "It's just been a rotten day. I'm sorry," she said, before he could reply. "Betty had some bad news this morning about Nate."

"Is he still in Peabody at the rehab center? Tucker and I went to see him about two weeks ago. He seemed pretty good."

Nate was an active member at church and a deacon there, along with Sam and his friend Tucker Tulley, a local police officer.

"His doctors decided he wasn't making any progress, maybe even doing worse. Betty is taking him home tomorrow. She's very worried. She's afraid he won't walk again."

Sam looked sad at the news, his mouth in a grim line. "Sorry to hear that. I'll go see him again. He could probably use some company. Do you think Betty will mind if I tell Reverend Ben? He might be able to help."

"Good idea. Betty won't mind. She has so much going on, she probably didn't even think of calling the church yet." As Sam made a note on his phone, Molly got another idea. "Hey, what if I set up a table out front and sell stuff from there? Hot cocoa and muffins and cookies?" she mused out loud. "Maybe we could have some Christmas music playing. Or hire a few high school kids to sing Christmas carols?"

"Sounds . . . fun," Sam agreed in a tentative tone. "You would need a permit to sell food on the street, though. I'm not sure how long it takes to get one of those either."

Molly sighed, avoiding his sympathetic gaze. "I'm talking crazy now, right? I'm scaling down my vision from a Parisian Belle Epoque café . . . to a pathetic bake-sale table."

She could tell Sam didn't want to laugh but couldn't help smiling. "That's our Molly. 'We shall *never* surrender,'" he said with a British accent.

Molly knew that quote, and even had a postcard with the words stuck in her desk blotter. "Well, it worked for Winston Churchill, didn't it?"

Sam met her gaze. "What's up, sis? Is it just this construction delay? You seem totally stressed out."

"It's just that there's so much going on right now. Betty's been away from the shop for over a month. She was working from home a little, but now she's totally disappearing. I'm sorry about Nate, I really am . . . but it's hard to manage everything on my own. Especially this time of year . . ."

Her voice trailed off. She didn't want to bore him, cataloguing her workload—signing up more business, running the Cape Light store, trying to get this place open. And they had barely started running the holiday parties.

Sam looked as if he wanted to know more, but a man covered in dust, wearing a hard hat, goggles, and a face mask looped around his neck, emerged from the basement and waved a gloved hand their way. "Hey, Sam . . . we need you downstairs."

Molly shook her head in dismay. "I don't even want to know what this is about. Don't even tell me." She zipped up her parka and hitched her tote bag over her arm.

Sam laughed and gave her a hug. "I'll work on that special permit, Mol. I'll do my best. But—"

"I know, you can't promise anything." Molly raised her hands in surrender as she headed for the door. "If they give you a flat-out no, try the bake-sale idea."

She was only kidding. She hoped he knew that. She waved good-bye to her brother and headed toward her SUV.

She turned for one last glance before she ducked into her car. The shop did look pretty from the outside, a warm yellow glow in the old-fashioned storefront windows. Even though it was a perfect wreck inside, in her mind's eye, Molly could still see that it would be something very special.

It was late afternoon as she headed back to Cape Light. The fragments of a slate-blue sky visible through a web of bare branches overhead promised snow and matched her mood perfectly.

She had to get back to the shop, even though the café would be closing by the time she reached town and the kitchen would be empty. She had a lot of calls to make, informing her staff of some changes in the schedule. She also had to start on the list Betty had left for her of potential clients. If she didn't follow up tonight, they might lose the extra last-minute jobs.

Better to get this over with now than try to call from home later, she thought. She rarely got much accomplished when she tried to work from home, between putting dinner on the table and little Betty and Matt needing her attention. Then, once the house calmed down, she always felt too tired to talk to anyone.

Her cell phone sounded and she saw that it was Matt. "Hi, honey. I was just going to call you. I have to work a little late tonight. I don't think I'll be home until about seven or so."

"What do you mean? You're not coming to the concert?"

Molly was confused. She had no idea what he was talking about. Then she heard her youngest daughter's voice in the background. "Daddy? I can't find my new tights . . ."

"Betty's tights are in our room, on my dresser," Molly told him automatically.

The holiday concert at school. Betty had been practicing her songs for a month. Molly had forgotten all about it.

"I didn't forget Betty's show," she added, quickly covering her tracks. "What time does it start?"

"Six thirty. But Betty has to get there earlier to practice. I'm going to bring some work and wait."

"Thanks for taking care of that, honey," Molly said sincerely. She was sure Matt could tell by now that she had forgotten. But he wasn't the type to make a big deal of things like this. He adored Betty and shared the child care as much as he could.

"Don't worry, I'll be there on time," she promised.

"Drive carefully. It's going to snow."

She said good-bye and checked the time, feeling torn between working on the phone calls until the last possible minute or heading home so she could change her grubby outfit and look more presentable. She did have an image to keep up around town.

The phone calls, she decided. She had to follow up tonight. There was a fancy blouse and blazer at the shop, tucked away for emergency meetings. With some fresh makeup, that would have to do.

So you won't be the best-dressed mom at Harbor Elementary tonight, she told herself. *Sneak in after the lights go down, no one will see you.*

It was Thursday afternoon, and Carrie sat reading in the outer room during Noah's appointment with Jeff Carlson. The small room was very quiet and still. She couldn't even hear a murmur of voices from Jeff's office, though she did occasionally hear his dog bark or Noah laugh out loud. At least they were having fun. A good sign, she thought.

She put the book aside and checked the time. She had to bring Noah to school tonight for a holiday show. He hadn't been in class very long but had already learned most of the songs his class was going to sing. He was excited and not feeling shy about getting up onstage. She was glad about that. Vera was excited, too, which Carrie thought was sweet, and when Noah invited Vera to come see the performance, she had happily agreed.

Noah hadn't really known any of his grandparents very well. Both of his parents passed away when he was a toddler, and Kevin's parents lived clear across the country in San Diego. It was good for Noah to have the kind of attention and delight of a surrogate grandma like Vera, who bestowed that attention so generously and so gladly. Carrie was more grateful for that every day and was coming to see their arrival at Vera's doorstep as an unexpected blessing.

A light snow had begun to fall, and she stepped to the window to watch. Jeff's house was secluded, the last on the street, and his property seemed large, blending in with a vacant stand of woods behind the house.

Large, feathery flakes fell slowly from the darkening sky, the low clouds a lavender-blue color. The flakes clung to branches and dried leaves, coating the brown clumps of grass. A dusting, the weather forecasters had predicted. It looked like it might be more than that already, but the silvery coating brightened the scenery so much, Carrie could easily forget all the practical problems it created.

"You can't be a sissy about snow if you want to live in New England," Vera said frequently.

Carrie turned at the sound of the office door opening. Jeff, Noah, and Elsie emerged. They all looked happy, the dog's tail wagging wildly, as usual.

"Hi, Mom," Noah greeted her, heading for his jacket.

Carrie smiled at him, and then at Jeff, who met her glance with a warm look. She wondered if he was just pleased with the session or happy to see her. For some reason, she felt herself blushing. She looked away, pretending to hunt through her big purse for her gloves.

"I'll see you soon, Noah. Have fun at school tonight." Jeff held on to Elsie's collar as Noah pulled on his jacket and mittens.

"Noah sang his songs for me," Jeff reported. "I think he'll do very well. And with very little chance to practice," he added, praising the boy.

"I was supposed to practice with him this afternoon. Thanks for covering that," she said.

Carrie suddenly wondered if she would see Jeff at school later, too, but felt awkward asking him. He was part of the faculty, in a way. But maybe as a counselor, he didn't come to events like this one.

And yet, she found herself hoping she would see him there—one familiar face in the crowd. *And that's all it would be,* she reminded herself. *It wouldn't be right to have any social connection to Noah's therapist . . . even if you were ready to date again. Which you're not.*

"Better put your hood up, honey. It's snowing," she said, turning her attention back to her son.

Jeff smiled, looking out at the snow. "I'd better take Elsie for her walk before it gets too deep."

As Carrie herded Noah toward the door, making sure he was properly zipped up, Jeff slipped a down vest on over his thick turtleneck and clipped on the dog's leash. She wondered if he intended to walk them all the way down to her car. She had parked on the road today, some distance down the long gravel drive, which had been blocked by a truck delivering firewood.

She hoped he did walk that way. It would give her a chance to ask about Noah's session. *Or just to talk to him?* a tiny voice chided.

Noah led the way, and Jeff followed with Elsie. They were soon out in the snow, and Noah went wild, running in gleeful circles around the front yard, his arms flung wide, head tilted back to catch big flakes on his tongue. His sneakers slipped and slid in the soft snow, though it was only an inch deep or so.

"Noah . . ." Carrie couldn't help but laugh at him. Jeff did, too.

"Nothing like watching kids in the snow. They don't hold anything back. They really know how to enjoy it."

Carrie turned and smiled at him. "Yes, they do. That's it exactly. Once you get older, you forget. You just think about the shoveling and the trouble driving. You don't really see the beauty of it, how amazing it really is."

He didn't answer for a moment, and she turned to him, wondering if he had heard her. She felt suddenly self-conscious, rambling that way. It wasn't like her at all.

But when she met his eye, she saw a certain light there that sent a rush of happiness through her. A connection . . . a real connection. Wonderful and surprising . . . and a little frightening, too. She wasn't sure she was ready for that.

"Well said, Carrie. That's so true."

She nodded, thinking that he, of all people, seemed quite aware of ordinary miracles, able to see the world through a child's eyes, since that was part of his life's work.

Noah was now picking up handfuls of snow and tossing them on his head. Elsie barked, excited by the boy's activity, wagging her tail and jumping around on the end of her leash.

"Slow down, Elsie . . ." Jeff tugged her back, but she pulled too hard, getting loose from his grasp and sending him falling backward.

"Jeff, are you all right?" Carrie quickly turned to help him. She could see in an instant he was fine. She reached out a hand and helped him up, both of them laughing again.

"I should have seen that coming," he admitted.

Suddenly they were face-to-face, Jeff so close she felt his warm breath on her cheek, their hands still grasped tight.

His wide smile faded as he stared into her eyes. Then he caught himself and pulled back, forcing a more self-conscious grin.

He quickly turned his attention to the dog. "Elsie, come back here. Come on, good dog," he called in a deep voice, though he sounded more cajoling than commanding, Carrie thought. He was just too kindhearted to get control over that dog. Luckily, Elsie had not gone far, her only goal being to reach Noah.

"I'll get her for you, Jeff," Noah called out.

"Thanks, Noah. Try to grab her collar," Jeff said.

"At least she's not running away," Carrie pointed out.

"Yes, thank goodness. When she gets loose I usually have to chase her for miles through the woods, especially if she catches the scent of a squirrel or a rabbit. It's not very good weather for that tonight. But now they each have a partner to play with in the snow. This capture may take a while," he observed with a smile.

Carrie watched Noah chase after Elsie, who ran at a carefully calculated pace, fast enough to elude Noah, but slow enough to dare him to grab her collar. She would stop and allow him to get close, then dart away again. For a big dog, Elsie was surprisingly fast and nimble.

Noah was having a great time, skidding around, falling down, and getting up. The dog would quickly trot over to check that he was all right, licking his face and making Noah laugh, then run off again.

"I hope Noah isn't making Elsie too excited. We'd better help him. We should get going anyway—"

"Oh, not yet." Jeff turned to her and touched her arm. "Let them play a few more minutes. I can never give her this much exercise."

Carrie smiled. "Sure, we can stay a few more minutes." They had plenty of time to grab a bite, change, and still get to the show on time. "It's good for Noah to burn off some energy before his show anyway."

Her hood had slipped off, even though she had pulled it up as they left the house. Jeff reached out to help her pull it up again, gently brushing snow off her hair as he did.

"Thanks," she murmured, afraid to meet his glance.

She knew he was looking at her and heard him clear his throat. She turned and met his mesmerizing blue eyes, feeling totally lost for a moment.

"I got her! I got her!"

They both turned to Noah, who was trudging through the snow toward them, holding Elsie by the leash. His cheeks were red and his panting breath made clouds in the air, but his smile was as wide as Carrie had seen in a long time. Elsie looked happy, too, and finally calmer, Carrie noticed.

"Great job," Jeff told the boy. "I would have had to chase her halfway to Maine by now. Thank goodness you were here."

"She's fast. But I finally tricked her. I lay down really still with my eyes closed, and she got worried. Then I grabbed her."

"That was clever." Carrie brushed snow off his hair and kissed his cheek. "Say good-bye, now. We really have to go."

"See you, Elsie." Noah pressed his forehead to Elsie's and gave her a kiss. Then he looked up at Jeff. "See you," he said waving up at him. Carrie could see that he liked Jeff even better now than last week, which was saying something.

"Good-bye, Noah. Good luck tonight. I'm sure you'll do very well."

Carrie said good-bye to Jeff, too, carefully avoiding his gaze for some reason. Though she did glance over her shoulder at him as she and Noah made their way down to her car.

It was darker now and she could hardly make out Jeff's expression. But she could tell his warm gaze was fixed on them, as if she were sensing more than seeing him there, his attention like a guiding, protecting light following them into the snowy night. A light she felt glowing in her heart now as well.

DESPITE OOZING NONSTOP CHARM AND EVEN OFFERING SOME DIScounts, Molly only closed deals for two parties after several hours of phone calls. She hurried from the shop, feeling stressed and annoyed that this quest had to be interrupted at all.

She slipped into the school auditorium just as the lights were going down. Betty's teacher, Mrs. Fischer, was announcing her class's performance, and Molly scanned the crowd for her husband. Luckily, Matt had picked seats on an aisle, so she was able to land without making any fuss.

He turned and quickly kissed her cheek. "I was starting to worry. Betty's class is coming out next."

"Perfect timing," Molly whispered back, so glad she hadn't missed it.

Matt was well prepared to save the performance for posterity, she noticed, his new video camera in hand—though he didn't quite know how to operate it, but wouldn't admit it—and a digital camera hanging from a strap around his neck as well, for emergency backup, she suspected.

She had to smile at his over-preparedness, but it was sweet to see him savor the moment. Betty was at an adorable age, and they both knew how quickly the years flew by. Before he could get the video camera set right, their youngest would be done with high school and off to college. *We might have some grandchildren by then,* she realized. With Amanda getting married next year, it was more than possible. Maybe Lauren and Jill would be married by then, too.

So much to look forward to, it boggled the mind. As Betty's class marched onstage and prepared to sing, Molly glanced at her husband and rested her hand on his arm. This was the true joy of her life, her family—her proudest achievement, her most cherished treasure.

I can't let these business problems drag me down, Molly reminded herself. *I have to keep things in perspective. So we miss out on a few holiday parties. Is that the end of the world? Is that what I'm going to remember on my deathbed? I have to count my blessings and look at the big picture.*

Like how cute Betty looks tonight in her red velvet dress, and how Matt didn't tie the sash right and her braids are kind of crooked. But she's still the prettiest little girl in her class . . . at least, she is to me. And how loud she's singing, when she was whispering the words at home all week.

I'll take a mental video of that . . . and save it in the photo album in my heart.

Chapter Eight

"Noah got into a fight? Is he hurt?" Carrie tried to stop her rising panic and focus on Mrs. Fischer's calm voice on the other end of the phone. It was Tuesday afternoon. Reverend Ben was in his office with the door closed, leaving Carrie free to talk. "When did this happen?"

"Right before the lunch break. In the cloakroom," Mrs. Fischer explained. Harbor Elementary School was an old building, and the old-fashioned classrooms had small anterooms where children stored their coats and packs.

"This isn't like Noah," Carrie said. "He's never had a fight at school before. Though he's sometimes been teased and been reluctant to stand up for himself," she admitted.

"I was surprised, too. I'm not sure how it happened. I haven't spoken to Noah and the other child involved yet. But I did want you to know that Noah is in the nurse's office. The other boy, Max Newton, struck him in the mouth, and Noah's lip is a little swollen. Nothing serious," Mrs. Fischer hurried to add.

"Oh, that doesn't sound good. Should I come to school and pick him up?"

"I don't think it's necessary, Ms. Munro. The nurse gave him an ice pack, and he should be fine. I don't think it would be a good idea for him to leave school over this," Mrs. Fischer said. "Both boys will get an extra assignment tonight as a consequence," she added. "But we can talk again tomorrow, after I've figured out what actually happened."

"I'd appreciate that, and I'll talk to Noah, too, when he gets back today. Thanks for calling, Mrs. Fischer."

Carrie hung up, feeling troubled. She stared at the phone, wondering if she should call Jeff. But she didn't even know what the fight had been about. Noah had just seen Jeff again yesterday and had another appointment on Thursday afternoon, possibly his last.

Though perhaps this fight at school would change that plan? Still, it seemed silly to call him now. What could Jeff possibly do? Though hearing his calm, thoughtful voice would certainly make her feel better.

She did like him. It was getting hard to deny it.

But Noah was the one who needed his help, and it would be best to wait to bring Jeff into it until she had all the facts—Mrs. Fischer's version of the story and her son's.

She tried to focus on work again, but all she could think about was poor Noah, sitting in school for the rest of the day with a swollen lip. Was he suddenly developing some of his father's traits—a quick temper and an aggressive personality? No, she told herself, he couldn't be; that simply wasn't Noah. So what *was* going on?

She glanced at the clock. Half past one. Noah would reach the church by three. She just had to wait until then; she had a good amount of work to finish before she left for the day. Reverend Ben had been very accommodating about her hours, allowing her to come in at eight thirty, instead of nine, and leave early, too, as long as she got her work done. It had saved her the trouble of figuring out after-school care for Noah, aside from playing basketball on Tuesdays. He had been seeing Jeff two days a week since she started, so Noah wouldn't have been able to take part in any club or other sports anyway. Once the holidays were over, and after Noah was finished with his sessions with Jeff, she would find something for him to do in the afternoons.

Jeff had mentioned that the end of this week would be a good time for them to discuss Noah and decide if he should have more sessions. Now, with this fight in school, Carrie wondered what he would recommend. She busied herself typing a letter.

Reverend Ben emerged from his office. "Carrie, could you run off this flyer and post it around the church when you get a chance? We should also include the information in this week's bulletin." He handed her an announcement about the Adopt-a-Family project. "The committee is worried. They don't seem to have enough gifts collected yet."

Christmas was close, only ten days away. Carrie could see why they would be worried. She quickly read the flyer. She already knew most of the information from hearing Vera talk about it. Working with a social services agency, the church had adopted an anonymous family in the area that was just about to move from a shelter to their own home. The committee hoped to fulfill the family's wish list—items for the new house and Christmas gifts. Carrie scanned the list. The few requested gifts were for the children, and most were what Carrie considered basic necessities—warm coats, gloves, scarves, and waterproof boots.

"I see requests for the children and for setting up their house," Carrie said. "What do the parents ask for?"

"Oh, the parents rarely ask for anything," Reverend Ben said. "They're just happy if there are gifts for their children under the tree. But we do send a few surprises just for them."

Reverend Ben's beard and sparkling eyes behind his wire-rimmed glasses suddenly reminded Carrie of Santa. Though the minister's hair and beard were reddish-brown, touched with gray, and he wasn't nearly as plump. It was more his warmth and kind personality that reminded her. She could easily see him playing the part.

"I'll take care of this today," Carrie promised. "But I may have to leave a bit early, if it's all right? Noah was in the nurse's office with a swollen lip. His teacher said it wasn't anything to worry about, but I might need to bring him home and give him another ice pack."

"Of course. How did he hurt himself? Did he fall down?"

Carrie shook her head, feeling embarrassed. "Mrs. Fischer said he had a fight with another boy in his class. She's not sure what happened. The other boy punched Noah in the mouth."

"Poor Noah. At least he doesn't have a black eye."

"Noah's never had a black eye . . . or a fat lip. He's never gotten into a fight at school, or anywhere, before. It worries me," Carrie admitted.

"Naturally. I'm sure you'll talk it over with him and try to get the whole story. But little boys do tend to settle things with their fists. I wouldn't worry too much. My son Mark had a fight like that when he was around Noah's age, and the two boys wound up being best friends."

"That's encouraging. Noah's only been in that class about two weeks, and he hasn't made any real friends yet. There are . . . other problems, too," she admitted.

"Really? What sort of problems? Noah seems very well-behaved whenever I see him."

Carrie didn't mean to unload her worries on Reverend Ben, but he was so easy to talk to, and so understanding. From the short time she had been working at the church, she could see he was a great support and comfort to his congregation. Perhaps he would be able to help her understand Noah's imaginary friend and what to do about it.

"I don't mean to take up all your time, Reverend Ben, but since you asked . . . Noah has been telling stories. Well, just one story, actually. He has an imaginary friend. But he talks about him, this friend, as if he were perfectly real."

"I see. So you're wondering if this imaginary friend of Noah's had anything to do with the fight, is that it? It's fairly common for children to have imaginary friends. I'm sure you know that."

Carrie sighed, knowing she had not told him the whole situation, the important part. "I do. The thing is, Noah thinks his friend is an angel. He even has a name—Theo. Noah even draws pictures of him."

"Really? How interesting." Reverend Ben wore a thoughtful expression, but somehow Carrie got the feeling that he believed Noah was telling the truth. Or at least, believed Noah's story was possible.

What had she expected? Even Carrie knew that the Bible was full of Scripture about angels. She guessed that most ministers probably believed in their existence, or at least the possibility of them.

"The name Theo is an interesting choice right there," Reverend Ben said. "Do you know what the name means?"

Carrie shook her head. She hadn't even thought to look it up.

"Theo in Greek means 'God,' but the name can often mean 'gifts from God.'"

"That is interesting. The name is uncommon, but I'm sure Noah heard it somewhere. Or read it in a book. He's a very big reader."

"Certainly, he could have heard it or read it somewhere," Reverend Ben agreed. "You said before Noah talks about the angel as if he were a person. Does Noah say he sees the angel all the time?"

"Pretty much. The angel does seem to appear when he's in trouble or needs help. Last week, the angel found his homework for him, under his bed. Reportedly," she quickly added. "He also said the angel helped us find our rooms at Vera's house." She found herself smiling; relating this aloud, it sounded so . . . well, preposterous. "I know I seem amused . . . and in a way, I am. It is amusing. Cute and charming and probably very harmless," she conceded. "But it's upsetting to hear Noah talk about the angel as if he's totally real and taking part in Noah's life. In my life, too."

Carrie didn't want to insult Reverend Ben and hoped he hadn't taken offense. "I know that most religious doctrines talk about such things—visions and messages and even miracles. I don't mean to sound irreverent or disrespectful," she assured him. "But I've never taken Noah to church very much. When this story interferes with his everyday life and relationships . . . well, it's not that cute anymore. It seems to be a problem."

"I understand completely, Carrie. And you haven't offended me in any way," he assured her. "I'm never eager to be drawn into the debate over whether angels are 'real' or not. There are libraries full of books on the subject. I'd say that territory is one of the mysteries of faith," he added. "But speaking more practically, about Noah . . . have you sought any help? A therapist or counselor?"

Carrie nodded. "Noah's been seeing the school psychologist, Dr. Carlson. Since I started working here, actually. Dr. Carlson doesn't think anything is seriously wrong, but he thought it would take a few sessions to make sure. So far, he thinks Noah just needs this imaginary friend for a while, and that he'll outgrow it. But I was worried it might be a sign of some deeper issue. I guess what I'm saying is, I still am."

"Jeff Carlson is a very good therapist," Reverend Ben said. "He's helped a lot of children and families that I know personally. He has a true gift with kids. It's a shame that he and his wife never had any of their own before she passed away."

"That is sad . . . I didn't know he was a widower," Carrie replied, taking in this unexpected information. She wondered when and how his wife had passed away. She must have been very young, which made the loss seem even more poignant. She also realized that it was Jeff who always asked the questions. He knew a lot about her and Noah by now, though she knew very little about his life.

"It was quite sudden," the reverend told her. "A car accident, about three years ago. But he's young. I expect he'll marry again at some point. And I would trust his take on the situation," Reverend Ben added, returning to the subject of Noah again. "Does Jeff have any reason to think it's a sign of something more serious?"

Carrie shook her head. "Not so far. I'll have to find out if this fight today at school is related. That would seem more serious to me than an angel finding lost homework or helping us find a new place to live or even helping me find this job."

She hadn't meant to tell Reverend Ben the last item on the angel's list of accomplishments. It had just slipped out.

"Did Noah really say the angel sent you here? Maybe there are some grounds for the boy's claims. That day you called and came in for the interview, Mrs. Honeyfield and I both decided that you were perfect for her replacement and that you had to be heaven sent."

She knew he was teasing, but his kind compliment made her smile again. "Thank you, Reverend. It seems a perfect job to me, too."

Before Reverend Ben could reply, they heard Noah at the open office door. "Hi, Mom. Hi, Reverend Ben."

"Hello, Noah, good to see you, son. Playing basketball today?" Reverend Ben asked him.

Noah nodded. "In a little while . . . I mean, I hope I am." He sounded subdued; it wasn't the usually high-spirited greeting he offered the minister. Noah glanced at Carrie, as if wondering if she wouldn't let him play because of what had happened at school.

"I'll come and watch you then," Reverend Ben promised. He slipped back into his office, offering Carrie an encouraging smile.

She got up from behind her desk and held her son's small face in both of her hands. His cheeks were cold from the outdoors, his eyes bright . . . he did have a swollen lower lip, a bit bruised with a tiny cut. "Does it hurt much?"

"Not too much. The nurse gave me an ice pack. Mrs. Fischer said she called you."

"She did. She told me you had a fight with another boy at school."

"Yeah. But it wasn't my fault," Noah said.

Carrie decided not to ask for all the gritty details yet. "Let's go into the kitchen and get you a snack."

Noah's expression brightened. He dropped his jacket and pack and followed her. Back in the church kitchen, she made him apple slices with peanut butter, along with a glass of milk and some chocolate chip cookies. She watched him wolf down the treat. "Don't eat so fast. You'll get a stomachache," she said automatically. "Didn't you have any lunch?"

He shook his head. "I was in the nurse's office a long time, and I only got to drink some milk after."

Carrie felt sorry for him and stroked his hair with her hand. He'd had a hard day. She was fairly certain that he was telling the truth—that the fight hadn't been his fault—but she needed to know more.

"Can you tell me what happened? You never fight with other boys, not that I know of."

"I don't, Mom," Noah said. "But Max started it. He's very mean. He finds kids' lunches in the coatroom and hides them. Then they can't find their lunch when it's recess, and he makes fun of them."

"I see . . . So you caught Max doing that and told him to stop? Is that what happened?"

"Not exactly. This girl in our class, Betty Harding, was crying because she couldn't find her lunch box. And Max was laughing, so I sort of guessed he hid it. My angel told me it was hidden behind a pair of boots on the other side of the closet, and I found it for her. And Max got real mad at me and called me a lot of names."

"That wasn't very nice of Max. Did you call him names back?"

Noah shook his head. "No. I didn't say anything. When I tried to walk by him, to get out of the closet, he punched me. So I punched him back . . . and Mrs. Fischer finally came. That's how it started, I guess."

"I see." At least Noah didn't claim that the angel swooped down and took part in the fistfight. But the angel did play a role, and not a small one either.

"So your angel told you where Betty's lunch was hidden. Are you sure, Noah? Maybe you saw Max hide it earlier in the day, and you forgot?"

She didn't mean to interrogate him, and she posed her question in a gentle tone. But she did hope to remind him of what may have really happened, unembellished by his imagination.

"I didn't see Max hide it. Theo told me," he insisted. "I'm not lying, Mom, honest." Noah seemed on the verge of tears.

"Okay, honey. I believe you. I do," Carrie soothed him.

She did believe that Noah was sincere. Though she truly doubted it had happened that way. She hesitated a moment, trying to figure out what to say next.

"We talked about having an imaginary friend, remember? It's fine to have one; a lot of children do. But an imaginary friend isn't real. He's just a pretend game. I'm proud that you tried to help that little girl," she said truthfully. "And that you have such a wonderful imagination. But it's important to be sure about what is real and what isn't. Do you understand what I'm trying to say?"

"I know, Mom. I am sure. Totally," Noah told her.

Carrie stopped herself from saying more. She had probably said too much already and had ignored almost everything Jeff had advised about dealing with the situation. But this latest episode had caught her by surprise.

Maybe I should have called him for some guidance on how to handle this, she realized. *Too late now.* She decided to call him after dinner, to give him a heads-up before Noah's next appointment. And maybe get some guidance for herself.

"Did you tell Mrs. Fischer that Theo helped you again?" she asked curiously.

"Sure. She knows about Theo."

A few of the boys who played basketball had wandered in. Noah had finished his snack, and she cleared away the dish and glass. "Better get your sneakers and T-shirt on. Looks like they're going to start." He hadn't mentioned anything about his lip. Perhaps it looked worse than it felt. Carrie hoped so. It didn't seem to be holding him back from wanting some exercise, which was a good thing.

Noah ran off to change, and Carrie went back to her office. She knew that Noah was not going to outgrow this overnight or even in two weeks. But she had been starting to believe that it wasn't a sign of anything more serious. Now, once again, she wasn't so sure.

MOLLY HAD BEEN AT THE SHOP, WORKING IN THE KITCHEN, SINCE SIX a.m. and had not even been the first to arrive. Her cooking helpers, Abby and Kira, were busily prepping the ingredients for several dishes that were going out in catering orders that weekend. Oscar was working on crescent-shaped meat pies with a savory Middle Eastern spiced filling. She hoped the recipe was up to his standards. She didn't have the patience for any more of his food snobbery.

A few new helpers manned the sink and ran from place to place under

Sonia's supervision. Molly could barely remember their names. She had also hired more servers to work at parties, but had no time to train them properly. At the parties last weekend, Molly had given up trying to supervise and had just squeezed her eyes shut, pretending not to see their screw-ups. If these parties were clumsy, amateur affairs, word would get around quickly. She would pay the price later, that was for sure.

Despite Betty's absence, they had muddled through the events with only a few glitches. But this weekend would be the real test. Molly could feel the pressure building, like watching a wave swell far out at sea, gathering power and height as it approached the shore.

Get a grip, it's only Tuesday, she reminded herself. *Three more days to cook and plan a strategy.* But by Friday afternoon, the giant wave of holiday parties would arc overhead and crash down on them. Would they sink or swim? She had no idea. She squeezed curls of herb-and-cheese filling from a pastry tube into tiny, flaky tart cups and hoped the effort would be worth it.

She had finally called the bank to ask about the extra loan, but it wasn't going to be easy or quick to find out if Willoughby's Fine Foods even qualified. A bank officer was looking into it and promised to call back.

"Of course, with Christmas coming, everything takes longer," the banker had reminded her.

"Of course. I totally understand," Molly had said politely. She hung up and wanted to kick herself for putting off the dreaded task for so long.

She checked the large baking sheet in front of her. The rows of canapés were filled and ready to bake. A timer sounded, and she ran over to the oven to pull out the first batch—then stared at sheets full of pale, raw pastries. Molly slammed the tray on the worktable and turned to her crew, who were scurrying in all directions, focused on their jobs, like a well-orchestrated dance.

"Who shut this oven off? I had three trays in there . . ."

It had to be one of the newbies. Molly was sure of it. She would trade in a dozen of them for one good worker like Sonia or Eddie.

Everyone in the crew glanced at her, most of them not missing a beat in their chopping or mixing. All of them shook their heads and murmured, "I didn't do it" or "Not me."

She hadn't meant to sound so snarly, but what idiot would shut the oven off today—in the middle of this chaos?

Oscar walked by without any response. He didn't even look at her. She recalled spotting him near the oven just a moment ago, taking out some meat pies from the bottom section.

Molly wanted an answer. "Did you shut off the oven, Oscar?"

Tall and gangly, he topped her by at least a foot, and peered down as if finding a bug in a bowl of cream. "Don't look at me. I took my stuff out and you put your trays in. End of story."

"End of story? Are you sure? I think you screwed up and shut it off. Maybe you can be more careful next time," she snapped.

"Get a grip. I didn't lay a finger on the oven controls. Which are all half-broken anyway. Why don't you get some new equipment in here before that old piece of junk blows up?"

Molly stared at him, feeling as if *she* were about to blow up. How dare he talk to her like that? She was the boss *and* the only chef around here, culinary school degree or not.

She had to tilt her head back to call him out but didn't miss a beat. "Don't you *dare* tell *me* to get a grip, okay? *You* get a grip. Get a grip on your *time card* and punch out. You're fired."

Oscar frowned, his mouth pulling to one side. She could tell he knew that he had gone too far, and she wondered if he might apologize.

He shook his head and laughed in an angry way, pulling his apron off. "Fine. This place is nuts. I heard you were cool, but you're actually crazy."

Molly had to hold back from grabbing a handful of raw cheese tarts and showing him just how crazy she could be.

The rest of the staff stood by watching, completely silent. Molly felt them all staring at her. "Show's over. Back to work, everyone," she said as the door slammed, marking Oscar's departure.

She heard some murmuring, but the staff quickly returned to their tasks. Except for Abby, who had recently begun dating Oscar. She had been chopping vegetables near the sink and now set down her knife. She walked up to Molly, gave her a long, hard, angry look, then pulled off her apron and tossed it at Molly's feet. "I'm out of here, too."

Molly stood back in surprise. Abby was a good worker. They would all miss her, especially right now. Molly gazed around, wondering if anyone else was going to quit in protest. She didn't think Oscar was very well liked, but you never knew . . .

Sonia came forward and clapped her hands sharply. "All right, everyone. We have work to do. Back to it."

The crew returned to their work once again. Sonia lightly touched Molly's arm, then walked up to the oven. She looked at the dial and then back at Molly, urging her forward. "It's still set to three-fifty. Is that what you put it on?"

Molly nodded bleakly. She had been in such a panic, she hadn't even looked at the temperature setting. She pulled open the oven door and stuck her hand inside—and felt only cool air.

"What in the world . . ." She turned to Sonia. "I didn't even look. I totally freaked and thought someone had turned it off."

"Yeah, we noticed," Sonia said sympathetically.

Molly glared at the traitorous oven. "It was preheated and ready to go. I heard the bell. It must have shut itself off," she admitted finally. "It must be broken again."

"Let me check." Sonia turned the dial off and turned it back on again. They both listened intently for the sound of the oven firing up. But there was nothing. "Sounds like it really died this time," Sonia said. "I don't hear a thing."

"I can't believe this! It's just not fair!" Molly twisted the oven dial wildly, tipping her head toward the open door, listening for at least a sputter. "Why did you do this to me? Today, of all days in the entire year. You stupid oven! You are a giant piece of junk!"

She waved her arms and accidentally tipped over a tray of the unbaked cheese tarts. Then, stumbling, she managed to step in them, squishing the pasty filling all over the kitchen floor.

"Mother of Pearl! What next?" She knew she was yelling now, out of control. Her entire staff stood staring, as if she were onstage. Or losing her mind. She twisted in a hysterical circle, staring back at them. "Clean up this mess! Does that not occur to you?" she yelled at no one in particular.

Feeling about to explode and melt down in tears at the same time, she stomped off to her office, the thick soles of her kitchen shoes leaving a trail of sticky footprints. She collapsed in the office chair, feeling embarrassed and guilty and awful. She had accused everyone and lost two of her staff at the busiest time of the year. Oscar might be obnoxious, but he hadn't done anything wrong, and he didn't deserve to be fired. *But that's what happens when you're totally stressed and freaking out about a hundred things at once. You're not thinking straight.* She just wanted to hide in a dark little hole somewhere, like a hermit crab.

For a long moment, she just sat there, her head buried in her hands. Why was this happening? It seemed like one disaster after another. Who was she going to call now to fix the oven? Whoever she found would probably just pronounce it officially dead and charge her for the honor.

There were only two repairmen in the area who fixed commercial appliances, and she now owed both of them money. Even if she could get one of them to come, she couldn't use the business credit card or even write a check from the business account, she realized. Not before they got in more receipts this weekend. The balance was too low after she bought all the food they needed for the party menus.

She stood up and began to pace the small office, not sure if she was going to scream or cry or do both. She took a deep breath. She would just have to pay the guy out of her personal account—and hope he didn't charge a fortune, because she wasn't so sure about that balance either.

Sonia peeked into the office as Molly tore through her big tote bag, hoping she had brought her checkbook today. Sonia seemed concerned but also looked scared, Molly noticed. Outside, the kitchen seemed very quiet. She guessed the staff were whispering and worrying about her. *Maybe opening two shops is too much,* they must be saying. *Maybe Molly is having a nervous breakdown.*

"Molly . . . are you all right?"

"Yeah. I guess so . . ." Her voice trailed off on an unconvincing note.

"Don't worry about Oscar. He's a total diva. I had a feeling he was going to make a big scene like that and quit sooner or later."

"I know, but . . . I shouldn't have accused him. And I shouldn't have fired him. And I shouldn't have screamed at all of you. That was so wrong. I was totally out of control." Molly felt bad about blowing up like an idiot at her crew. She needed them now more than a drowning man needed a life raft.

"What about the oven? Should I call somebody?" Sonia asked.

"I just called that guy we usually use . . . and left a message on his cell." Molly hated herself for lying, but she still didn't know what to do. "I'll try the other guy. I have to look for his number."

"Okay . . . but I was just thinking . . . what about Chez Chandor?" Sonia said, mentioning the French restaurant next door. "They don't open until five. Maybe Alain will let us use his oven for a while?"

Molly stared at her and realized her eyes were wet with tears. She dabbed them with a tissue. "Good idea. We helped him when his freezer broke last summer. He owes us one."

"I can call if you want. My brother-in-law is the manager there. Alain knows me."

"Would you? That would be great." The perks of living in a small town. Molly felt grateful and relieved to have Sonia deal with Alain Chandor. She feared that she might get too emotional and start crying to her neighboring restaurant owner. That would make for great gossip flying around town.

Molly shut her office door and took a few more deep breaths. One disaster at a time, she told herself. But she truly wondered if she would make it to Christmas without her wheels falling off entirely.

By the time Molly emerged from the office, the kitchen floor was clean and her crew was working smoothly. There was little evidence of her blowup, except for the sight of her staff running in and out of the back door with trays of canapés, either ready to bake or hot from Alain's oven.

The small oven in her shop was still working, bless its stalwart little heart, and she had managed to negotiate a visit from a repairman who said he would take a quick look just to tell if the oven was worth fixing, and wouldn't charge for the call if the oven was over the hill.

"It drives me crazy every time I think of those two brand-new ovens up in Newburyport. Still in their crates," she confessed to Sonia. "If only we could bring just one of them down here."

"That would solve the problem for a little while. But then you would need another new oven up there, right?" Sonia replied in her logical way.

Not if that store never opens, Molly nearly replied. But she caught herself just in time. It wasn't that dire yet, was it? They would make enough profits in this party season and get the loan extension to carry on as planned. She didn't even want to think about abandoning the new store yet.

Her kitchen crew was efficient, considering the situation, she thought. But five o'clock was approaching, and Alain needed to cook for his own customers.

Sonia returned with the last trays of canapés. Alain followed her, dressed in his cooking whites. The red bandana covering his head, his jaunty walk, and his small neat beard reminded Molly of a pirate.

"Hey, Alain . . . I was just coming over to say thanks. You really saved my bacon. This stupid oven is driving me crazy. I have to get a new one—as soon as I get through the holidays."

"No problem, Molly. Happy to help you out. I thought you just had that oven fixed last week. What's wrong now?"

Alain turned to the culprit and opened the top door, peering inside like a doctor asking a patient to open wide and stick out his tongue.

"I don't know." Molly shook her head in dismay. "It preheated fine, then just went cold on me. The repair guy last week replaced the thermostat. Maybe something else is wrong now."

Alain continued his examination, looking in the top section and then the bottom, then turning the dial up and down again. "You got a flashlight? Let me take a look under the hood. I might be able to see something."

She handed him the flashlight they kept near the door for emergencies. Alain knelt on the floor and popped the metal cover off the front of the oven, then bent low and swung the light around a moment.

"Ah . . . I see what's going on," she heard him say.

"You do?" She bent over, too, but couldn't see a thing.

"The new thermostat wasn't wired very well." He turned and looked up at her. "It must have shook loose, from banging the doors open and shut. I can fix it if you've got a pair of pliers?"

"Sure thing. Let me find some." Molly ran to the cupboard near the sink and pulled out a toolbox, then handed it down.

Alain picked out a pair of snub-nose pliers and a long, thin screwdriver, then bent low again and worked inside the oven, holding the light with his other hand.

"I think that should do it. Let's see." He put the cover back in place and stood up, then twisted the dial on top. Molly stood very still, holding her breath. She could hardly stand the suspense.

A moment later she heard the pilot light spurt to life and the oven jets kick in. Alain did, too.

"Voilà!" Alain tossed his hands in the air and smiled as Molly's staff broke out in applause. She spun around, surprised to see they had all been watching.

"Alain, you're a genius. I owe you, big time." Molly leaned over and gave him a hug.

"That was nothing. You can pay me back with your delicious pastry," he said with a shrug. "Can I feature the pear tart as a dessert special tonight?"

"Absolutely. Take some napoleons and cream puffs, too," she insisted. She waved at Kira to box up some pastries for Alain.

Once Alain was gone, she turned to her crew. "I'm sorry for the meltdown today, guys. I know I totally lost it. This oven nearly pushed me over the edge. Let's put all this craziness behind us. We have a big week and an even bigger weekend coming up. Let's stay calm and march on. I know we can do it," she told them, trying hard to resume her trademark "never surrender" attitude.

Sonia, who was standing closest, patted her shoulder. "Don't worry, Molly. We know it's hard for you without Betty around. We're all behind you."

Molly quietly thanked her. She knew that was true. Her staff—

what remained of it—was staying the course. They were a well-trained, hardworking group of professionals—most of them—and she wouldn't take her stress out on the kitchen like that again. Deep inside she wondered if even their loyalty and hard work would be enough to get the business through to the new year.

MOLLY DIDN'T GET HOME UNTIL MIDNIGHT. THE HOUSE WAS SILENT, and she crept into the kitchen and made herself a cup of chamomile tea, the usual remedy she gave her daughters when they were anxious and couldn't sleep. She felt exhausted but knew she wouldn't fall asleep easily. She pulled out her lists and files from her tote bag, checked off the work the crew had accomplished today, and looked over what still had to be done by Friday.

Down two employees now, she reminded herself. *Because of your bad temper.*

"Molly? When did you get in?" Matt stood in the kitchen doorway in his bathrobe, yawning, his hair mussed from sleep.

"A few minutes ago. My stomach is a little queasy. I'm just having some tea."

"You look exhausted, honey. I thought you would be home on the early side. You said you were going to work on your speech tonight, for the awards dinner."

"Oh . . . that. Yikes . . ." Molly sighed. "I didn't even make a hair appointment yet." And she had no idea what she was going to wear. After the initial excitement, she had tossed the invitation aside, feeling the dinner was a long way off. Or maybe it had just gotten buried on her desk, under piles of more urgent and troubling bills and paperwork. It didn't really matter now what she had done with the invitation. The reality was that the awards ceremony was this coming Friday night, just three nights away.

"Hey, you look as if I just said you have an appointment for a double root canal. You deserve to be honored by your peers, and you deserve a night off." He stood behind her and rubbed her shoulders, and Molly let her head flop.

"Maybe I can get Jill or Lauren to write the speech for me. I did enough homework assignments for them when they were little," she recalled.

Matt laughed. "Very true. But make sure you ask them tomorrow. You don't have much time to pull that together. What you need now is some sleep. You can't run yourself into the ground, or you'll be no good to anyone. I know you have to pick up the slack for Betty being out, but you're working much too hard."

Molly sighed and glanced at him. She was tired from working what felt like a double share. But she also knew she usually thrived on the pressure at this time of year, strangely drawing even more energy from the breakneck pace.

She knew in her heart what was really draining her. She was so worried about the business and the mess she had made of the finances. She met Matt's glance, wanting so much to tell him—but feeling so ashamed.

"Hey . . . what is it? Is something else wrong? You look like you're going to cry."

She swallowed back a lump in her throat. "I just have a lot on my plate. All the work in the kitchen, running the staff, and getting ready for these parties. The oven broke today and I blew up . . . and two people no longer work here."

"Wow. That *was* a bad day."

"Yeah, you might say. Aside from all that . . . well, Betty usually does the books and handles all the financial stuff, and I'm just not very good at it," she confessed. "In fact, I totally stink. I've made a big mess of things since she's been gone. I'm in over my head there, Matt. It's not pretty."

He shook his head sympathetically and rubbed her shoulders again. "Don't you have an accountant who handles all that? I'm sure Betty doesn't do everything. Just give your bookkeeping over to the accountant for now. Until Betty comes back."

She glanced at him. He didn't get it. He didn't understand what she was trying to say. *Maybe because you're not being totally honest with him?* a little voice pointed out.

She had made a mess of their finances in a way that no accountant could solve. Unless it was an accountant who gave out small business loans.

"It's more . . . complicated." She couldn't manage to explain anything else. It was late and she felt so drained and tired, she couldn't push herself to make this confession tonight, not even to Matt.

She might have to ask Matt for a loan from their savings, when all was said and done. How she dreaded that. Not that he wouldn't want to help her and Betty, but . . . it would be such a huge sign of failure to her. It would feel as if she were hanging a sign around her neck that said, HAD IT ALL . . . SCREWED IT UP.

And with Amanda's wedding coming up, she wondered how they were even going to afford to bail out Willoughby's. She rubbed her forehead, feeling a sudden headache coming on. She walked to the sink, took out two aspirin, and poured a glass of water.

"How about giving a few parties to another caterer? Someone you trust who needs the business," Matt suggested. "Wouldn't that take a load off? Especially if you just lost two employees."

A nice idea, but she couldn't afford it. Scant as the profits looked right now, the business needed every penny.

"I really can't do that. Quality control." Not entirely a lie, but hardly the real reason. "We have a reputation to keep up."

"Well, think about it."

"I will. Why don't you go back up? I'll be along in a minute."

"Okay, but don't be too long. Even Super Molly needs some sleep." He kissed her cheek and left her alone again.

Super Molly did need some sleep. That was one suggestion she couldn't contradict. The big weekend loomed. She piled her schedules, lists, and budgets together and shoved it all back in the file.

She hoped the shop's financial picture looked brighter by next week, though she was not sure that would be the case at all.

Brighter or not, I have to talk to Betty about this. I can't put it off any longer.

Chapter Nine

A frosty coating of snow, left over from the flurries last week, still covered the ground, Carrie noticed. She had her boots on, and so did Noah, who ran ahead through the woods leading Jeff's dog, Elsie, on her leash and halter.

Carrie walked side by side with Jeff, the rhythm of their steps matching. Jeff had ended the session a few minutes early today and suggested that they all go for a walk while it was still light outside.

It was a perfect winter afternoon, windless and not even that chilly for mid-December. The light was fading quickly, the clear sky turning dark blue high above while piles of white clouds at the horizon were streaked with golden and rose-colored sunlight.

"I like to take a walk outside at the end of the day," Jeff told her. "It clears my head."

"So do I, when I can. Henry David Thoreau said, 'A walk is a blessing for the whole day.' Well, he actually said, 'An early-morning walk'—but I think it's true any time of day."

"I do, too," Jeff agreed. "So, do you read a lot of Thoreau?"

"Not recently," Carrie admitted. "But I used to. He was one of my favorites in college."

"Did you study philosophy?"

"I was an English major. I wanted to be a teacher . . . but I had to leave school in my junior year." She felt self-conscious confessing she hadn't even earned a four-year degree, while Jeff had probably gone to college for double that time.

"That's too bad. I think you'd be a great teacher, Carrie. You've done a wonderful job with Noah," he said sincerely. "You can finish a year of credits easily, once you and Noah are settled. You have plenty of time."

She could tell he was trying to encourage her, and she appreciated it. "I've always hoped to go back. I would like to find a career path that's more fulfilling than being a secretary or a waitress, or working in a store. I've had a lot of random jobs over the past two years." *Sometimes more than one at the same time, just to make ends meet.* But she didn't say that; she didn't want him to feel sorry for her. "I guess each job was interesting in its way. I like dealing with people one-on-one. But at the end of the day, I'd like to feel my time and energy are adding up to something more than just a paycheck. I'd like to feel as though I was really helping people, making a difference in someone's life."

Jeff must feel that sort of satisfaction all the time, helping children and families with his work.

He nodded. "Some people say that's the key to true happiness—not money or fame, but feeling that you're making a contribution. Of course, we help other people in millions of ways: giving helpful service at a store or being a really good waitress . . . or even keeping the church office in order. That's a contribution, too," he pointed out. "But I do know what you mean. It's all in your perspective, your feeling of satisfaction. That's very personal."

Carrie nodded and glanced at him, but fell quiet again. Sometimes she hardly recognized herself when she was with Jeff. She rarely talked so openly or seriously with anyone. Even when things had been good with Kevin, they never talked like this. But she also felt as if she and Jeff were always laughing. It wasn't all heavy talk and ponderous confessions. Being around him was somehow very comfortable and exciting at the same time. She couldn't really remember feeling this way with any other man before.

She caught herself, suddenly embarrassed. She hadn't even asked him about Noah yet. "I'm sorry to go on about myself like that. I should have been asking you about Noah. What do you think now, after all his sessions?"

It was the day they had set for Jeff to give a summary of his visits with Noah and tell her if he thought Noah's angel was a sign of some deeper issue. She wondered now if that was the real reason he had suggested the walk.

"I spent some time last night going over my notes about the sessions we've had these last two weeks. And I did carefully consider the fight he had at school," Jeff added. "But my extended contact with Noah has not changed my initial impression at all. I believe the angel is an imaginary friend, even a guardian figure. But I don't see it as a sign of anything more than Noah feeling the need for an ally—or for greater safety right now. Which, all things considered, is understandable, as we've already discussed."

He glanced at her to gauge her reaction. Carrie kept her gaze fixed on the path. "So you don't see any deeper problem? Nothing at all?"

"No, not at all. It's not impeding him socially or impacting his everyday functions or his safety in any way. I'm even willing to say I think this fantasy is helpful to him. It gives him an expression and outlet for the stress he's been under. And it's certainly a benign way for him to vent that. He could be having nightmares or headaches—or acting out with angry behavior. There are any number of ways he could deal with the disruptions in his life, instead of creating an imaginary friend."

"I never even considered that," she admitted. "When I look at it that way, the angel does seem harmless. And a much better choice than nightmares or headaches."

He glanced at her with a thoughtful smile. "But I can tell that you don't agree completely. That's all right. You're entitled to your opinion."

Carrie sighed and kicked a clump of snow with her toe. "Honestly, I don't know what to think anymore about the angel. I lie awake asking myself what's the most important thing in my life. It's Noah, keeping him safe and happy." She stood with her hands sunk in the pockets of her parka and watched her son, just up ahead, leading Elsie along by her leash as she carried a big stick in her mouth.

She turned back to Jeff and shrugged. "And he does seem happy and he is safe . . . and I think he knows he's loved. So I could be worrying for no reason."

Jeff smiled at her, understanding. "That's just what mothers do. That's sort of your job description."

"Yeah, I know. Sometimes I work a double shift, though. That's not good."

"You wouldn't be the first," Jeff assured her. "But that does bring Noah's counseling to a close, for now. Christmas is coming. Maybe you should just see how it goes for a few weeks. If it seems to be worse or more troubling for some reason, just call me and I'll be happy to see him again. Or I could recommend some colleagues in the area. I really wouldn't be insulted if you wanted another opinion."

She had thought of that, too, early on, but certainly not lately. "I trust your opinion," she said truthfully, "even if I don't entirely understand what's going on with Noah. You're the expert here, and you've helped both of us," she added. "Thank you."

She could tell from his expression her words had moved him. "It's been my pleasure to work with your son. He's a wonderful kid." Jeff smiled at her, but she noticed a wistful light in his eyes.

"Thanks. He thinks you're pretty cool, too." Her words made Jeff's smile widen. She thought he was pretty cool herself but, of course, couldn't say that. She felt relieved by Jeff's conclusion, happy to confirm the angel was nothing to worry about. But also sad that they wouldn't be coming here anymore.

But that couldn't be helped. And it wasn't as if she would even feel ready to go on a date if he wanted to see her socially. But she did enjoy his company; she couldn't deny that. And she had a feeling he knew that, too.

They had come to a spot in the path that was blocked by a large fallen tree trunk. Noah and Elsie had jumped over it easily, but it was bigger up close than she had realized.

Jeff climbed over, then stood on the other side, reaching out a hand to help her as she climbed up. "Watch out, it's slippery."

"I'm okay," she said, then suddenly lost her balance as she tried to jump down.

He caught her, with both hands around her waist, and when she landed, they stood very close, face-to-face, staring into each other's eyes. Carrie thought he was about to kiss her, and she held her breath, frozen in place.

The sound of Noah laughing and Elsie barking broke the spell, and they quickly drew apart.

"Noah . . . are you all right?" Carrie walked ahead on the path. She could see Noah easily, though he was twenty or thirty yards ahead.

"Elsie tried to catch a squirrel. She practically climbed up a tree," he reported.

Jeff grinned. "I'd better go get her—before she pulls him up into a tree." He walked ahead quickly, and Carrie followed.

When she and Jeff reached Noah and the dog, they decided to turn around. It was starting to get chilly, and the sun had almost gone down. Tiny points of light appeared in the darkened sky above, and Carrie could already see the moon rising on the horizon.

Noah noticed it, too. "Look, Mom, the moon and the sun are out at the same time." He turned, looking at the sunset before them and then at the rising silver orb behind them.

"That's right. I didn't even notice," Jeff said, looking pleased by the sight.

Carrie met his gaze but didn't reply. She didn't want to break the peaceful silence that had fallen over them. She held Noah's hand, walking alongside Jeff and Elsie.

She recalled something Jeff had said the first time they spoke—something about how seeing the world through a child's eyes renews us. She suddenly understood and felt an uncommon peacefulness, as deep and indescribable as the dark blue sky above.

As if the entire universe were in perfect harmony, always had been, always would be . . . and she was as much a part of it all as a star in the night sky.

MOLLY MANAGED TO BOOK AN APPOINTMENT TO HAVE HER HAIR DONE Friday morning, as soon as her favorite salon in town opened its doors. In fact, her hairdresser, Tina Hartley, who owned Hair by Tina, had insisted on opening early just so Molly could be accommodated.

It was the week before Christmas and, of course, they were fully booked, Tina had explained. "But I've got to get you ready for the red carpet, Molly. I can't wait to see you get your award. Of course, I voted for you," she added, as she was also a member of the local business owners' group.

Molly appreciated both favors, though she actually dreaded the banquet. She felt like such a fraud. How could she be getting an award? It seemed totally ridiculous now. *I should be honored with the award for Biggest Business Screwup in Town,* she thought. *That would be more realistic.*

But there was no help for it. She had to go through with the entire charade. She would deserve an Academy Award if she managed it.

She decided to put in a little time at the shop before she went over to Tina's, and as she drove down Main Street she spotted her brother's truck. It was barely seven a.m., but Sam was usually at one of his jobs by now.

She pulled up and got out, hoping to catch him for a quick word. They had been missing each other's phone calls, and Molly was eager to know if he'd won his battle with Newburyport Town Hall for the special inspection and certificate. If further prodding was needed, it was always best to plead with her big brother face-to-face. Molly knew that by now.

No news is good news. You have to think positively, she reminded herself as she headed for the big barn Sam used as his workshop, behind The Bramble antiques store.

She met Sam coming out of the shop, carrying a beat-up canvas bag full of tools. He tossed it into the back of his truck as he greeted her. "Hey, Molly. I was just on my way to Newburyport. We've got all the new Sheetrock in place, and the mold situation is practically under control."

Molly felt a bit of hope rising. "Finally, some good news. That's encouraging. How are you coming with that limited permit? Can I at least open the counter area next week? Puh-leeese, Sam, please say yes." Molly had her fingers crossed and even squeezed her eyes shut, wishing.

She heard Sam chuckle at her theatrics, but the tone of his voice dashed her hopes. “I’m sorry. I tried my best. I called everyone I know up there in town hall and everyone I know who knows someone. The building inspection department is really strict. It’s either all or nothing.”

“Come on, Sam. There’s got to be someone. Are you sure you pulled out all the stops? I just can’t believe it. There’s got to be some way to manage this . . .”

She could tell by the expression on Sam’s face that her voice was getting loud and her famous temper was showing. And when he spoke, it was in the kind of calming voice that parents used to defuse their children’s tantrums. “I know it’s not the news you want to hear, Molly, but just slow down and take a breath. When I tell you that I called everybody and then some, I am not just making excuses—”

“I didn’t mean to imply that you were. But maybe there’s somebody you didn’t think of. Or some other way around this? Maybe you could—”

“There’s no other way,” he cut in, his tone sterner. “I wish you would just trust me and let go of it already. That department moves like a glacier. You could get a decision from the Supreme Court faster than from that gang, believe me.”

Molly took a breath. Her brother, famous for his patience, was starting to get annoyed.

“I know you had your heart set on an opening by Christmas, and I’m sorry the construction didn’t go as planned,” he went on. “But that’s the way it is with these projects. It’s not a cake that you put in the oven and set the timer and *bing*, it’s done.”

For a moment, Molly had felt she was being unfair. But Sam’s last comment pushed her buttons, and she shot back without thinking.

“If you’re trying to say I’m far more efficient at what I do than you are, I agree. It’s hard to believe that one simple renovation job can have so many unforeseen disasters and lose so much time in the schedule. And you still stand there so calm and collected, and tell me it’s just the way it is." She paused, taking a moment to mimic his stoic personality. "I just don't believe that, Sam. Every day that store stays closed is costing me a truckload of money. I think you owe me some explanations."

"I *owe* you explanations? Are you kidding? Nobody in their right mind would have picked that place. It was a broken-down wreck. But you insisted, in your usual Molly-steamroller style. Against my advice and Betty's," he reminded her. "And now you have the nerve to tell me it's my fault the place is taking a long time to get into shape?"

He paused for a breath, but not long enough for her to answer before he continued, "If you think it's that easy, why don't you find another contractor? One with a magic wand in his toolbox that he can wave over that mess. And maybe he can wave it over the building inspector, too, while he's at it."

Molly felt all the anger drain out of her, replaced by total shock. "Are you quitting on me? Right in the middle of this?"

Sam swallowed hard and crossed his arms over his chest, his voice at a reasonable level once more, but his attitude not at all comforting. "Maybe the only mistake I've made with this job is taking it from you in the first place. I love you, Molly. You're my little sister. I want to help you when I can. But I'm not going to stand here and have you berate me just because *you* weren't realistic—and didn't listen to a word I said about the actual amount of time it would take to fix that place up. That's the way I see it."

Molly's first urge was to yell back again, but all she could do was stare at her brother bleakly. She knew what he said was true. Her timeline had been wishful thinking, or at least the best possible outcome if every single repair went smoothly and perfectly to plan.

Unfortunately, too many items on the list had not gone to plan. And some things—like the mold—had never been in the plan at all. But she had refused to accept that.

She shook her head, unable to answer him for a long moment. Finally she said, "All right . . . quit if you want. It doesn't matter now anyway. I don't think that place will ever open."

It was her most secret fear, spoken aloud for the first time. A horrible thing to hear, and yet, somehow, a relief.

Now it was Sam's turn to look shocked. "What do you mean, it won't open?" He sighed and shook his head. "I'm not walking off the job, princess. I just said that to blow off some steam. And scare you a little," he admitted. "I'm sorry."

"Yeah . . . I know. But I'm not trying to scare you. I wish . . . I wish I was . . ." she sputtered.

It had been easier to keep up a brave front when Sam was angry, but now that he was looking at her with such concern, Molly felt herself melt down like a puddle of chocolate ganache. She started crying and couldn't help herself. She covered her face with her hands.

"Molly . . . what is it? What's wrong? Is it just because the new store isn't opening by Christmas? I'm really sorry. I know you had your heart set on it."

She felt Sam's hand on her shoulder and finally looked up at him. "No . . . it's not that. Not *just* that." He'd handed her a tissue, and she dried her eyes and took a shaky breath. "Oh, Sam . . . I've made a mess of everything since Betty left. We owe money all over town, and I could barely afford the supplies for all the parties that we're catering. I've had to skimp a bit on quality ingredients," she admitted—at least a felony in her book. "The renovation has gone way over budget. I've been so extravagant, and we didn't plan for all these unexpected costs . . . and I dipped into our regular account to cover it. I thought I could pay it back once the new store opened. And it would be all fine by the time Betty got back. But the shop in Cape Light is behind with its usual earnings, and even our party business has fallen off this year."

She paused to take a breath. Sam kept his gaze fixed on her, his expression neutral but concerned. He didn't interrupt, and she decided to tell him everything. Down to the last embarrassing detail.

"I'm paying out money as fast as it comes in, Sam. I don't know where it goes. I don't know how Betty kept us in the black all these years. I could hardly afford to get the oven fixed when it broke down last week," she confessed. "We're hanging on by our fingernails. It's so scary. And I don't know what to do . . ."

Sam stared at her and sighed. He ran his own business, and she knew he understood.

"I thought something like that might be going on," he said at last. "I just didn't think it was such a tangle. I feel so bad for you, Molly. Honestly. No wonder the delays on the shop are making you crazy."

"Yeah, well. I think they actually have put me over the edge. Not your fault," she added quickly. "Just sayin'."

Sam cracked a small smile, but it was quickly replaced by a look of concern. "Betty doesn't know any of this?"

Molly shook her head. "I tried to tell her. I had it all planned. But when she got to work that morning, she had just heard that Nate wasn't really recovering, so of course I couldn't tell her then. I just haven't had a chance since to go see her and talk about it. I haven't even told Matt yet," she confessed.

"You've been carrying a heavy load, haven't you? No wonder you're so stressed out. But there's got to be some way out of this. Even if it hurts a little. Weren't you going to apply for a bigger loan for the renovation?"

"I did call to find out if we'd qualify. But the bank hasn't gotten back to me yet—about whether we qualify and for how much. They might not be able to tell us until after Christmas. I was waiting to find out before I told Betty what was going on. At least that would soften the blow."

"I don't think you can wait, Molly. You've already waited too long," he added honestly. "If something like this had happened to Betty, or to Matt, wouldn't you want to know?"

"Yes, of course . . . Oh, I know I haven't been fair. I know it's not my best moment by a long shot. But this is the way business goes sometimes. I've been in holes before. I've always climbed out of them, one way or another. But this time is different. It's like I'm in the hole and I'm digging, but the dirt just keeps coming and coming, piling on top of me again."

She looked back at Sam, suddenly terrified. "What if I've ruined everything? What if we lose the entire business now—all my investment, and Betty's, too? I'm just so ashamed. I feel like such a failure."

"You? A failure? Never," he insisted. "You're a true success story, Mol. You've just hit a bump in the road. You need some help. Everybody does, at one time or another."

"Oh, Sam. It's nice of you to say that. But I don't feel like a success lately. I feel like a fraud, a big phony. I have no idea how I'm going to get on a stage tonight and accept some award for Business Owner of the Year. What a lie that is. Maybe that's why God is punishing me," she said suddenly. "I'm just a big phony and He wants everyone to know. Maybe I'll be struck by lightning on the podium when I make my speech."

"Hey, you're just talking crazy now, Molly. God isn't punishing you," Sam insisted. "It just doesn't work that way. You must know that by now."

"I never thought so. But since we're telling the truth here, I have to admit, I feel like Job in the Bible. I mean, if Job were a caterer," she added, making Sam crack a grin.

Molly had some faith, but Sam's was stronger. He had always been that way, and she admired him for it. People turned to Sam for strength and guidance, and he was often able to help them. It was a gift, she thought, the way his artistry as a woodworker was a gift.

"Come on, Molly. It's not that God is punishing you or singling you out for rough treatment. Difficult times are part of life. We all go through them. The upside is that He's always there to help you if you're open to it—if you ask for His help and give Him a chance. Our lives are filled with spiritual choices, Molly. Maybe that's what you should be taking away from this rough patch."

Molly shook her head and rolled her eyes, resisting this spiritual advice. Still, she felt she had to be honest. "I have said a prayer or two. In my way," she qualified. "I didn't get any great answers—except for our neighbor, Alain, fixing the oven. *That* was a miracle," she had to admit. "As for the rest of it, I wouldn't be melting down right in front of your eyes if God had answered my prayers, Sam."

Sam gazed at her a moment, then said, "Did I ever tell you the joke about the guy on the desert island?"

"I don't remember . . . Do you really have to tell me now?" she teased.

"Just bear with me a minute. You'll like this. There was this guy stranded on a desert island, and all he did all day was sit on the beach and pray for God to save him. The first day, a giant turtle swam up to the shore and offered to carry the guy to safety. But he told the turtle to go away. 'God is going to save me. I don't need a turtle,' he said. The next day, a fishing boat drops anchor and offers to take him off the island, and then the next day, a cruise ship, and the day after that, a seaplane—"

"Okay, okay, I get the idea. So what's the punch line?" Molly rushed him along. She hated the way Sam told a joke, slowly drawing out every line for effect.

He seemed unfazed by her comment. "Every day the guy kept telling anyone who came, 'God is going to save me.' Finally, the man died of starvation. His soul went up to heaven and he met God. 'I prayed to you every day on the beach. Why didn't you save me?' he told God. 'Are you kidding me?' God said. 'I sent you a helicopter, a seaplane, two boats, even a giant sea turtle. What were you waiting for?'"

Sam met her glance and started chuckling. Molly had to laugh a little, too. "That was cute. So, what's the point? Should I hide on an island and take the first sea turtle?"

Sam ignored her tart reply. "You have to ask for help, Molly, and let God work through other people. Trust Betty. Trust Matt. Give them a chance to be a channel for the help that you've prayed for. God isn't going to send a bolt down from the blue to ruin your speech—or to help you. But that doesn't mean He isn't listening."

She met his serious glance and looked away. What he said made sense—especially if you had faith. But Molly wasn't sure her faith was that strong. It was so hard to put herself out there, to trust that everyone could understand and forgive her. Molly just sighed. Finally she said, "If only the new shop would get hit by lightning. Some night when no one would get hurt. At least we'd be able to collect the insurance."

"Don't try to sidetrack me with your stand-up routine," Sam said quickly. "And take off your cape and boots. You need to come clean with Betty and apologize. That's the first thing you need to do to solve this problem. At least you've confessed your mess to me," he pointed out. "It will be easier the next time," he promised.

Molly was feeling a tiny bit better from his pep talk, but at the mention of confessing this all over again to Betty and Matt, she felt a sudden sour knot in her stomach. As if she might throw up.

Sam noticed it, too. "Hey, don't look so bleak. You can do it. You're great at going out of your way for anyone and everyone who asks you for help. Now it's your turn. Try to look at it that way?"

Molly wasn't sure that perspective worked for her either. But Sam did know her well. That was her role, the Statue of Liberty, a lady alone on an island, holding a light up for the rest of the world. Sometimes her arm did get tired, but it was so hard to stop.

Still, she knew what she had to do. Sam was right. She wasn't going to get anywhere with this problem if she kept hiding. She just couldn't solve it on her own. She had to face that now.

"I'll do it. I'll talk to them. First chance I get," she promised. "And I'm not going to bug you about opening this shop anymore. I know you're doing your best. It will open when it opens."

If it opens, she added silently.

She expected her brother to say, *In God's time, not ours.* One of his favorite reminders. But instead he just patted her shoulder. "You never know, Mol. Maybe I'll surprise you."

She sure hoped so. But she decided not to say that either.

A MILLION EXCUSES FOR DUCKING OUT ON THE AWARD CEREMONY RAN through Molly's head as she dressed for the event. Most involved faking some illness or injury. But with Matt around, she knew she would never get away with that.

That's the trouble with being married to a doctor. You can never fake a sick day, she thought.

She fussed over her outfit, her stockings, her makeup and jewelry, while Matt called upstairs several times, worried about being late. Finally, he appeared in the bedroom doorway, looking distressed but very handsome in his best navy blue pinstripe suit, a silk tie, and a dressy white shirt that required cuff links.

"You look so handsome, honey. You could wear that suit on Amanda's wedding day."

"My daughter will probably require a tux or even tails," he replied. "Speaking of Amanda and Gabriel, they're waiting for us. She just sent me a text asking if we left yet."

Molly ignored the question. "Oh . . . nice. Then they made good time." Amanda and her fiancé had come down from Portland for the dinner. Her older daughters weren't able to come home, and little Betty was too young. She and her babysitter were already watching a movie downstairs.

"Yes, they did, but we're going to be very late if you don't get a move on. The cocktail hour is going to start soon."

"I know. I'm almost ready," she claimed.

"Do we need to pick up Betty Bowman?"

"No, she's coming on her own. If she can make it."

"I hope she can," Matt replied quickly.

Molly nodded. She knew Betty wanted to come, but she wasn't sure she could leave Nate alone. Molly had mixed feelings about seeing her best friend and partner in the audience, applauding her. Next to Matt, she wanted Betty there most of all. But Molly also knew that every time their eyes met she would feel sad and guilty.

"Can I help you with anything?" Matt was losing his patience; she could tell by his tone.

"Zip me up. This dress has a funny little catch at the top." She had already gone through all her formal wear, feeling uncomfortable in everything. Finally, she had settled on a black silk wrap dress, cocktail length and flattering to her figure. She couldn't even remember when she had bought it, but it was still sort of in style.

"Very pretty," Matt said as she smoothed out the fabric.

"It'll do. I didn't have time to shop." She'd had neither the time nor the heart. Though most people would have splurged on a new outfit for a night like this one.

She pushed at her curls with her comb, trying to get her hair right. "I really don't like the way my hair came out. Do you?"

"Your hair looks fine. It looks great. It doesn't look any different at all to me."

"You just contradicted yourself like . . . five times in one sentence, Matt."

"You look beautiful. That's what I meant to say. Are you nervous about giving your speech? Is that it?"

"It won't be much. I'm keeping it short and sweet."

She had scribbled out random remarks today—a mixture of thank-yous and happy talk—then emailed the mess to her daughter Jillian, who was the best writer in the family. Fortunately, Jill had been happy to translate the rambling sentences into English without changing them too much.

"Just speak from your heart, Mom. You're good at that," Jillian had said when she'd called to wish her mother luck.

Good advice, Molly thought. *But if I really follow it, I'll end up shaming myself right off the podium.*

"Okay," Matt said. "You're not nervous. And we all know you're not shy—you bask in attention." He frowned. "But something is making you drag those high heels tonight."

Molly put down the comb and met his eyes in the mirror. "It just doesn't feel right, getting some big award. I don't deserve it."

"Nonsense. Of course you do. You're a real success story in this town, honey. Everybody knows that. And everybody loves you," he added.

She had to smile at that claim. "Not everybody, Matt," she corrected him, thinking of her creditors and Oscar. "But it is sweet that you think that."

"Anyone who really knows you," he amended. "I'm very, very proud of you, Molly. You amaze me every day. My life would be utterly boring if I'd never met you."

Molly pretended to be fussing with an earring; she didn't want Matt to see that she was very moved by his words, actually close to tears. He really did believe in her. He put her on a pedestal of some kind. She had never gotten used to it—her amazing good luck that this wonderful, accomplished, and loving man loved her. She dreaded disappointing him, confessing her mistakes and failure. She hated knowing that very soon, she would appear so diminished in his eyes. No longer amazing or wonderful. Just a big failure. And a liar, to boot.

"That's very nice of you to say," she murmured. "Thanks, honey."

"You don't have to thank me. I should tell you that every day, not just on the nights when you're getting awards." He came up behind her and dropped a quick, warm kiss on her cheek. "I'll start the car. It's pretty cold out. Please come right down? Or we really will be late."

"I'll be right there," she promised, watching him go.

She stared back at her reflection, relieved to have one last moment alone. She rearranged the long strand of pearls that hung from her neck. Fancy jewelry had never been Molly's weakness, but the pearls meant something to her. A pearl necklace was the only piece of jewelry she had ever really wanted; a set of genuine pearls, not the costume kind you can buy in any department store.

Pearls were classic, elegant, and pure luxury, she thought. Lillian Warwick and her kind were rarely seen without them. Molly had bought the necklace for herself years ago, soon after she married Matt and moved to the beautiful house they still lived in. She believed then that she had finally arrived. She had come through her struggles and made something of herself, and owed apologies to no one.

I arrived, she thought wistfully. *But I didn't stay long at the party.*

She slipped off the pearls and put them aside, choosing instead a thin gold chain with a small heart charm—a gift from her girls, who had saved up babysitting money and allowance to buy it for her a long time ago. A modest piece, but she felt drawn to it when she needed some courage—and needed to remember that, no matter what, she was truly loved.

Molly finally went downstairs and put on her best coat and black leather gloves. She kissed her youngest daughter good night and gave the sitter some last-minute instructions.

She slipped into the car next to Matt and shut her door. "Let the games begin," she said, sounding much heartier than she felt.

"That's the spirit." Matt smiled and nodded. "This is your night, Molly. Just relax and enjoy it. You have a lot of fans out there. I'm glad to see you recognized for all you've achieved, and all you've done for the town and the church community."

She had been generous to their community, happily supporting any cause that came to her attention, knowing firsthand how it felt to be blessed with a hand up. But she still didn't feel she deserved all the praise and attention. She had turned into a phony, just the sort of person she detested.

Molly turned to Matt, longing to tell him everything. But she just couldn't do it.

By the time they reached the Spoon Harbor Inn and made their way into the reception, the cocktail hour was just about over. Molly found herself working her way through the crowd, like a politician in the last hours of a big campaign—exchanging hugs and loud, happy greetings. Shaking hands and accepting good wishes all around.

She had barely caught her breath and sipped the drink Matt had handed her when a chime sounded, indicating that it was time to start the dinner.

Emily Warwick, the mayor of Cape Light, was going to present the award, and now she came over to walk Molly into the dining room. "Congratulations, Molly," she said. "I'm so happy for you. We couldn't have chosen a more deserving person."

"Thank you. I appreciate you saying that, Emily." Molly knew Emily was sincere. She'd been one of Molly's earliest supporters, willing to hire her when no one else was, even championing Molly in the face of Lillian's disapproval.

"We'll make the presentation right away, before dinner is served," Emily explained. "I hope that's all right with you."

"No problem. Let's just get it over with."

"Don't worry. I'll keep my remarks short and sweet," Emily promised, sensing Molly's unease.

Molly smiled in answer as Emily patted her arm in a comforting way. *Emily thinks I have a case of nerves because I'm speaking in public,* Molly realized. *She could never guess what's really eating at me.*

Molly waited in her seat on the stage as Emily took the podium and the crowd quieted down. The room was packed with well-wishers and even more familiar faces from town than Molly had imagined would turn out. Which made her feel worse.

Even her arch restaurant rivals, like Charlie Bates, had come to congratulate her. Her good friend Alain Chandor was there, of course. And just about every business owner on Main Street had come. Even Grace Hegman, who owned The Bramble antiques shop and was practically a recluse. Molly noticed her sitting with Claire North, who didn't own the Inn at Angel Island but managed it on her own now.

Molly's family and closest friends filled practically all the seats at one large table up front—Matt, along with Amanda and Gabriel, and Jessica and Sam. And her parents, Marie and Joe Morgan, whom Molly had invited as special guests. Dan Forbes, the former publisher of the *Cape Light Messenger* and Emily's husband, was there as well.

There were three empty seats at the table, too. One for Molly, one for Emily, and one for Betty, who had not yet arrived. Molly wondered if she was coming after all. Maybe Betty wasn't able to find anyone to stay with Nate. On one hand, Molly felt bad that Betty wasn't there . . . and on the other, she was relieved. Of all the friends, acquaintances, and family here tonight who would soon be staring back at her, Betty would be the hardest to face.

Emily had begun Molly's introduction, and Molly forced herself to focus and take a few deep breaths to calm her nerves.

"—and everyone in Cape Light knows Molly. Or thinks they do," Emily was saying. "What many do not realize is just how this amazing, accomplished, and generous woman came to be the success story that we all know and love. Working hard in two, or even three, jobs to raise her young daughters as a single mom. Baking nights and racing around town to make deliveries each morning. But never giving up on her dream to someday own and run her own thriving business . . ."

Molly blinked and stared at the carpet. She hoped Emily would wrap it up. She couldn't listen to her praises being sung for much longer before she'd jump up and scream. All she could think was, *I'm no success story, believe me . . . Just the opposite, it turns out.*

Emily was soon smiling at her, holding out the award, and Molly walked up to the podium as the audience applauded wildly.

It took a few moments for the room to settle down. Molly cleared her throat. "Gee . . . thanks, Emily, for that wonderful introduction. You make me sound like Superwoman, Julia Child, and Angelina Jolie, all wrapped into one. Okay, maybe not Angelina," she added, and everyone laughed.

She stared down at her notes, the words blurring before her eyes. "I really just want to thank everyone for this great honor. First, to the Cape Light Merchants' Association, my fellow shop owners and friends, who make it such a pleasure to run a business in our wonderful town.

"The most important thing I've learned over the years of turning my dream into a reality is that nobody does that alone. I certainly didn't. I have to thank everyone who helped me on the way. My family, of course, especially my husband, Matt, who is always in my corner, no matter what," she said, catching her husband's eye. "My parents and my brother Sam, who, by the way, made a lot of those early-morning muffin deliveries and should definitely get some credit."

"And ate my fair share of the goods," Sam called out.

Molly laughed. "How true," she agreed. She paused, waiting for the laughter to subside, and suddenly noticed the door at the back of the room open as Betty Bowman quietly slipped inside.

Betty remained by the door, leaning against the wall, trying not to call attention to herself. But when Molly caught her eye, Betty greeted her with a wide, bright smile and a tiny wave, wishing her well.

Molly felt teary. *I was doing so well, too, carrying out this charade.* She felt her voice choke up and wasn't sure she could continue.

The room went silent as Molly stared down at her notes a moment, collecting herself. She finally looked up and forced a smile.

"And I know I would not be here tonight, selected for this special honor, if it wasn't for my wonderful partner and dearest friend in the world, Betty Bowman." Molly gestured toward Betty. "Betty was the first person to encourage me to start my own business. Then, about ten years ago, feeling a little bored with the real estate business, Betty offered to help out at Willoughby's. That was one of the luckiest days of my life," Molly said honestly. "We soon became partners and . . . Well, the rest is history, as they say."

And a story that might end very abruptly and very soon, Molly silently added.

"I truly appreciate your recognition and good wishes tonight. But please, no more applause for me," she said. "I'd like to recognize and applaud my partner, Betty Bowman, and share this honor and award with her."

The audience rose from their chairs, first to applaud Molly and then quickly turning toward Betty, too. Betty waved her hands, willing everyone to stop. Molly left the stage, walked to her friend, and gave her a big hug.

"That was sweet of you, Molly. But honestly, it's your night. I told you that I didn't want to share the spotlight. You shouldn't have," Betty gently scolded her.

"Sorry, but you deserve it," Molly replied. *And that should be the worst breach I've ever made in our friendship,* she added silently. She sighed, feeling the weight of all she had to tell Betty. But knowing that tonight was neither the time nor the place.

CHAPTER TEN

DESPITE HER LATE NIGHT AT THE AWARD DINNER, MOLLY was up and out at the crack of dawn on Saturday morning. She drove toward the village, bleary eyed but determined, facing twelve parties that would kick off at noon that day and wind down late Sunday night. It was the weekend before Christmas, always one of the busiest party weekends of the year.

A nickel-gray sky hung low, heavy with moisture and clouds. The forecast was uncertain, with a possibility of snow flurries or icy rain that would likely start late in the day.

Molly hoped it would hold off or even blow out to sea. Bad weather only complicated her crew's loading and unloading of their catering vans. But just like the postal service, as she had often told her employees, "'Neither snow nor rain nor heat nor gloom of night . . .' will keep us from delivering great parties."

Molly tried to summon up some Christmas spirit. She pictured herself a little like Santa with a merry—though overworked—bunch of elves, shuttling around town in two catering vans and her own SUV to six locations today, two this afternoon and four in the evening. She kept her clipboard close at hand, reviewing the plans for each event and noting reminders each time she paused at a stop sign or a traffic light. As much as they tried to prepare in advance, there were some dishes that had to be made fresh or even cooked on the spot.

When she reached the shop, she found Sonia in the kitchen, along with an early-bird crew. Molly greeted them, psyched to rev up her team like a championship-winning coach.

"Hey, guys, thanks for coming in at the crack of dawn. Looks like everything is under control. We're going to hit the deck running today and just do it. I know you can," she added in her best fearless-leader voice. She consulted her clipboard. "The first van should go out at eight thirty, to the luncheon in Salem."

"We've got that order set. We've already started packing the van," Sonia confirmed. "How was the banquet last night? Sorry I couldn't make it."

"That's all right. It was fine, a real town booster thing. I think it was just my turn."

"You're too modest, Molly."

"Not really," Molly said honestly. "If we get through this schedule, *that* will be something, and I'm giving everyone in this kitchen an award."

Oscar's replacement, a new prep cook named Tim, stood at the worktable, making a pile of vegetable curls to garnish the platters. "Meat pie by meat pie, Molly," he announced. "That's how we'll do it."

If only it were that simple, Molly thought. Even though the day required her full and complete attention, Molly's business worries buzzed around her head like a swarm of gnats.

Of course there had been no time last night to tell Betty about the situation. It was all smiles and compliments, hugs and congratulations, from her friends and family.

I really can't talk to her until Monday, Molly thought. *I'm not making an excuse. I don't have a minute, even if I had the stomach for it today,* she decided, looking over the schedule again, which was color coded with highlighter markers—yellow for her events, pink for Sonia's. And one or two that were still ominously blank.

Monday. That's the day. I'll send her a text right now and tell her I need to visit.

But when Molly pulled out her phone, she found a text message from Betty.

> Sorry to bother you on the BIG day. But I had a strange call from the bank yesterday afternoon. Didn't get to mention it last night. We didn't apply for a loan again, did we? Must be some mistake. Just wanted you to know I'll call and follow up today. You looked gorgeous last night, by the way. So glad I made it, at least for a little while.

Betty signed it with Xs and Os, making Molly feel even worse.

The bank had called Betty . . . What a disaster. But it did make sense. Betty had handled the original loan for their company; her contact information had probably popped up first in the bank's computer.

Molly's mind raced, wondering what the banker had said. Did the bank tell Betty that they'd been rejected for the loan? Molly winced at the thought. But from her note, it didn't sound that way. At least no one had told Betty the whole story yet.

Molly found Betty's number and started to call. Then stopped. Better not to get into this on the phone. They had to talk face-to-face. Today. There was no putting it off any longer. She went back to the text message screen and tapped out a reply.

We should talk. I can stop on the way to the Elks Lodge. Around 5 or so? Let me know if that's okay.

Molly knew that stopping at Betty's meant she would be stretched thin, leaving one job early and getting to the next one late. *I'll have to ask Sonia to cover for me for a little while. Or put Tim in charge?*

Either way, it had to be done. Sam might even say, "*Someone* is trying to send you a message."

Molly rolled her eyes skyward as she began her own morning tasks in the kitchen. *Okay, God, I'm finally paying attention. Please help me out when I see Betty?*

CARRIE WAS THE FIRST ONE UP ON SATURDAY MORNING, THOUGH SHE usually found Vera in the kitchen first, up every day bright and early. Carrie set up the coffeemaker and mixed a batch of pancakes for Noah. The smell of his favorite breakfast soon drew him downstairs.

"Pancakes? Yum. Can I have bananas on them?"

"That's fine. Here, you can slice it yourself." Carrie gave Noah a banana, a plate, and a very dull knife, happy to have him busy while she cooked.

Vera ambled down the stairs and joined them a few minutes later. She was still in her bathrobe and slippers, Carrie noticed, which was unusual for Vera.

"Would you like some pancakes, Vera? I made plenty."

"Maybe later, dear. I'm just going to have some tea for now. I'm feeling a little chilled. I must be coming down with something."

Vera sniffed and dabbed her nose with a tissue. She did look a little pale, Carrie thought, and seemed quiet as well.

"Maybe you should go back to bed. I'll make you some tea and toast and bring it up to your room."

"Would you? That would be so nice. A little more sleep today would help. I feel sort of achy, not quite right," Vera admitted, touching her forehead.

"You should probably spend the day in bed. Maybe you'll shake it off."

"I wish I could . . . but I have to get out later, at least for a little while. I promised the committee I'd collect more donations for the Christmas family." Vera took the flyer from a pile of papers she kept on the counter and put her reading glasses on to look it over.

Carrie knew the flyer by heart. She had run off plenty of copies at church last week. She turned back to the pancakes and flipped a few that were bubbling around the edges.

"That's what I get for putting off a big job until the last minute," Vera murmured. "Maybe some stores will be open tomorrow."

"Don't worry, I'll go around for you," Carrie offered.

Vera looked surprised by her offer and very relieved. "Would you really? But I can't ask you to do that for me. You must have a list of things to take care of on your day off."

"It's no trouble, Vera. Honestly." Even working full time at the church office, Carrie found herself with much more free time than she'd had at Helen Vincent's house. "I'll go down Main Street and ask around a bit. Noah can help me."

Her son's head popped up at the sound of his name. He was reading a book at the table as he shoveled in bites of pancake. "What are we doing?"

"We're going to help Vera collect donations for the Christmas family. She has a bad cold." Carrie sometimes wondered if Noah heard half of what was going on around him; he was often so lost in a book or his own imagination. She slipped two slices of bread in the toaster for Vera. "I wanted to help with that project anyway," she said. "I almost forgot about it."

"If you really don't mind, I'd be very grateful." Vera left the flyer on the table and headed back to the stairs. "I don't think there's much I can do today except get back in bed."

"I'll be right up with your tea. Let me know if you need anything at the drugstore. I'll get it for you when we go out."

Vera nodded but didn't reply. Carrie heard her sneezing as she headed up the stairs and sighed with sympathy. The water in the kettle had come to a boil, and she returned to the stove and fixed the tea.

"You don't have to come with me if you don't want to, Noah. Maybe there's some friend at school, or in Essex, you'd like me to call?"

Noah thought a moment. "There's this boy named Henry. He's my friend now. We ate lunch together this week and he picked me in gym for his kickball partner . . . I think he's having a birthday party or something."

Carrie didn't know what a kickball partner was, but the news of Henry's birthday was encouraging. A real child, in Noah's class. Nothing imaginary about him . . . she hoped. "Sounds like he does want to be friends with you."

"Max hid his lunch one day, too. So Henry liked that I stood up to him."

"When is the party? Did he give you an invitation?"

Noah thought a moment. "I think so . . . it might be in my backpack." He ran over to his pack, which hung near the coats by the door, and riffled through it, finally presenting a piece of wrinkled paper to Carrie.

She read it quickly. "Noah, this party is today. When did Henry give this to you?"

Noah shrugged. "I don't remember . . . Can I go?"

"Sure, if you want to. Let's see . . . it's bowling and pizza and a sleepover." She glanced over at him. "What do you think? I can pick you up after the bowling and pizza if you don't want to stay over." She knew he was sometimes shy with large groups of kids, especially if he didn't know them well.

"It's okay. I'll sleep over. I bet it'll be fun. Henry says he has a finished basement with a Wii."

"Sounds like a great party. I'm glad you remembered," she said with a smile. "I'll call Henry's mother and tell her that you're coming. We'll have to get him a gift today, too."

She was so glad to hear Noah had made a friend. She loved spending time with him, but the Christmas break would be a long one for both of them if Noah didn't have any children his age to play with.

"Maybe Henry will be around over the vacation and you can have some playdates," she said.

"Yeah, I hope so." Noah's expression seemed suddenly thoughtful. He slid a bit of pancake around his plate, wiping up extra syrup. "Do you think we'll ever see Jeff and Elsie again?"

The question took her by surprise, though the truth was that ever since Wednesday night, she had been wondering the same thing—if and when they would see Jeff again. Would he call and ask her out? She had often felt he was attracted to her, but she didn't want to get her hopes up. She was sure there were ethical boundaries about dating a patient's parent. Then again, Noah wasn't officially his patient anymore.

Still, maybe he still wasn't allowed to date her, or there was some rule about faculty dating parents? Or maybe it was too soon for him since his wife had passed away. Or maybe it was too soon for her, she reasoned.

Well, you've covered all the reasons why he can't date you, Carrie, a little voice inside her teased. *Are you that afraid he might call? Or just trying to soften the blow in case he never does?*

She didn't even know if she was ready to date yet. Her marriage to Kevin had left her feeling wary of men, wary of letting someone close again. But Jeff was different. She felt very comfortable with him, as if he were a friend. Noah seemed to think of him that way, too.

Jeff had spoken to Noah about their sessions ending in a careful, kind way. He explained that even though they wouldn't have their afternoon visits anymore, he would always be happy to help if Noah ever wanted to talk about anything that made him unhappy or bothered him. Noah had seemed to understand at the time, but now Carrie wasn't so sure.

"Do you think we'll see them?" Noah was impatient for her answer.

"I don't really know, honey," Carrie said honestly. "We might run into Jeff around town, I guess. Or you might see him around school."

Noah didn't seem satisfied with that. "I liked playing at his house. And playing with Elsie."

Carrie nodded and touched his hand. Chester the cat was friendly, but he didn't tolerate playing or even petting for very long. Elsie was a much more playful four-legged companion.

"I'm sure you did. Jeff is a nice man . . . and Elsie is a great dog." She had fixed Vera's tray and was ready to take it up to her. "If you help me today, we can have lunch at Willoughby's or the Clam Box," she offered. "And I'll take you to the playground. There's going to be a lot to carry," she said optimistically. "I'll need your help."

"I can help. Theo can, too. Getting people to donate, I mean. Not carrying stuff."

Noah hadn't mentioned the angel for a day or so. Carrie had hoped Noah's imaginary friend was fading. But, recalling her last conversation with Jeff, she did try to understand it in a new way. She reminded herself that this was Noah's way of feeling safe, and she did want him to feel safe and happy.

"I guess that's good. Because I'm a little shy at asking people for donations. Even for a good cause," she admitted. "So I'm happy Theo's helping, too."

VERA HAD MADE A LIST OF THE ITEMS CARRIE WAS SUPPOSED TO ASK for and told Carrie which stores to visit in town. "I was assigned a lot of household goods. The family is just getting out of a shelter and into a house, so they need a lot of practical, everyday things. Krueger Hardware and Variety Store should have most of this stuff. But Mr. Krueger isn't exactly Santa Claus," she explained, handing over the list. "You may need to go up to the turnpike to some big store and see if you can get the rest there."

"I'll try my best," Carrie had promised. It was a long list. Carrie doubted any store owner would donate this much. But she already planned to buy a few things herself and donate them. She could also go out tomorrow afternoon and try to get more.

In town, Carrie and Noah parked near the harbor, then headed down Main Street. The village looked very pretty decorated for Christmas. All along Main Street the stores were decked out with beautiful decorations and displays. A miniature train in the window of the toy store chugged its way through a tiny snow-covered town. In the window of the vintage clothing boutique, mannequins dressed in 1950s evening gowns gathered 'round a Christmas tree covered with tinsel and shiny ornaments. The florist's shop displayed poinsettias and wreaths and pine garlands, all decorated with gold and silver ornaments. Everything was festive and sparkling, and Carrie felt some of the excitement of the season lift her heart.

She thought of her own Christmas shopping, too. She hadn't done much yet, just bought Noah a few practical gifts that he needed. He didn't believe in Santa anymore, which was one of the reasons she wondered about the angel. But he had asked for a few things—LEGOs, a model spaceship, and a book about dogs.

Aside from Noah, she didn't have many people to buy things for. But she wanted to bring Helen a gift, put a few small surprises for Vera under her tree, and find some small gift for Reverend Ben, too. Carrie realized her list had grown a bit the last few weeks, which made her smile. Everyone they had met in Cape Light had been so nice to her and Noah. Including Jeff, of course. Though it would be a little too forward to buy him a gift, wouldn't it?

It would have to be very impersonal and nothing expensive. She considered the problem as she and Noah wandered into Krueger's, hoping to speak to the owner about the donation. But the store was very busy. Carrie couldn't even catch the attention of a salesperson. She decided to look at the items they needed and maybe toss a few in the cart.

"Let's see, we need a broom, a mop and a pail, lamps, and lightbulbs."

"Those are weird things to want for Christmas," Noah said as they walked down a narrow aisle.

The store was called Hardware and Variety for good reason, Carrie thought. It was packed with a wide and random variety of items—just about everything you would need for a home and the great outdoors, from fishing reels to frying pans and beyond.

"This family is moving to a new house," Carrie explained. "They've been homeless and living in a place called a shelter. So they don't have all the regular things you need in a house, to keep things clean and neat and all that."

"That's sad," Noah said. "We don't have our own house, but we share a nice house with Vera now."

It did seem as if they shared the house with Vera, maybe because Vera had been so welcoming and generous to them. She did truly want them to feel at home with her.

"Yes, we do. We should count our blessings," Carrie said, not even knowing where that phrase had come from. She rarely said things like that aloud, though lately she had felt very blessed to have wound up here in Cape Light. *It must come from working in the church,* she thought with a smile.

They had reached an aisle with gardening supplies and birdseed. "Nothing down here," Carrie said, still looking for the owner or store manager. "Let's go down another aisle."

"Hey, Mom . . . look at these birdhouses. Aren't they neat?"

Carrie turned and backtracked to where Noah stood, transfixed. The birdhouses were unusual, handmade, and carefully painted. Each one had a theme. One looked like a miniature schoolhouse, and another like a bank. Another one had clapboard and all the trimmings of a fancy Victorian house, and still another looked like a small church.

"Whoever makes these has a good sense of humor," Carrie said.

"I bet Jeff would like one. He likes birds. There's a bird feeder by the window in his office, and there's a bird book there, too, so when the birds came by, we could look them up."

That sounded like Jeff, she thought with a smile. "I think it would be a nice present for him. But we have to concentrate on the family now," she reminded Noah. "Let's find the manager and ask if he'll donate some things. Maybe we can buy some to give, too."

She took Noah by the hand and led him back toward the front of the store. They came to the end of the narrow aisle and turned—to find themselves about ten feet away from Jeff. He was looking over the snow shovels and didn't notice them.

Noah broke away from Carrie and ran toward him. "Hi, Jeff!"

Jeff looked up and smiled. "Noah, my man. How are you?" He raised his hand and Noah gave him a high five.

"We're good. We're shopping for a Christmas family. That's a family who's getting a new place to live and they need stuff. We're collecting it for them at church."

"Yes, I know." Jeff smiled gently at him, and Carrie remembered that he was part of Reverend Ben's congregation, though she had never seen him there. "That's a nice thing to do on a Saturday."

"We're helping Vera. She has a cold."

"Oh, I see . . . That's too bad." He looked up from Noah and met Carrie's glance, greeting her with a warm smile.

"Hello, Jeff. I guess Noah's filled you in on our shopping trip—"

Before she could say more, Noah spoke up again. "We were just talking about you, Jeff," he said brightly.

"Really?" Jeff looked pleased at that news. As he looked over at Carrie, she felt herself blush. Which seemed to please Jeff even more.

"Noah was telling me about the bird feeder outside your office window," she said in a matter-of-fact tone.

He nodded. She wasn't sure if he believed her. He did look amused.

"Well . . . nice to see you. We have to find the store manager and see if he'll give us some donations," Carrie said. "Come on, Noah. I'm sure Jeff has a lot to do today."

She wasn't sure why she was suddenly so eager to leave Jeff. She had been thinking about him a lot the past few days, ever since Noah's last appointment. But she suddenly felt so awkward . . . and obvious. It was silly. Just a silly crush. A girlish fantasy about her son's doctor. What was she thinking? He wasn't even interested in her that way.

Jeff looked surprised as she started walking away. He took her arm. "Wait, don't go. Let me help you. I know Frank Briggs, the man who manages this store. Let me speak to him for you?"

When Carrie didn't answer right away, Jeff persisted. "I heard about that project at church and wanted to get involved, too. I meant to call Claire North but never got around to it. See, it's a lucky coincidence that I ran into you. Now I can do something."

Carrie didn't know what to say. Part of her liked that idea very much, and another part felt awkward and self-conscious.

Noah had no such conflict. "Great. Let's go find that guy you know. We were looking for him everywhere . . ."

Noah and Jeff marched off, and Carrie had no choice but to follow. Jeff found his friend mixing a can of paint and quickly explained their mission. Carrie showed him the flyer and the list.

Frank Briggs glanced at the flyer but looked doubtful. "Well . . . I can see it's a good cause, and I'd like to help you out. But I have to talk to Mr. Krueger, and he's not here right now."

George Krueger, the man Vera had warned was not very open-handed. Too bad, Carrie thought, because Mr. Briggs seemed willing to donate.

"Is he coming in at all today?" Carrie asked.

Frank shook his head. "He's gone out of town. Just left this morning. Family business."

Carrie was disappointed. "We don't have much time to do this. We've left it for the last minute, I'm afraid."

"Can you call him up and ask him?" Noah asked.

All the adults looked down at him. Carrie hoped Frank Briggs didn't think her son was rude.

Frank thought it over, but he didn't look very hopeful. "I guess I can try. I've got to warn you, though; Mr. Krueger never picks up when he's traveling. He doesn't even leave his phone on."

It was sounding more and more like a long shot. Carrie felt disappointed. They could drive to the turnpike to one of the big-box stores, but it wouldn't be as much fun. And there were other stores in town they wanted to shop at.

"We can walk around a few minutes and come back, Frank," Jeff suggested. "I'll buy a few things on the list and donate them."

"I will, too," Carrie said.

Carrie rolled the cart and Noah jumped on the front, hitching a ride as they headed down the first aisle, where they picked out a plastic trash pail and sponges.

In the next aisle, Jeff found a lamp he liked. He held it out for her to see. "What do you think of this one? It would be a good reading lamp."

"It would," Carrie agreed. "It's a good height . . . but I don't really like black. How about the brass finish?"

Jeff looked back at the display. "That is nicer. Let's get that one." He put the box in the cart and picked out the right lightbulbs. Then he picked out a toaster, too. "Four slices. They need fast action in the morning to get out of the house in time."

"Toast with peanut butter," Noah suggested.

An older couple passed and glanced at them. The woman smiled and Carrie could tell that she thought they were a family, out on their Saturday morning errands.

The notion gave Carrie a wistful feeling. *Now I'm getting like Noah, caught up in fantasies. Better get a grip, or I'll be imagining angels, too.*

When they came to the end of the next aisle, Frank Briggs was there to meet them. He had a cell phone in his hand and was staring at it as if it had come alive.

"It's the strangest thing. I was still mixing the paint and didn't even get a chance to look up the number. And Mr. Krueger called me. He never calls me when he's traveling . . . not once in twenty-five years."

Jeff glanced at Carrie, sharing a secret smile. Noah was smiling, too, and very widely.

"That is a coincidence," Jeff remarked. "Did you ask him about the donations?"

"He said it was fine, anything you need on the list. He's happy to help. 'That's what Christmas is about.' . . . His words, not mine," Frank clarified, looking quite surprised at his boss's message. "Of course, I agree."

"Thank you, Mr. Briggs," Carrie said. "Thank you so much."

"Don't thank me," Frank Briggs insisted. He shook his head, stared at the phone again, and slipped it into his pocket.

"Vera told me not to expect much from Mr. Krueger. He must have caught the Christmas spirit this year. That was very generous," she said to Jeff as the three of them headed off to do the rest of the shopping.

Jeff nodded. "I didn't expect much myself, to tell you the truth. But it's nice to see that people can change for the better."

Noah stood by the brooms, testing bristles on the palm of his hand. "That's what Theo said. He's very proud of Mr. Krueger."

Jeff looked thrown off balance by the remark. He glanced at Carrie to check her reaction. She shrugged. Maybe now he understood how disconcerting Noah's remarks about his friend could be. As if Theo were right here with them in the store aisle.

Carrie glanced down at the cart, almost full now, wondering if she was giving Theo a ride today, as well as Noah. An angel would probably be very light. As light as . . . well, as a feather, she realized. Theo could probably sit right in the cart or hang on the side, like Noah did, she reasoned. For a second she tried to picture it, her son and his angel.

"Sponge or rag top?" Jeff held up mops, his question drawing her back to reality.

"Sponge, I think. I'll get this doormat for them. It's cheerful." Carrie picked up a mat for outside the front door, covered with red birds and the words WELCOME HOME!

"Very nice," Jeff agreed.

They worked their way to the front of the store, the cart full, including the shelf on the bottom, and Jeff holding a few items as well.

"How are we doing? Anything left?" Jeff peered over her shoulder, disturbingly close for a moment. Carrie could hardly focus on Vera's thin, curly handwriting.

"I think we're done here. But I still have to stop at a children's clothing store, and I thought a few toys would be nice."

"I love to buy toys." His look of anticipation lit up his handsome face. "Maybe we can go get lunch someplace in town after."

"Okay . . . sure." That had been her plan, too. She was glad he wanted to join them. It felt good to know he wanted to spend more time with them.

Jeff's attention was suddenly drawn by the snow shovel display at the front of the store. "Here's something they could use. A good heavy one, with a sharp blade."

He picked out a metal shovel with a curved handle. Noah ran over to help him, but was soon distracted by a pile of plastic snow saucers. He pulled one down and kneeled in it, crouching and squinting, as if he were at the top of a snowy hill.

Jeff laughed at him. "Noah, what are you doing?"

"I wanted to see if it was big enough for me. It's the perfect size." He looked up with a beguiling grin.

"It is," Jeff agreed. "We should get one for the kids in the family. And one for you, too," he added quickly. "My treat."

"Thanks, Jeff!"

The deal was done before Carrie could protest. "You don't have to do that, Jeff. I'll get it for him."

"I insist. He's been a big help this morning. And I can check Noah off my Christmas list now."

He was being very polite and graceful about this, Carrie thought. She didn't really think Noah was on his list. He certainly couldn't buy gifts for all his patients. And Carrie wasn't really comfortable with the idea of him spending money on Noah—but it was only a few dollars. And Noah looked thrilled.

"What colors should we get?" Jeff asked Noah.

Noah thought a moment. "Theo likes blue. But I like orange better."

"How about blue for the kids in the family and orange for you?"

Carrie sighed. She had never heard Noah say he disagreed with the angel before. She wasn't sure if that was good or bad.

Jeff didn't seem to notice as he pulled two saucers off the pile. Noah wanted to carry his and balanced it on his head. Jeff tossed the other one on the cart along with the snow shovel. "I guess we're done."

"Definitely. But this haul will never fit in my car. I'll take some now and come back for the rest later, or tomorrow."

"I'll take the rest. My car is right out front," he said. "I can bring it to church tomorrow."

That seemed a good solution. It was nice to have help, Carrie realized. She was used to doing everything on her own, which often took a lot of strategy and effort.

"Look at all this stuff." Noah rolled his eyes. "We don't have to wrap it, too . . . do we?"

Carrie laughed. "Not all of it, but some. I think someone else at church volunteered for that job."

Noah looked relieved.

"You're going to be real heroes at church tomorrow," Jeff said as they headed to the cash register.

"We just wanted to help Vera," Carrie replied, though Jeff's comment made her realize that Vera might be too sick to get to church tomorrow, and even if she felt better, she would never be able to fit all these items in her small car. Carrie realized that she was now obliged to attend tomorrow's service. Well, at least Noah will like that, she thought. He had not liked skipping last Sunday.

"Are you coming to church, Jeff? You helped, too," Noah pointed out.

"I think I will," Jeff said. "I need to drop the gifts off anyway."

"Will you sit with us? We sat in the back last time, in the middle section," Noah said, obviously hoping Jeff would look for them.

"Absolutely. Save me a seat. I'll find you." He tousled Noah's hair and glanced at Carrie. She felt herself blush and looked away.

She had been afraid Noah would say something like that . . . but of course Jeff understood that her son was hungry for male attention. Of course Noah would act this way.

I just hope he understands that it doesn't mean I feel the same. Though in her heart she knew that Noah's guileless reactions to Jeff matched her own feelings. If only she could be as open and forthcoming as a seven-year-old boy . . .

After stowing the gifts in their cars, Carrie, Noah, and Jeff headed for the other stores in town. Shopping for the last few items on the list went quickly. By the time they finished, they were all very hungry and ready for lunch. Noah wanted to eat at Willoughby's, which the adults quickly agreed was a good choice. They all liked the soup, sandwiches, and salads there. And the cookies. Carrie knew that Noah was angling for a stop at the playground, too.

She kept expecting Jeff to leave. Surely he had errands or other plans for the day? But he seemed content to follow along, even happy to go to the playground after lunch, too.

"We can stay a little while," Carrie told Noah. "But it looks like it's going to snow. And you have to get ready for Henry's party."

"Let's just stay until it snows," Noah suggested. He started toward the monkey bars. "I can go all the way across just using my hands, Jeff. Want to see?"

"Can you really? I could never do that when I was your age." Jeff glanced at Carrie over his shoulder and smiled as he followed Noah.

Carrie stood back, hoping Jeff didn't mind giving Noah so much attention. But he did seem to be enjoying himself as he watched Noah's athletic feats . . . and also grabbed him by the waist a few times to keep him from falling to the ground.

She sat on a bench nearby, sipping hot cocoa. A light breeze lifted off the harbor. A few tiny snowflakes had begun to fall, so fine it was almost hard to notice them. Or maybe it was her good mood that made her less mindful of the weather. She felt relaxed and happy, as if she had done something really worthwhile with her time today—and she'd had such a wonderful time with Jeff, doing it.

She checked her phone to see if Vera had called and noticed it was later than she thought. The day had just flown by.

She stood up and walked over to Jeff, who was standing at the bottom of the slide while Noah climbed up the ladder on the other side. "I'm afraid we have to go," Carrie said. "Noah has a birthday party for a boy in his class. Bowling, pizza, and a sleepover."

A flash of disappointment crossed Jeff's face, but he quickly smiled again. "Wow, sounds like fun. I hope you have a great time, Noah."

Noah had zipped down the steep slide while the adults were talking and suddenly appeared in front of them. "I'm not very good at bowling, but Theo said he'd help me."

Carrie glanced at Jeff but otherwise didn't react. She was relieved that Noah didn't make a fuss about leaving the playground. Or leaving Jeff.

"Can I beep the car open?" Noah asked. It was one of his favorite jobs now, unlocking the car with the remote on her key chain.

"Sure." Carrie handed him the keys, knowing he was cautious enough not to run into the street without her at his side. Her hatchback was parked just a few cars away, and she and Jeff followed.

"I can't thank you enough for your help today," Carrie said. "And for lunch," she added, since he had insisted on treating them.

"You're very welcome. But I should be thanking you. I got to do a good deed for Christmas—and spend the day with you and Noah. That was a gift for me, too," he added, catching her glance and holding it.

Carrie didn't know what to say. His words touched her heart. Did he really mean that, or was he just the poetic type? Maybe a little of both, she thought.

"See you tomorrow," she said quickly. "But it's fine if you can't make the service. As long as the gifts get there by Monday, Vera said."

"I'll be there. I promised Noah." Jeff's tone was definite. "Can I see you again sometime, Carrie? For dinner or a movie?"

Some evening, without Noah, he meant. *As in a date.* Carrie felt flustered. She had wanted him to ask her out . . . but now that he had, she felt tongue-tied.

"Noah isn't my patient any longer, so there aren't any ethical issues for me," he added.

"Uh . . . yes, that's right, I guess." She paused, acting as if she hadn't already considered that problem. "I'd like that very much," she said finally. "You can call me anytime."

He smiled, looking pleased by her answer. "Well . . . is tonight anytime? A friend gave me two tickets to a concert at Lilac Hall. I've had them a few weeks and forgot all about it. I was planning on going alone. I'd be very happy if you could join me."

"Tonight?" That was short notice. But Noah was taken care of, sleeping at his friend's house. "Sure, I'd love to. What kind of music is it?"

"It's a big swing band, playing Christmas songs and standards. The concert is in the great hall. They decorate it beautifully for the holidays. Have you ever even been up to the mansion?"

Carrie shook her head. "I've heard it's magnificent, but I haven't had a chance to go up there."

"You'll enjoy it, then," he said. "I can pick you up at seven. Will that work out with Noah's party?"

"Yes. Sounds perfect."

He seemed about to lean down and kiss her cheek, but—mindful of Noah watching them—he reached out and squeezed her hand instead. "Good. It sounds more than perfect to me."

MOLLY HAD NOTICED A LIGHT SNOW STARTING TO FALL IN THE LATE afternoon, and by the time she emerged from a party in a large, stately home in Hamilton, it was coming down heavily.

Hamilton was horse country, famous for its polo grounds and breeding stables. The host and hostess were definitely fans, with a stable and riding ring on the grounds of their riverfront estate.

The mansion's tastefully decorated rooms had served as the perfect backdrop to the holiday gathering. Like a scene from a British costume drama, Molly thought. Except that the last-minute servers she hired were more suited for roles in a comedy.

She had tried not to stress too much, correcting them when she could and covering up as well. She kept thinking of the funny stories she wanted to tell Betty—then remembering what she really had to tell her, as soon as this party was over.

The hostess had seemed pleased when Molly said good-bye, which put Molly somewhat at ease. Though she did hope none of the elegant guests complained later.

The next party on her list, the annual Fire Department soirée at the Elks Lodge up in Topsfield, was a much more relaxed event. Molly wasn't nearly as worried about high expectations or bad reviews there.

But she had to stop at Betty's in between. She was resolved now to get it over with.

She left the Hamilton mansion just as the cleanup had begun and found herself pelted by a wintry mix of snow and freezing rain.

"Great. This day is getting better and better," she muttered. The windshield of her SUV was coated with a crusty, icy layer—and so were the side windows and mirrors, and the back window. She leaned into her open car, searching for the brush and scraper, and could only see abandoned food containers, chafing dishes, and other equipment filling the space.

She did find a pair of Matt's huge, waterproof gloves, and she put them on and set to work with her hands. A few minutes later she finally got into the driver's seat and slammed the door. She was wet, cold, and weary, in body, mind, and spirit. The snow was falling so fast, it had practically covered the vehicle again—except for the areas on the front and rear windshields that were kept clear by the wipers and defroster.

Molly took a moment to text Sonia, at another location, and Tim, who was still inside the Hamilton home and about to pack up the van. *It's a mess out here. Be careful driving, everyone,* she warned them. Then she dashed off a note to Betty. *Just leaving Hamilton. I should be there in a few.*

She put her phone aside and carefully backed out of the long driveway. Once on the road, she settled in for the ride back to Cape Light. It was slow going, and Molly glanced at her watch uneasily. She could stop and text Betty again and say that she was running behind schedule and couldn't stop after all. With the bad weather, Betty would definitely understand.

But Molly wiped that excuse off the slate. She had to step up and do the right thing. Betty deserved to know what was going on. Molly felt awful, knowing that the bank had already given her some hint.

It makes me look so sneaky, she wailed inside.

Well . . . you have been, another voice reminded her.

But not intentionally, she knew. She had held back out of consideration for Betty, because of Nate's illness. That wasn't the entire reason, though. There was also Molly's pride, her own stubborn, willful, persistent streak that had often gotten her out of tight spots. Still, she should have stepped back and looked at the big picture—before it became such a big mess.

Molly sighed, wondering how she was going to explain this. It was not going to be easy. Not one bit. *How will I even start the conversation?*

Molly saw a red stop sign fly by. Too late to even slow down. She cruised through the intersection, jolted from her wandering thoughts. That was bad. *Pay attention to the road!* she scolded herself. She was used to driving in snow much worse than this, but the icy mix was making the short trip challenging.

All of a sudden, the windshield wiper on the driver's side didn't flip up in rhythm with the other one. Molly worked the controls a little, hoping to get it going. The wiper was probably stuck under a chunk of ice, the coverage was so heavy.

She pulled over to the side of the road, got out, and cleared it off with her glove. There was nothing really holding it down. Not that she could see.

She slid into the driver's seat again, even wetter and colder than before, and turned the wipers back on.

No luck. It was totally dead.

I can't believe this . . . What next?

She slapped her hand on the steering wheel and honked the horn by accident. There wasn't another soul on the road to hear it. She sat there a moment, trying to decide what to do. She could call Sonia or even Matt to come get her. But that meant she would have to leave her SUV, with all the equipment, here in the middle of nowhere.

It was better to keep driving back to Cape Light. *I'm at least halfway there. I'm not even that far from Betty's. I'll go there, spill my guts, then deal with this stupid windshield wiper.*

"All right, God," she called out. "I'm going, see? You don't have to break something else in the car to remind me of what an idiot I've been."

She remembered what Sam had told her: It doesn't work like that. God isn't punishing you . . . But He is there to help when you ask for it. Right now, she didn't quite believe that. She felt singled out for lousy luck and distress.

She drove along slowly, leaning as far as she could to the passenger side in order to see out the windshield. *Which is ridiculous and unbelievably dangerous,* some small, persistent voice told her. *You have to pull over and call for help.*

But for some reason, she ignored it.

Luckily, the road was empty, and Molly slowed to a crawl, encouraged when she passed the gates of Lilac Hall. "Almost there. Only a few miles more," she told herself. But the sound of her voice was shaky, and she realized her hands were shaking, too.

She turned on her hazard lights and continued, navigating slowly around a curve in the road. As she tried to straighten the big vehicle out again, she heard a crunching sound. Before she knew what was happening, a thick veil of snow and icy slush slid down and covered the entire windshield. *The snow from the roof of my car,* she realized. *I should have cleaned it off before I left Hamilton!*

But it was too late. She was totally enclosed, staring at a blank white wall where before at least a tiny part of the road had been visible.

Molly hit the brakes, trying to maneuver the SUV to a stop, not even knowing if she was steering off the road. The SUV went into a spin, turning in a wild, wide circle. She felt herself pushed back against the seat, her seat belt tightening so that she could hardly move.

She screamed as the vehicle flipped to one side, skidding forward in the snow, then bumped along and slammed into something very hard. *A tree,* she thought, right before her head slammed into something hard, too. And she blacked out.

Chapter Eleven

Molly heard voices speaking quietly next to her bed—Matt's voice and someone else's, a young woman. Jill or Amanda? *I've been taking a nap, and they want me to get up and cook dinner,* she thought, her eyes still closed.

A rambling, bizarre dream continued to unreel inside her head. *Oh, I'm in a movie theater, and the people sitting next to me are talking.*

"Molly? Can you hear me, honey? Can you open your eyes now?"

"Shhh . . . I'm trying to watch this," she mumbled, her eyes still shut.

"Open your eyes, honey. It's me, Matt." His tone was still gentle but more insistent.

Molly blinked. Her eyes felt dry and scratchy, as if grit had blown in them. But when she tried to lift her arm to wipe the feeling away, it felt heavy and achy, as if it were attached to a brick.

She opened her eyes wider, feeling alarmed. She tried to sit up in bed, but she could barely move, seized by aches and pains all over. Matt gently touched her shoulder and held her back.

"Stay still, honey. You're hooked to the machinery."

Machinery? Molly turned her head, finally realizing that she was in a hospital bed, not at home in her lovely bedroom. The lights were very low, and she was sheltered by pale green curtains. She could hear machinery beeping and saw a thin tube taped to her arm.

Matt sat on a chair close to her bedside, leaning toward her, his expression a determined smile, despite deep lines of concern that were etched on his forehead and the corners of his mouth. It was the way he looked when he was worried about a very sick patient, she realized. *Which, this time . . . is me.*

"What happened? What's going on?" Molly could barely get the words out; her tongue was thick and her mouth horribly dry.

"You had a car accident. You drove straight into a tree on the Beach Road. Right near Lilac Hall. Thank goodness that SUV is built like a tank. It flipped over . . . but it saved you."

Matt paused and Molly remembered now—driving with one wiper in the icy snow. Then the snow from the roof sliding down over the windshield. Why hadn't she just pulled over? Her own idiocy.

"You have a concussion. And your wrist is broken and your left side is badly bruised. Your ankle is taped, but it's just a bad sprain." He swallowed hard. Molly saw the fear in his eyes. "It could have been much worse, Molly. Thank God you're all right."

Molly just nodded. Trying to reply, to form words, seemed too much of an effort. What could she say anyway? That she had been a total idiot?

She felt as if she had been hit by a truck—that had backed up and run her over a second time. But she knew what Matt was trying to tell her. She could have been killed today. All because she was so stubborn and willful.

All because she had been so distracted and so determined to see Betty . . . because of the financial mess she had created.

And what about all the parties? Who was dealing with all that now? Was all their business this weekend canceled because of this? Were they going to lose that, too?

Molly raised her good arm and touched Matt's hand. "I have to tell you," she managed. "It's . . . important."

Matt leaned closer and held out a glass with a straw. "Here, have a drink. You look parched."

Molly gratefully sipped some water. Matt hovered over her, watching her every movement, her every breath. He was such an angel. How was she going to tell him what she had done? He took the water away and she stared at him.

"I'm so sorry . . ." she finally managed, the bits of her confession flying around in her head like white swirls in a snow globe.

"I know, I know . . . You should not have been driving around in that mess at all and rushing, I bet, to get to another party—"

"Not that," she managed, shaking her head though the movement was painful.

He sat quietly, stroking her hand. "What is it, honey? Don't upset yourself. You've had a bad accident. A real shock . . ."

Molly sighed. She felt tears well up in her eyes. Matt dabbed them with a tissue. "Amanda and Gabriel are coming down tomorrow to see you," he said in a comforting tone. "She wanted to come tonight, but I told her not to drive down in the snow. We don't need them in a fender bender, too, right?"

Molly nodded, feeling her nerve and her last drop of energy drain away.

A nurse suddenly appeared at the foot of the bed. "How's the patient doing, Dr. Harding?"

"She's coming along." Matt's tone was official, though he stared at Molly in a very unofficial, loving way.

"It's time for pain meds, Molly. I'm just going to add them to this drip. You're going to feel sleepy in a few moments. Don't be alarmed. Dr. Croft thinks it best if you don't move around much tonight."

"That's your orthopedist," Matt explained. "He's very good. I'm glad he was on call when you came in."

Molly watched the nurse inject a solution into the portal of her IV. It sounded as if the dose was going to send her back to sleep. She glanced at Matt, and he stroked her hand.

"Just relax, honey. You don't have to be Superwoman tonight, okay? You must be hurting all over. Just close your eyes and sleep for a while. I'll be right here when you wake up."

Molly tried to reply. She squeezed Matt's hand, wanting to squeeze out a few words, too. But she could only mumble, already feeling the effects of the drug.

"Whatever it is, it will be all right. The main thing is that you're okay. You're going to be fine. Please don't worry about anything now, honey."

She met his gentle gaze and gave way, her eyes drifting closed as a warm, dark quilt of sleep moved over her.

Henry's mother came by at six o'clock to pick up Noah, as she and Carrie had planned. Noah ran out with his backpack and a gift for Henry, hardly remembering to kiss Carrie good-bye. Carrie walked him down to the minivan, which was already full of boys, and chatted with Barbara Newton for a minute or two. Henry's mother seemed as responsible and pleasant in person as she had on the phone, and Carrie had no qualms about sending him. Making friends and keeping busy with children his own age was just the thing Noah needed right now, especially if he was going to forget about his angelic pal.

Once Noah was gone, Carrie brought a tray up to Vera with some soup, crackers, hot tea, and a baked apple.

"Oh my. You didn't have to go to all that trouble, Carrie," Vera admonished her, as if she had cooked a five-course meal. "But this does look delicious."

"It was no trouble. I'm going out in a little while. I don't think you should get out of bed if you don't have to." Vera still had the chills off and on, and had been running a slight temperature during the day.

"I'm not going anywhere fast. Even though I slept all day. Don't you look lovely," Vera added. "Where are you going, out to dinner?"

"Yes, I am. With a friend. He had an extra ticket to a concert at Lilac Hall, and we're having dinner afterward. I've never been to any events there. Do you think I'm overdressed?"

Vera took Carrie in with an assessing glance. Carrie's plum-colored knit dress was one of the few nice things in her closet, a leftover from the time before the divorce. "Not at all. People dress up for that place. It's like a castle. You look just right," Vera said. "I'm sure your friend will think so, too," she added with a knowing smile.

Carrie felt herself blush a bit but busied herself, taking away an empty cup and saucer. "If you need anything, just call," she reminded Vera. "I won't be far."

"Don't worry about me. I'm just going to watch a movie and go to sleep. Again. I'll feel better tomorrow," she said hopefully. She paused as a few dainty sneezes shook her frail form. "Though I do think I may skip church, especially if the weather's bad."

"That might be a good idea. I'll bring the donations. Most of the packages are still in my car. And my friend . . . who helped me today . . . will bring the rest."

"Does this friend have a name? I don't think you mentioned it."

"Jeff . . . Jeff Carlson," Carrie told her, standing in the bedroom doorway.

Vera looked surprised, then pleased. "I know Dr. Carlson. He's a very fine man."

"I don't know him well, but . . . yes, he seems to be." Carrie didn't know what else to say. She could just imagine how nice Jeff was to the senior ladies at church, like Vera, Claire, and Sophie. They probably had a fan club for him.

"I haven't been out on a date in a while. I'm a little nervous," she admitted.

"Understandably. And it's a first date, I gather. But I bet he's nervous, too," Vera reminded her. "Once you get settled and the music starts, you'll both relax. It will be fine."

Carrie smiled and sighed. "Yes . . . I think so."

It had always been so easy to talk to Jeff when she considered him Noah's therapist. Now that the situation had changed, it felt different. It didn't really make sense. They were still the same two people.

But something had shifted. She had felt it today, even before Jeff asked her out. She had wanted him to ask her out, but now that he had, she felt nervous and wondered if it was such a good thing after all. As much as she did like him. Or maybe because she did like him so much. And Noah did, too.

"Noah doesn't know we're going out. I guess I'd rather he didn't. For now, anyway."

Vera nodded. "I understand. I won't mention it."

"Thanks." Carrie felt relieved. If the date turned out to be a flop, she wasn't sure who would be more disappointed, she or Noah.

"I won't be late. I'll try not to wake you."

"You have fun. It's nice to see you so happy, Carrie," Vera added.

Carrie felt herself blush again. She did feel happy. And hopeful. Despite her case of first-date nerves. She bid Vera good night and went down to wait for Jeff.

She opened the door as soon as he knocked. He smiled at her, looking very handsome, she thought, in a camel hair overcoat with a suit and tie underneath. He had a close shave and had maybe even found time for a haircut.

"I'm all ready. Just need to put on my coat," Carrie said as she greeted him. He stepped into the entryway as she found her good wool coat, gray with brass buttons. He quickly stepped forward to help her. "You look very pretty, Carrie."

"You look nice, too. I almost didn't recognize you . . . in a suit, I mean."

Oh, dear . . . that hadn't come out the way she'd meant it, at all. It had been a long time since she had done this . . . this dating business. She hoped she wouldn't be an awkward mess all evening.

"It was the only piece of clothing I could find without paw prints on it," Jeff admitted, looking down at himself.

She laughed with him, forgetting her self-conscious feeling. He stood quietly, wearing a small smile as she pulled on leather gloves and tossed her dressy scarf around her shoulders—a sheer silky fabric with black velvet flowers scattered across.

"Watch your step out here. It's icy," Jeff warned, taking her arm. They walked carefully down the path to his car.

"I noticed that before when Noah left. I should have come out and shoveled."

"Not in that outfit, I hope?" Jeff teased her. "I'll do it for you later and put some salt down. I have some in my car." He quickly changed the subject before she could thank him. "Was Noah excited for the party?"

"Was he ever, bouncing off the walls when we packed for the overnight. Mrs. Newton seemed very nice. I do admire her, having all those boys at her house all night."

"It will be your turn soon. Maybe she'll give you a few pointers. I am pleased to see Noah making friends," he added as he opened the passenger-side door of his car for her.

"So am I. It does help me worry less," she admitted.

"I'm happy to hear that, too."

Worry about the angel, she had meant. She knew he understood but was glad he had not gone into it. She didn't want to be talking about Noah's situation all night and decided if Jeff brought it up, she would change the subject.

She'd never been alone with him without Noah, she suddenly realized, and this was a chance for her to get to know him more. To see if the chemistry she felt in his company was real. Noah wasn't the only one who could get tricked by a wishful imagination. But glancing over at Jeff as he drove through the snow-lined streets, she doubted that was the case here at all.

Though Carrie had worried over what they would talk about once the topic of Noah was sidelined, she soon realized that was another silly fear. As they passed through the stone gates and headed up the long drive toward Lilac Hall, Jeff told her a bit about the mansion's history and about the family who last lived there.

Carrie had heard a lot about the estate but had never visited the grounds of the Historical Society Museum, which took up a wing of the mansion now. They followed a line of cars around the circular drive and left the car with a valet before entering the mansion.

It was just as grand inside as she had imagined, like one of those great country estates in historical movies. Carrie gazed around wide eyed as Jeff, holding her arm, guided her to a vast gallery room at least two stories high.

The walls were gray stone with long windows all around; a stone courtyard visible outside was now covered with snow. The medieval-looking room was decorated for Christmas with boughs of fresh greens swooping across the walls. Pale white urns held small fragrant bushes draped with burgundy velvet ribbons.

A stage had been set up at the far end of the room, and chairs stood in neat rows. They took their seats and Jeff gave her a quizzical look, as if wondering what she thought of the place.

"It's really very splendid, isn't it?" she said. "I couldn't imagine living here, though. It would be like living in a museum or a castle."

"I know exactly what you mean. Magnificent, but a bit cold for my taste, too. So we agree on decorating. That's good to know." He nodded to himself, sounding very matter-of-fact. Carrie glanced at him and caught a teasing light in his eye.

The lights dimmed and the tuxedo-clad musicians came out onstage. They were all very talented and played the pieces with what seemed like genuine pleasure. Most of the songs were familiar holiday favorites, but performed with a jazzy flair. Carrie loved the full sound of the trumpets and clarinets. A female vocalist in a long black evening gown sang in a deep, smoky tone and was totally enthralling. Jeff enjoyed it, too, and often turned to her to comment with a glance or share a look of admiration after a solo.

Carrie never minded going to the movies or even to performances of live music on her own, though she could rarely afford the luxury. But it was much more fun to share it with someone, she realized; she had forgotten just how much.

On the way to the restaurant, they talked about the selection of pieces and the performers. Carrie didn't know very much about music, mainly just what she liked. She'd had a college roommate who was a music major and had played a lot of classic jazz and blues, music Carrie still listened to when she had the chance. Jeff, however, knew a great deal; it was obvious the moment he started talking about the concert.

"How do you know so much about music, Jeff? Do you play an instrument?"

"I used to play the piano. Mostly classical, though I dabbled around. I've always loved music, but I loved psychology more," he explained. "My wife was a real music buff. She played the French horn. She wasn't professional, but she was quite good. She passed away three years ago."

"I'm sorry. How long were you married?" Carrie didn't want to seem rude, but she was curious.

"Almost eight years. We met in college. She helped put me through grad school. She died very suddenly. It was . . . a great shock."

"That must have been dreadful . . . You don't have to talk about it if you don't want to. I don't mean to pry."

"I don't feel as if you're prying. I want to tell you," Jeff said. "She died in a car accident. At first I was devastated. Then I was sort of adrift—for a long time, only my work felt real to me. We were very close. We shared a lot. I've learned to be on my own again, and I'm past my grieving. I know she wouldn't have wanted me to mourn forever. She wasn't like that. When I look back on our marriage, I'm not sad anymore," he assured Carrie. "I appreciate even more what we had—and what I hope I can have again someday. I'm going to try." He turned to her. "What about you?"

Carrie was caught off guard. She wasn't sure what he was asking and gave him a puzzled look.

"How do you feel about marriage, Carrie? Has your experience with your ex-husband soured you on it?"

Carrie thought about the question a moment. "I was unhappy with Kevin most of the time we were married. But I can see how marriage can be a wonderful part of life. I see happy couples all the time, like Reverend

Ben and his wife, Carolyn. I know it's possible . . . I'm just not sure I know how to make that happen. Or even how to pick the right person," she admitted. "I wasn't so good at it last time."

Part of her couldn't believe she was confiding in Jeff like this, baring her soul. But something about him made her feel so comfortable, and she did want him to know how she really felt about things. Important things . . . like the answer to his question.

She shrugged and sighed. "I guess my answer is, I don't really know how I feel about marriage now. I'm not sure I have the right radar or something to pick a person who will be different than Kevin. I did love Kevin when I married him; I believed we would stay married forever. I still feel . . . tricked, or as if I did something terribly wrong."

Jeff nodded thoughtfully. "I understand. But I'm not sure it's a matter of radar. I think it's a matter of time."

"You mean, in time I'll feel differently?"

"Well, yes. But I really meant that you'll learn to trust your radar when you meet someone who can show you, over time, that he's worthy of your trust and that he's very different from your ex-husband. And that won't happen overnight," he added.

"No . . . it won't," Carrie agreed. She had a feeling Jeff was talking about himself and their relationship. She already had feelings for him that went beyond simple attraction. She could barely believe that she was feeling this way about any man.

It was too soon . . . wasn't it? She didn't know him well enough. But Jeff was right; it was a question of trust. Of trusting him—and her own judgment.

They arrived at the restaurant Jeff had chosen, a very charming-looking, long flat building near Essex Harbor, which Jeff explained was the site of an old fish market.

Their dinner passed quickly with much lighter conversation. She learned a lot about his past, and he learned a lot about hers, too. But they also talked about less personal topics, like books and films. Carrie had a lot to say about the former, and Jeff seemed impressed with her eclectic taste in literature.

"The next time I need a good book to read, I know who to call," he said as they shared a dessert, a slice of double-fudge cake—which they had both zeroed in on immediately upon reading the menu, also sharing a weakness for chocolate.

"I'd be happy to put together a stack of recommendations for you. Though I've only unpacked a box or two of my favorites at Vera's."

"You won't be at Vera's forever. Pretty soon you'll have your own place, with as many bookcases as you want."

"I hope so. Mrs. Honeyfield now says that she won't be back until the third week in January at the earliest. So I don't have to look for a new job just yet. Noah likes Cape Light better than Essex. So we'll try to stay here. I certainly don't want him to have to change schools again."

"Yes, that's important," he agreed. "What about you? Do you like Cape Light better, too?"

"I do," Carrie said. "It's a very pretty place, and everyone's been so nice to us." *And I met you,* she added silently. Making sure to catch herself in time before she said it out loud.

Jeff didn't answer for a moment, spooning up a last bite of cake. "I'm not surprised by that. You're an easy person to be nice to, Carrie."

Carrie met his glance. She didn't know what to say, disarmed again by one of his compliments. But the waitress came by to ask if they wanted anything else, and Jeff asked for the check.

Carrie checked her phone, just in case Noah or Vera had tried to get in touch. She was surprised to see how late it was. Hours had flown by. *And I didn't worry about Noah once,* she realized. When was the last time that had happened? She could hardly remember.

When they reached Vera's house, Jeff insisted on walking her to the door. "I'll come by tomorrow and get this ice off the walk," he said. "I'll bring some road salt, too."

"You don't need to do that. Vera said she has a handyman who takes care of the shoveling. He couldn't make it today for some reason. He'll be here tomorrow."

Jeff still looked concerned. "All right. If it's taken care of. But if he doesn't come again, let me know."

Carrie nodded as she found her key. She could just imagine telling Vera about this gentlemanly offer. He had a fan club, definitely, she decided.

"So I'll see you at church tomorrow. Is Noah coming?"

"Yes, he wanted to. Though he'll probably be a zombie after the sleepover. I'm picking him up on the way."

Jeff nodded and smiled. "Good. He should take some credit for all that shopping, too. He was very helpful."

"He was," Carrie agreed. Not to mention Theo. But she had managed not to mention the angel all night and was determined to keep the promise she had made to herself.

Distracted for a moment, she didn't realize how close she and Jeff were suddenly standing. He put his hands on her shoulders and gazed down at her. "I had a wonderful time tonight. Thank you for coming with me."

"I did, too. Thank you for inviting me."

"My friend gave me the tickets a while ago. I'd forgotten all about them. Then I found them this morning, stuck in a book I'd put aside. I imagined myself sitting at the concert with you . . . but I didn't know how I could ask you so last-minute. Then I ran into you and Noah today at the hardware store, and it seemed such a perfect coincidence. I knew I had to find a way." He shook his head with a wondering expression. "It's sort of funny, right? But our evening was just as I'd imagined it. Even better."

Carrie was surprised at his admission, which was so honest and sweet. When he dipped his head to kiss her good night, she closed her eyes and found herself melting into his embrace.

She had also imagined spending time with him alone, without Noah. And it had been even better than she had imagined. When she finally stepped back, she was surprised at her reaction. While she had expected Jeff to kiss her, she had expected to be much more nervous, even tense and self-conscious. But it had not been at all like that. Just the opposite, in fact. It had been so easy and natural between them. As if she had known him for years, instead of just a few short weeks.

"Will you have lunch with me?" he asked suddenly. "Sometime this week . . . maybe Tuesday?"

It was all Carrie could do not to shout, "Yes!" Instead, she said, "I'll have to check my calendar, but that sounds really nice . . . Good night, Jeff. And thanks again."

She went inside and shut the door, then leaned back against it for a second. She felt breathless . . . and so happy, she thought she might float up to the ceiling, like a balloon.

Good thing Noah isn't home tonight, she realized as she hung up her coat and headed upstairs to her bedroom. *If he was still awake and saw me now, he'd be asking way too many questions.*

WHEN MOLLY FINALLY WOKE UP AGAIN, EARLY-MORNING LIGHT WAS slipping into her hospital room through the gauzy curtains. She saw Matt asleep in an uncomfortable-looking chair, his head thrown back at an angle and a thin cotton blanket barely covering half of him.

Poor guy, she thought as her body stirred. Pain shot through her left side and arm, causing her to catch her breath. *Poor me . . . What did I do to myself?* Molly suddenly felt so mad at herself, and so frustrated she wanted to cry.

Matt stirred and woke, blinking at her. "Hey, you're awake again. When did you wake up?" He rose from the chair, tossing the blanket aside, and walked over to her bedside.

"A few seconds ago." It was still hard to talk, but it was a little easier than before. Molly tried to clear her throat, and her sense of confusion. "What day is it?"

"Sunday," Matt told her. "You've only been here overnight."

"Do I have to stay much longer?"

Matt practically laughed at her. "I should have expected that question. The Unsinkable Molly Willoughby." He shook his head. "Yes, you have to stay here a day or two more, at least. If you think you're going to jump out of that hospital bed and go back to work on crutches, or roller skates or whatever, forget it. Sonia called last night. She wants you to know that they have everything under control. When I called Betty and told her what had happened, she was very upset. She said she was going to find someone to stay with Nate so she can take over for you this week as much as she can. She wants to come see you this afternoon."

"Betty . . ." Molly murmured. "I was on my way to her house when I had the accident. Did she tell you that?"

Matt shook his head. "Not that I remember, but I've been calling so many people these last twenty-four hours. She might have mentioned it. I thought you were driving up to Topsfield, to the Elks Lodge?"

"I was. But I needed to stop and see Betty in between—" Molly paused and took a breath. "Matt, I have something to tell you. Something serious."

He looked at her with concern. "What is it, Molly? What's wrong?"

"I'm having some problems with the business. Financial problems," she forced herself to add. "Ever since Betty left. Well, I've messed things up completely. I've overspent on the renovation of the new store, and it's not even done. And I've also gotten behind on paying bills. And overdrawn on our credit line and our charge accounts . . ."

She watched Matt's expression as he heard her out, calm and focused. "I knew that something has been bothering you the last few weeks. More than the usual holiday pressure. And you told me your books were a mess. But how can it be that bad? The shop is crowded with customers, night and day."

"We're taking in good receipts, but it flies out even faster. The new shop has turned out to be a total money pit. We've used up our loan and then some. And we fell behind on our party business this year." She sighed. "Betty's been so busy with Nate since he had his fall. I wanted to tell her, a few times. But something always came up. I was going to her house yesterday. That's why I kept driving, even though the wiper was broken on one side—"

"The wiper was broken? In that awful weather? And you didn't have the sense to pull over?" Matt looked at her with disbelief. "You're so single-minded sometimes . . . honestly, it scares me."

"I'm sorry. I know it was dumb. I wasn't thinking."

"I'll say. What would you say to me, or one of our girls, if we told you that?" he demanded. "That we kept driving in a snowstorm with a broken wiper?"

"I'd be upset. Very," she added, knowing Matt looked like a Buddha right now compared to how she would react to that confession.

He sighed and took her hand again. "I don't mean to scold you. That's the last thing you need right now. But if we ever lost you, I don't know what I'd do. You're not indestructible, you know."

Practically, she wanted to say. The police officer who arrived on the scene said it was a miracle she had survived the wreck. She sighed and bit down on her lower lip to keep from answering. She knew he was right.

"I just felt so bad about Betty not knowing. And everything was getting worse. Last week, it seemed like it all just crashed in on me. I never meant to hide things from her."

Matt nodded and stroked her hand. "Of course you didn't, sweetheart. Please don't cry. You're still in shock from the accident. I'm sure this situation just seems much worse right now than it actually is."

She glanced at him, her vision blurred with tears. He was so sweet to comfort her like this. "Believe me, it's bad. I let it go too long, Matt. It's a mess."

"Okay, it's a mess. But no matter how big a mess it is, please try to get some perspective. You could have been killed yesterday, Molly. We could have lost you forever. Business problems don't matter much compared to that."

He handed her a tissue and she wiped her eyes. "I know. But lying in this bed only makes me feel worse about it. At least when I was working, I felt like I was doing something to solve it—or trying to."

Matt sighed and brushed her hair back gently with his hand. "Even Super Molly gets grounded once in a while. Even if it takes driving straight into a tree." She nearly smiled but couldn't. "Do you want me to tell Betty for you?" he offered gently.

Molly was touched by the gesture but didn't consider it for a second. "That's so sweet. But I couldn't. It's my mess. I have to step up and tell her."

He sighed. "I knew you'd say that. Think about it. I want to help you with this. You and me, we have resources—retirement accounts and equity in our house. If you need it, use it," he said. "It's not a problem for me."

"Matt . . . you're so dear." She touched his cheek with the fingertips sticking out from her cast. "I'm hoping we don't have to raid our own piggy banks. But we might," she added sadly.

"All right. One step at a time. When you tell Betty, she might be upset for a while. But I'm sure she'll understand, and you'll figure it out together."

"I hope so, too. I keep trying to imagine how I would feel if she told me something like this. It's an adult portion," she said with a shaky breath.

"It's not going to be easy," he conceded. "But you'll clear the air and go on from there. Give her a little time. I know Betty. She won't stay mad at you."

"I hope not, Matt. She's my best friend in the world. I feel like I've really let her down. That's the worst of it."

Matt nodded and lifted her hand to his lips for a quick kiss. "I know, honey. It will work out, I promise."

Molly sighed. There was nothing left to say. She was grateful for Matt's understanding and comfort. But she still feared that Betty would not take the news nearly as well. What if they weren't friends after this anymore? She blinked back tears as she tried to imagine her days without Betty.

"Hey, now . . . no more waterworks. All this crying isn't good for you," Matt urged her, handing over the tissues again. "How do you feel?" he asked with concern. He was her doctor again—a very loving one.

"My head still hurts. And I feel tired again." Their conversation had sapped her of whatever energy she'd had when she'd woken up.

"Go to sleep, then. Rest. I'll tell the nurse not to disturb you."

Molly nodded and closed her eyes. She held on to Matt's hand and drifted back to sleep.

Carrie was not surprised when Vera decided to stay home on Sunday morning and take care of her cold. Carrie checked in with Noah by cell phone, to make sure he still wanted to come to church. He was sure, and was even packed and ready, waiting for her.

She swung by the Newtons' house, picked him up, and got to church early enough to empty out the gifts from her car. Sam Morgan and Tucker Tulley, the deacons for the day, ran out to help her, making very short work of the job.

"Wow, look at all this stuff. Is this all for the Christmas family?" Sam asked Noah.

"Yup. Mr. Krueger donated most of it," Noah explained. "We bought some, too . . . and Jeff, Dr. Carlson, I mean, is coming with more. He helped, too . . . and so did Theo," Noah added.

Carrie quickly handed him a package. "You can carry this one, Noah. Take it inside and leave it in the church office with the others, okay?"

She hated to feel as if she were tricking Noah to keep him from saying more about the angel. But it was so . . . embarrassing, in some way. They were new here, and she didn't want him to be known as the boy who thought he was talking to an angel.

"Nice work, Noah." Tucker patted Noah on the shoulder as he clasped the package to his chest. "You and your mom are really helping that family to have a great Christmas. You should be very proud."

"We are," Noah replied. Carrie wasn't sure if he was talking about her and Jeff, too. Or about himself and Theo. But she was glad he was now focused on his task and did not continue the conversation.

They were early, and the sanctuary was almost empty when they walked in. But Noah picked a seat in the back row anyway. Carrie knew why; he had told Jeff yesterday to look for them there. Once they were seated, Noah knelt on the pew, facing the back door, keeping a watch for his friend.

Carrie was looking forward to seeing Jeff, too. Though she also felt a little nervous. Recalling last night, she felt surprised at how much she had opened up to him, and how much he had shared with her. Even though she had always felt comfortable around him and found him easy to talk to, the sudden closeness—after being on her own so long—felt a little frightening. But in a good way, she reminded herself. Like trying something daring but also fun and exciting—like a giant waterslide or a hot air balloon ride.

And yet it was all a bit overwhelming. She felt swept off her feet and, sweet as that sensation might be, thought she might hang back a bit today. This was all happening so fast. Carrie needed to slow down and catch her breath.

She focused on the church bulletin, noticing she had made a typo or two. Nothing serious, thank goodness. Reverend Ben was so easy-going; even if he noticed, she was sure he wouldn't even mention it.

"Jeff's not here yet. Maybe he forgot." Noah's voice drew her attention. He was still keeping a careful watch, though most of the seats around them had filled up.

"I'm sure he didn't forget. I'm sure he'll be here," she added, suddenly realizing that she did believe that, and could never have sounded so sure of Noah's father.

A few minutes later, the music director sounded the opening chords of the first hymn, and the choir stood at the entrance to the sanctuary, robed and ready to walk in. Carrie gently tapped Noah's shoulder and indicated that it was time for him to turn around and sit down, facing front.

He did so reluctantly, staring down at his lap, then glancing at the seat he had saved for Jeff, with his coat and hat neatly piled on top. Carrie had seen him carefully guard it once or twice.

She sighed, wondering if she had been wrong about Jeff. Had he decided not to come this morning, even after promising Noah? She hoped not. This was what she had worried about—Noah getting so attached to Jeff and already feeling disappointed.

The choir took their places on the risers, and the hymn was soon concluded. Reverend Ben welcomed the congregation and began the morning's announcements.

"Excuse me . . . sorry . . ." Carrie turned at the sound of Jeff's voice. He was easing into the row, seeking the empty seat next to Noah and smiling down at them. Looking a little sheepish, she thought . . . and totally adorable.

"Jeff, here's your seat," Noah said in a loud, happy whisper. "I saved it for you." Noah whisked away his jacket and hat so Jeff could sit down.

Jeff grinned and tousled his hair. Carrie noticed that the front of his jacket was all wet and his khaki pants were wet up over his knees. "Sorry I'm late. Elsie got away from me, and I had to chase her through the woods," he whispered back.

"That's okay. I knew you'd come." Noah shrugged, as if he hadn't worried at all.

Carrie smiled at Jeff over Noah's head. She'd had her moment of doubt, but now that he was here, she felt inexplicably happy. Was this what people meant when they said someone could make you light up inside? Carrie felt as if she were glowing.

It was an intergenerational service, so the children didn't go off to Sunday school after the children's sermon. Which was a good thing, Carrie thought, because Noah probably wouldn't have left Jeff's side anyway.

When it was time for Joys and Concerns, Sam Morgan asked for prayers for his sister Molly Harding, who had been in a car accident on the Beach Road Saturday night. "No major injuries, thank goodness. But she's pretty banged up and has a broken wrist and a lot of bruises," he reported. "Her SUV flipped right over and plowed into a tree. It's amazing she survived."

His news sent a ripple of concern through the sanctuary. Even Carrie knew who Molly Harding was, recalling how she and her family had lit the Advent candles a few weeks ago. Life was so unpredictable, wasn't it? She said a silent prayer for Molly's recovery . . . and also thanked heaven for her own unexpected blessings.

"Does anyone have any good news that they would like to share today?" Reverend Ben asked a few moments later. Noah began waving his hand wildly. Carrie felt a jolt of alarm, not knowing what he would say.

"Yes, Noah. Do you have a joy to share with us this morning?" Reverend Ben walked closer, happy to call on her son.

Noah stood up. "I have a new friend." Carrie held her breath and glanced at Jeff. "His name is Henry. He had a birthday party yesterday."

Carrie felt almost slack with relief, so glad that Noah had not announced anything about Theo.

"A new friend? That is a blessing. Happy birthday to Henry," Reverend Ben said.

"And," Noah continued, "me, Mom, and Jeff collected a ton of stuff for the Christmas family yesterday. It took up two whole cars."

"That is a blessing. Thank you all very much," Reverend Ben said, taking in both Carrie and Jeff with his warm glance.

"It was nothing. We were just helping Vera," Carrie explained.

She felt as if everyone in church had turned to look at them, the three of them, thinking she and Jeff were officially a couple. Though they had only had one date together. But wasn't that what made it official—appearing out in public like this? Attending church together with her son?

Carrie hadn't realized she would be making such a statement by meeting Jeff at the service this morning. And she had never dreamed of the curious and approving looks that sitting with him this way—along with Noah's announcement—would inspire. It was more than she was ready for.

She snuck a glance at Jeff, wondering if he felt the same. He looked quite comfortable, smiling back at everyone and leaning over to help Noah find the right page when the next hymn began.

I'm making too much of this, Carrie thought. She had gone out on a few dates since her divorce, but she had never liked anyone nearly as much as she already liked Jeff. She had never even introduced Noah to any of those men.

Maybe that's what's making you uncomfortable. It's not what other people think or feel about seeing you and Jeff together. It's your own confused feelings about him.

"MOLLY, YOU POOR THING! OH, MY GOSH . . . I FEEL SO BAD FOR YOU!" Molly turned to see Betty sweep into the hospital room, her arms filled with a huge bouquet of flowers. Her heartfelt sympathy and the look on her face made Molly feel so guilty, she just wanted to disappear.

Molly was washed up and in her own bathrobe, sitting in a chair, having been moved from her bed with the help of Matt and two nurses. Matt had fallen asleep in his chair during her catnap, and she had persuaded him to go home and rest awhile, which he finally did, very reluctantly.

"Oh, boy . . . you must hurt all over," Betty said.

"I do," Molly admitted. Every body part screamed in protest as she sat in the chair, but the nurses said it would be good for her. Molly hoped compliance would help her get out of the hospital sooner. Besides, she had promised Matt she wouldn't be difficult and stubborn.

"My nose isn't broken, they said. But I have some stitches in my head. They shaved a patch of hair—"

"Yeah, I see."

"Very attractive, right? I guess if I get some piercings, it could work for me." Molly touched the bandage on her nose and one on her head. "You know that old joke where the fighter says, 'You should see the other guy'? Well . . . I *am* the other guy," she joked in a halfhearted way.

Betty smiled but also shook her head with sympathy. "Cute, Molly. Your hair will grow back quickly. Don't worry, you still have plenty."

"I'm probably not going to be able to do much cooking for a while." Molly held up her cast, then sighed, knowing that she had to get to the real problem, to say what she needed to say. Betty might not have much time. "Thanks for the flowers, Betty. They're beautiful. You shouldn't have."

Betty put the bouquet aside and pulled up a chair to sit facing Molly. "You shouldn't have run yourself ragged, trying to be in three places at once," Betty countered. "I bet you've been lying here worrying about the shop since they rolled you out of the emergency room."

That was true. But not exactly the way Betty meant it.

Before Molly could reply, Betty said, "I spoke to Sonia last night, and I stopped at the shop this morning. Everything is under control. I have a neighbor staying with Nate a few hours today, and I'm going to get more help this week so I can check on the parties and help Sonia supervise. She's great, but she can't do it all on her own."

"She's wonderful," Molly agreed, "but I don't think anyone can do it all on their own."

"The point is, I don't want you to worry about a thing. You've done more than your share these last few weeks. You've been positively heroic, holding things together."

Molly could not stand another second of Betty's praise and gratitude. "Betty, stop, please! I have *not* been heroic. More like . . . horrific," she insisted. "I was on my way to your house yesterday to tell you—I've screwed up everything. I've messed up the shop's financial situation completely."

Betty frowned. "Messed up the books, you mean? I did go online once and glanced at the accounting program. It did look a mess. But that was never your thing, Molly," she said lightly. "I'll work on it. I'll figure it out—"

"That's not what I mean, exactly," Molly cut in, pushing herself to make it clear, though her body ached painfully with every breath. "I've let a lot of bills slide. And I used up the entire loan for the renovation and had to dip into our reserves. That's why the bank called. I was trying to find out if we could borrow more money."

Betty stared at Molly, as if she wasn't sure she understood. "You were trying to get a bigger loan? Without telling me anything about it first? Without even bothering to ask my opinion?"

"I was just trying to find out if we even qualified," Molly explained.

Betty touched her hand to her forehead, looking suddenly dizzy. "So that wasn't a mistake after all." She stared at Molly. "Well, guess what. We don't qualify. We were turned down," she said curtly. "The bank already told me. But I thought it was all a big mistake." Betty's blue eyes were hard as she said, "What else haven't you told me?"

Molly felt sick to her stomach, and that had nothing to do with her injuries. "I've been dipping into our reserves to catch up on our overhead—and payroll. I kept thinking we'd catch up by now, at the holidays. But we haven't. I thought when we opened the new store and did all our party business, we'd be fine again. I never meant to keep it from you, Betty. Honestly."

Betty's expression changed from anger to confusion to total disbelief. "I cannot believe you spent the entire loan for the renovation. That was supposed to cover our new hires and supplies and the first few months of the lease, until we got rolling."

"I know. I don't know how it happened. There was the mold problem. And I overspent a bit on the fixtures, too, I guess."

"You guess? You don't know?" Betty's voice rose on a sharp note. Molly had never seen her so angry.

"I should have told you," Molly admitted sadly. "I should have pulled you in a long time ago. I tried. That morning you came in and told me Nate had gotten a bad report from his doctors? I was all set to tell you then . . . but how could I? You were dealing with so much. And it all seemed so much more important. I know it sounds stupid now, but I was trying not to burden you with anything else."

Betty grew quiet, staring coldly at Molly. "I know I've had to be away a lot, and I have been very distracted, even when I've been in the shop. But honestly, Molly, it's my business, too. I trusted you. It's like going on a long car trip with someone and trusting them to drive part of the way. Maybe I did take a little nap. If it was too much for you to handle, you should have told me. What were you thinking?"

Molly swallowed hard. "I don't know. I never meant to deceive you. I thought I could handle things until you got back. I really did think I could right things on my own. But I was fooling myself. I see that now. I'm so very sorry."

Betty did not look placated. In fact, she looked even angrier. "That's you all over, Molly. Always thinking you can tough it out. You can push through like some pioneer woman. 'No guts, no glory.' Well, that's not always a good thing. Not when other people are affected," she said tersely. "With Nate sick like this, we are depending on that business. We have no other income, and this is a serious blow for us," she added in a harsh tone. "I can't even think now about what we should do. I think it's best if I just go."

She grabbed her coat and scarf off the chair. "I'm going to the shop to look over the books. I may have questions for you."

Her cold tone stung Molly deeply. As if the idea of talking to Molly ever again was very distasteful.

"I'll be right here," Molly said in a small voice. "I'm not going anywhere for a while."

Betty didn't reply. She turned and walked out of the room without a backward glance. The beautiful bouquet of flowers—roses, Peruvian lilies, snapdragons, and tulips, all of Molly's favorites—had fallen on the floor. Betty had not even noticed, and Molly gazed sorrowfully at it, unable to rise and rescue the battered blooms.

The sight made her think of her beautiful friendship with Betty and how that was ruined now, too. Something so lovely and rare, carelessly trampled underfoot.

Chapter Twelve

Vera was feeling much better on Monday morning and came down to the kitchen dressed and ready to start the day. "A couple of days in bed were just what I needed to kick that bug. Thanks for taking such good care of me, Carrie. You're a dear."

"It was nothing. I'm glad to see you better in time for the holidays."

"You and me both," Vera agreed, making herself a cup of the strong tea she preferred in the morning. "I have a lot to catch up on. Cookie baking, for one thing." Her tone was serious, taking Noah in with a meaningful look. "I could use a helper, too."

"I can help you." Noah's face brightened. He was a helpful baker, but really shone as a taste tester, Carrie knew.

Carrie wanted to do some baking for Christmas with Noah, too. Some gingerbread people, maybe, and sugar cookies. "We can both help. That will be fun. I'll pick up some ingredients at the store on my way home from work."

"Very good," Vera replied. "We can start after dinner. I have to run over to the church this afternoon to wrap the gifts for the Christmas family. Would you like to help with that, too?" she asked Noah.

"I'll try. But I make the paper all wrinkly," he replied.

"You can put the bows and tags on, then," Vera suggested. "'Many hands make light work.'"

Noah looked as if he wasn't sure what she meant, but he smiled and shrugged. "Okay, Vera. I'll help you."

CARRIE HAD ALMOST FORGOTTEN THAT VERA WAS COMING TO CHURCH to wrap gifts until the volunteers from the Adopt-a-Family Committee gathered in the conference room next to her office, late in the day. She wondered if Noah would make good on his promise. There were no basketball games going on today, but he looked very engrossed in a new book about outer-space adventurers. Was spending time immersed in aliens and robots better than imagining his own private angel? she wondered. She had not heard him talk much about Theo for a few days now, not since the shopping trip on Saturday.

Vera popped out of the conference room. "Are you going to help us, Noah? We're not up to the bows yet, but I'll let you know." She turned to Carrie. "We're still trying to find the wrapping paper. I know we had several big rolls left over from last year. I think we put them in the closet."

Vera turned to the big office closet, which was mainly used to store stationery and office supplies. Carrie rose from her chair. "I may have seen wrapping paper in there," she recalled. "I think it's way on top, though. Let me help you look."

Carrie was much taller than Vera and could see most of the items on the top shelf of the closet by stepping back and getting up on tiptoe. "I do see it. But I'll need the ladder to get at it."

"Vera, did you find it?" Carrie heard Claire North call from the conference room. Vera ran back to the conference room. "Carrie found it in the closet. She's going to get it down for us."

Carrie headed to the other side of the office, where the ladder was tucked away between two file cabinets. She was pulling it out just as Reverend Ben walked in.

"Here, let me help you with that." Reverend Ben took the ladder from her. "What are you up to? Changing a lightbulb? The sexton can do that."

"Vera needs something from the top of the closet, a big package of wrapping paper." Carrie pointed to the shelf.

Reverend Ben opened the ladder and checked the supports. "I'll get it down. No problem." He set his hands on the edges of the ladder and started to climb up.

Noah suddenly tossed his book to the floor and ran over to them. "Reverend Ben, come down!"

Reverend Ben had just put one foot up on the ladder's first rung. He glanced down at Noah with a curious expression. "What is it, Noah? What's wrong?"

"The ladder is broken. Look, the step near the top . . . it's loose. It won't hold you," Noah insisted.

Reverend Ben took his foot from the bottom rung and stepped back, tilting the ladder toward him to inspect the rung Noah had pointed to. Carrie moved closer, too, and saw the minister test the step, shaking it. It easily came loose in his hand, a rusty, twisted screw hanging from each end.

"My goodness . . . you were right." Reverend Ben stared at the broken rung and back at Noah again.

Carrie felt her chest tighten. She leaned down and peered at her son. "Noah, how did you know that? Did you see someone break the ladder—last week, maybe?" She held her breath, guessing Noah's answer but not really wanting to hear it aloud.

Noah shook his head. "No, Mom. Theo told me. He warned me. Just now. I was thinking so much about my book, I almost didn't hear him."

Carrie stood up and looked at Reverend Ben. She had already told him about Noah's angel, and she was certain from the minister's expression that he remembered exactly who Theo was.

"Yes, your mom told me that you communicate with an angel sometimes," Reverend Ben said in a remarkably casual tone.

"I do. His name is Theo," Noah added. "He likes coming to church with me. He liked your sermon yesterday."

Reverend Ben couldn't help smiling at the compliment. "Well, high praise indeed." He nodded with a thoughtful expression. "Please thank Theo for the compliment—and the warning. I could have certainly hurt myself very badly."

"I'll tell him. But it's okay. He likes helping everyone. That's his job," Noah replied.

"Yes, that's just what I've heard," Reverend Ben agreed.

"Noah? Could you please bring us another roll of tape?" Vera called from the conference room.

"There's one on my desk, in the little basket," Carrie told him.

Noah quickly ran to do his errand for Vera and disappeared into the conference room.

Carrie turned to Reverend Ben. "Well, now you've heard firsthand about the angel. Noah hasn't mentioned it for a day or so. I thought he was on to outer space."

"Apparently not," Reverend Ben replied. He closed the ladder and put the broken rung on top of a file cabinet. "Personally, I'm glad Noah's angel is still communicating with him."

"Do you think he's psychic or something? He seems to get premonitions about things."

Reverend Ben gave her a quizzical look, as if angels and psychic powers were equally plausible.

"I just find it very hard to believe that there really is some celestial spirit talking to Noah, smoothing his way, rearranging the world to help him. To help both of us." She winced as she realized what she had just said. "I'm sorry. I hope that didn't offend you."

"Not at all," Reverend Ben assured her. "As you know, I don't feel able to confirm one way or the other, with absolute certainty, that angels exist—or don't exist. But I will tell you that I believe in God and believe that He wants to help us, to smooth our way where He can, to express His infinite love for us, His creation. Therefore, I don't find it unreasonable, or even illogical, to accept that God may have some helpers carrying out His work."

Carrie smiled in spite of her worries. "That sounds very reasonable when you explain it that way. But it's hard when it's actually happening. Especially out in public like this. I don't want Noah to be known as the boy who talks to an angel," she added in a whisper, glancing over her shoulder at the conference room. "It would make things even more difficult."

Reverend Ben nodded, and Carrie could tell he understood her concern. "I agree. That sort of attention wouldn't be very good for Noah. If anyone asks why I've retired this old wooden ladder, I won't go into details. I'll just say that a rung came off in my hand. Which is true," he added, his small blue eyes crinkling at the corners as he smiled.

Carrie was grateful for his promise, but before she could reply, Vera poked her head out of the conference room. "Any luck with that wrapping paper?"

"I need a different ladder," Reverend Ben replied. "There's another in the choir room. I'll have it down for you in a minute."

Carrie walked back to her desk, feeling grateful that Vera had not witnessed Noah's warning. Vera was the sweetest and most generous soul in the world. But Carrie had no doubt that if Vera had been in the room—with all good intentions—news of Noah's angel would already be spreading through Cape Light.

A close call, but no harm done. And if the angel had managed that, too, Carrie had to admit she was very grateful.

As much as Carrie did not want to make her conversations with Jeff center around Noah, when they met for lunch the next day she told him the story about the ladder and the warning from Noah's angel.

"I spoke to Reverend Ben about it. I know he won't tell anyone what happened. But if it had been Vera, or someone else at church, I might be protecting Noah from TV reporters right now. At the very least, he would be gossiped about—singled out as an odd duck, a boy who talks to angels." She wrapped her hands around her coffee mug, as if seeking comfort from its warmth. "I wouldn't like that kind of attention focused on him."

"Nobody would like that," Jeff said sympathetically. "And luckily, that didn't happen."

"Not this time," Carrie replied. "But if Noah keeps believing in this Theo, who knows what he'll say—and where and when. He's just a little boy. He doesn't understand about discretion or unwanted attention."

"Hiding his true feelings or ideas, you mean?"

Carrie didn't exactly like the way Jeff put it. "Well . . . yes, I guess I do mean that. A person can't just walk around the world saying everything he thinks and feels out loud all the time. You need to have some filter."

"Yes, that's true. But I do think it's wonderful the way children are so naturally honest about their thoughts and feelings. The world might be a better place if we were all a bit more spontaneous and open."

"It would be," she agreed. "But I'm just talking about this angel story. And it is a story, Jeff. Maybe Noah is psychic or highly intuitive. Or something else that we just don't understand is going on. Even you seem to agree he's talking about an imaginary friend. I'm just not sure if I've done the right thing, being so accepting. I don't want this very sweet, comforting idea to backfire on him and make him the object of ridicule at school . . . or anywhere else."

She could tell from the way he leaned back in his chair and tipped his head to one side that he was trying hard to listen without interrupting. But he didn't agree.

"I know it sounds like I've slipped back to square one," she admitted. "Maybe I have. The situation yesterday with the ladder threw me again. I'm not sure I'm doing the right thing—the best thing—for Noah," she said finally.

Jeff didn't answer for a moment. He stirred his coffee and took a sip, then set the cup down again. "I won't argue with you, Carrie. You know what my opinion is, professionally and personally. You need to do what you think is right for your son. I'll give you some names of other therapists if you'd like to get another opinion, though you probably won't be able to get an appointment until after the holidays."

"Probably not. But I do think we should do that." It was a hard admission to make. It was almost as if she were saying that she no longer trusted Jeff's opinion in this matter. She sighed, feeling she had more to say to him and not knowing how to begin.

He reached across the table and took her hand. She was surprised at the gesture, relieved to see he wasn't angry with her.

"I'm not offended. It's fine. Are you worried about that? Please don't be. I *want* you to bring Noah to another specialist. I think it's a good idea."

Carrie nodded. "Okay. I'll do that then."

He tried to catch her eye again, but she avoided his glance. After a moment he said, "What are you doing for Christmas? Do you have any plans?"

"We've been invited to Reverend Ben's house for Christmas Eve," she told him, surprised at the question. "It was very thoughtful of them to include us."

"I'm sure you'll have a good time. Reverend Ben has at least two or three grandchildren. Noah will have some company." He paused, as if he had something more to say but wasn't sure he should. Then he added, "I'm having my sister and her family over on Christmas Day. Would you like to join us?"

Carrie took a breath and forced a smile at the very unexpected question. She wasn't sure how to respond. It was incredibly sweet, she thought. She knew he was concerned that she and Noah would be alone on Christmas. But she and Jeff had only had one real date. It wasn't that she didn't like him. She was completely charmed by him, and so was Noah—and that was what scared her. What if they got closer and it didn't work out? Having dinner with his family; that was one of those classic steps for two people getting closer. It seemed too much, too soon, and pushed some panic button inside her.

He watched her, waiting for her answer. She struggled to find the right words. "That's very nice of you, Jeff, to include us. But I'm not sure. Can I think about it?"

"Of course you can. No pressure. It's going to be a very relaxed day, jeans and sweaters. Some dinner and games with the kids."

"It sounds perfect. I'm sure you'll all have a great time . . . I'll try to figure out our plans and let you know," she promised, thinking it would be much easier to decline over the phone, instead of face-to-face like this.

"Sure. You can tell me Christmas morning if you want." He paused. "Anything else on your mind, Carrie? Besides Noah, I mean? You seem . . . miles away."

Carrie met his gaze, then looked away. Should she be totally honest with him? After his invitation, it seemed she had to be.

"I'm confused, Jeff. About a lot of things. About Noah and his angel . . . and about our relationship, too, I think. It's just moving so quickly. Too quickly for me."

"It's moved quickly for me, too," he admitted. "I really care about you, Carrie, you and Noah. Look, if coming for Christmas dinner with my family seems like too much, just forget I ever asked. We'll get together after the holiday, take Noah skating or something."

Do you have to be so understanding and wonderful? Carrie wanted to ask. Because it was suddenly clear to her that the problem wasn't meeting his family on Christmas. And that she couldn't take him up on this new invitation either, much as she wanted to.

"It's not really the Christmas thing," she said, her voice all but breaking. "It's me and Noah and the fact that he's got to be my priority. I can see how attached Noah already is to you, and that worries me. What if this doesn't work out? Noah will be crushed. I hadn't really thought this through before, but now . . . it makes me feel irresponsible, to put him at risk like that, especially after . . . I took him away from his father."

Jeff sat back. He looked sad and caught off guard. "I see," he said quietly. He shook his head, as if amazed at his own foolishness. "And I thought caring for you and Noah was a good thing."

Carrie felt tears welling up and blinked them back. "It is," she said. She stared down at the table, unable to meet his gaze. "I can't tell you how much the time we've spent together means to me. Being with you makes me happy," she said simply. "But that's the problem. I need to slow things down a bit and feel sure of what I'm doing."

She finally looked up at Jeff, afraid that he would be angry or hurt. Would he think she had led him on in some way?

He did look upset for a moment, and a bit stung. But very soon, the same gentle warmth and understanding that had drawn her to him in the first place shone in his eyes again.

"I understand," he said. "Or I think I do." He shrugged. "I was just thinking of the two of you, alone on Christmas. And I do want my sister to meet you," he added. "But there's plenty of time for that, I hope?"

Carrie nodded, relief surging through her. He wasn't giving up on her. "Of course there is."

"Well . . . when you say 'slow things down,' what do you mean exactly? Take a break from seeing each other?"

Carrie hadn't thought things through this far. It was hard for her to put her request in such definite terms. Part of her didn't want to take a break from seeing Jeff at all. Another part insisted that she had to—if not to protect her own heart, then at least for Noah's sake.

"I don't know . . . but maybe a few weeks? I just know I can't do this now."

He nodded, looking unhappy again. "All right. If that's what you want," he said. "I know you've been disappointed before, Carrie. And it does seem as if we hardly know each other. But I trust my feelings for you. I hope someday you can, too."

His words surprised her. She had expected something very different. But she'd never known anyone like Jeff before.

She took his hand. "Thank you for understanding. You said it yourself the other night. It will take time for me to trust someone new . . . and trust my own judgment again."

He shook his head ruefully. "I did say that, didn't I? It's hard for a doctor to take his own medicine. But I'll do my best."

Carrie didn't answer. She had gotten her way, but it felt like a hollow victory. She believed he would try his best. But what if that wasn't good enough? What if he grew tired of waiting and she lost him? Lost this chance for a relationship with such a wonderful man, and the connection between them that seemed so strong and loving?

But the wounds and worries that had driven her to push him away were too strong. Besides, it was too late. Their course was set. She couldn't take back her words now, even if she wanted to.

WHEN MOLLY GOT HOME FROM THE HOSPITAL ON TUESDAY MORNING, her three older daughters—Lauren, Jillian, and Amanda—were there to greet her. They were all home early for Christmas, and their beauty, energy, and chatter were the perfect prescription for what ailed her.

They set her up on a couch in the family room, adjacent to the kitchen, where Molly was able to be in the middle of all the action.

"I'll make your lunch," Amanda volunteered. "I have to learn how to cook soon. Would you like an omelet or something special?"

Molly rolled her eyes. "As if I haven't been trying to teach all of you all these years. Why don't you start with a sandwich, honey? Anything you can find in the fridge, I'm not fussy. I can't remember the last time I went food shopping."

It seemed as if she had been gone from the house for weeks instead of days. The girls had tried to clean up for her homecoming, she could see, but the house still didn't look as neat as she kept it.

"I'll go shopping right after lunch," Jillian offered. "After that, we'll put up some Christmas decorations. What happened to you, Mom? The house is bleak. You're usually like Mrs. Claus or something."

Molly had fallen behind in her decorating, just like everything else this year. If it hadn't been for little Betty, they wouldn't even have the tree up yet, though it hardly had any decorations on it.

Molly shrugged. "The elves canceled on me. What can I say?"

"Go easy on your mom, please. She's been through a lot," Matt told their daughters. "And she's been very busy with her business the last few weeks. You can all decorate the tree together. That will be much more fun anyway."

As soon as he had brought Molly home, Matt had disappeared into his home office—a man cave with medical books, Molly called it. He had fallen behind in his own work the last few days, and seemed relieved that the girls were around now to help him take care of her.

But now he had emerged to join them. He walked over to the couch and looked down at her. "Do you need anything, honey? The doctor gave me some pills for the pain."

"None of that for me." She was still aching all over, but the discomfort seemed like nothing compared to her broken heart and defeated spirit.

She had told Matt about her conversation with Betty, but aside from that, they had not spoken about the business. Nor had she spoken to Betty again. But the only way out Molly could see was to sell Willoughby's Fine Foods, the café and the catering business—the business had a lot of value even if their bank account didn't—and never even open the doors of Willoughby's Too.

"I'll put the pills in the medicine chest," Matt told her. "Just in case you feel worse later."

"Did he give you any pills to make me look better? I'm afraid to have people see me like this. All of you, don't let anyone come over if they call, okay?" she called out, hoping her daughters heard her. "Too bad this accident didn't happen right before Halloween. I look perfect for a Zombie Parade."

"Oh, Mom." Amanda turned from the kitchen counter, where she was busily preparing a stack of sandwiches and a big salad. "That's the last thing you should be worrying about right now."

"True," Molly said. Though she couldn't resist taking a peek at her reflection in the big mirror hanging on the opposite wall over the fireplace. She still had a bandage across her nose, a black eye, and a shaved patch on her scalp a few inches above her ear. Her left wrist was broken and her right ankle sprained, requiring a soft cast and a cane.

I look as bad as I feel inside, she thought, then realized that she felt even worse inside.

"Of course people want to see you, Mom. Don't be silly. They know that you've been in an accident." Jill brought her a sandwich and a cup of tea and set it up on the end table.

It wasn't just looking like a disaster; Molly didn't feel like socializing. She stared out at the snowy backyard, wishing she could crawl in a hole in a big tree and not come out until the spring, like a chipmunk.

The girls were soon finished with lunch. Jill and Amanda decided to go the supermarket together and then pick up their little sister at the elementary school. Matt had gone back to his home office. Lauren offered to stay with Molly. "I'll go up to the attic and get some more decorations down," she said.

"Good idea, honey. The Christmas boxes are all marked, on the far end by the suitcases."

After the girls had dispersed, Matt came down, dressed for work in a suit and tie. He walked over to the couch and sat down with her. "I thought I'd go into the office awhile. There's a little boy I may need to admit to the hospital. He may have pneumonia."

"You should go. Don't worry about me. The girls are watching me."

"I know. But it's hard for me to let you out of my sight," he said, and Molly felt a pang of guilt. The accident had been nearly as hard on Matt as it had been on her.

"I'm fine," Molly assured him. "I just look like a total wreck."

"A beautiful wreck. And you'll look perfect again in no time," he insisted. He leaned closer and put his arm around her shoulders. "I know you haven't heard anything from Betty yet. But give her time."

"Maybe I'm not the most patient person in the world," Molly admitted.

Matt just rolled his eyes. "Listen," he said, "I know you want to solve this. I also know how much you love that business, Molly. It's your fifth baby. It's your heart and soul. But please, don't do anything rash."

Molly sniffed. "I've been thinking and thinking about this, and I can only come up with one solution. We have to sell the shop. It's the only way. I'm going to call Betty as soon as I can and tell her—if she'll even speak to me."

"That's exactly what I mean," Matt said. "I do think you need to talk things out with Betty, but maybe not today. I'm going to see our accountant after work. He may have some ideas. Maybe there's some way we can help the business stay afloat for a while—until the profits catch up."

"Matt . . . you don't have to do that. I don't want you to ruin your retirement or add another mortgage to our house over this. It's not fair to you," she insisted.

He stood up and patted her good knee. "I'm just getting some ideas. It never hurts to ask. We have to keep an open mind."

"We also have to be realistic," Molly pointed out.

"'Hope for the best'? 'Never surrender'? 'Pick up our skirts and plow on'?" he reminded her. "Aren't those the things you always say?"

The mental picture of Matt in a pioneer-woman skirt finally made her smile. "Maybe I need to find some new sayings," she muttered.

He leaned over and kissed the top of her head. "Try to stay out of trouble until I get back tonight, okay?"

Molly nodded and leaned back on the pillows, sipping the hot ginger tea Jillian had made for her. It felt odd to have everyone in her family waiting on her like this. She was always the one who took care of all of them. And the house, too, and the cooking and shopping and cleaning. She was just The Mom; it was part of her job description. She had never thought about it much before; she had simply been happy to do it all and do it well, most of the time.

But now she was as immobile as a beached whale and not used to it one bit. She closed her eyes, wondering if she should try to read a book. Just for some distraction. But she knew that she had no concentration now and no interest in TV.

I could make a Christmas list, but someone has to go shopping for me. I hardly have any gifts yet for anybody. Christmas is . . . three days away?

I think I'll just sit here. And feel sorry for myself, Molly decided. *I don't seem fit for anything else right now.*

"MOM? AUNT BETTY'S HERE . . ." LAUREN CALLED TO HER FROM THE entryway. Molly woke with a start. Someone had covered her with an afghan, and she could tell by the light in the room that she had been asleep for a while. She struggled to lever herself up on her cane just as Betty walked into the family room.

"Betty. I didn't expect you," Molly said honestly. She knew that she sounded strangely formal but couldn't help it. She wasn't sure how to talk to Betty anymore. Everything was upside down between them.

"I was going to call, but I was in the neighborhood, so I thought I'd just drop by." Betty's voice was cool and curt. "Matt told me you were coming out of the hospital this morning."

"Yes, they let me out, thank goodness. I couldn't stand much more of that place."

"Well, I'm glad you're well enough to be home," Betty said in the same curt tone. "We need to talk, Molly."

Molly nodded, fearing the worst but knowing they had to get this over with and read their poor business its last rites, declare the patient officially deceased. The sooner the better, she supposed.

Lauren had gone back up to the attic to sort out the Christmas decorations, and the others would not be back for a while. They had some privacy, Molly thought. It shouldn't take too long.

Molly sat back down on the couch and braced herself. "So, what do you think? Or maybe you've already found a buyer?"

Betty sat down in the leather armchair across from her. "I have to be honest with you, I *was* looking for a buyer. After I saw you on Sunday, I was ready to spit nails. I was ready to put a sign on the front door of the shop and sell out, lock, stock, and barrel, to the first offer. Even Silver Spoon."

Molly winced. "Okay, I deserve that."

"You do. And I'm still sort of steamed at you. But I've had time to think it over, to sit with this. And to get some perspective," she added. "And this situation isn't entirely your fault. It's true that I've been focused on Nate for a long time. To tell you the truth, I even got distracted with him the last few days while I was trying to think all this out," she admitted. "He's making some progress, Molly, slowly but surely. While I was ranting and raving about you, Nate got up out of his wheelchair on his own and was able to move around with the walker—the first time he's even come close to walking since October. That shut me up pretty quickly."

"Betty, that's great news! That's amazing!" Molly couldn't help but grab Betty's hand and squeeze it with happiness.

"Well, we're not entirely through the woods yet. But it definitely made *our* situation—which is mostly sorting out some difficult finances—look small in comparison. You didn't get into this mess overnight, and we won't figure our way out in one fell swoop either. I know we're both tempted to just take the easy money and call it quits. But I've thought it over, and I really don't want to do that. Not unless we absolutely have to. I don't think I'd be happy in the long run. I don't think you would be either."

Molly knew she would feel devastated if they sold the business, but she only wanted to do the right thing. "I don't think you should worry about my feelings," she replied carefully. "I wouldn't blame you if you wanted to sell. And you certainly don't need to decide right now."

"I know I don't, but I have decided," Betty said. "First of all, I have to admit, I've been very disengaged from the business for the past two months or more now. It's all been on your shoulders, and if the situation had been reversed, I'm not sure if I could have handled the whole enchilada either. Maybe I would be sitting here confessing some huge screwup to you. I mean, could you imagine if I had to be in charge of the cooking and baking?" Betty paused, her eyes wide. "We wouldn't have lasted a week, no less this long."

"It's nice of you to say that. Honestly . . . but it didn't happen that way. I'm the one who messed up everything. I should be the one to make amends. Matt is seeing our accountant tonight. I want to pay you back for all the money I've lost—"

Betty interrupted her. "I've been going over the books for the last two days, Molly. We'll need to borrow a computer from NASA to figure it out. But until then, we have to look at all our options. Let's just think about this and have some patience, okay? You drove our business off the road," she acknowledged, "but maybe we don't have to junk it entirely. Maybe we can patch it up and get it rolling again? But that's not a one-woman job," she clarified in a serious tone. "We both have to commit to it—and get past all the blame."

Molly couldn't quite take in what she was hearing. "Oh, Betty . . . it's so good of you to give me another chance. I can't tell you what that means to me. But I'm afraid it's too late. I don't see how we can patch it up and keep going." Molly looked down at the cast on her arm and the bandage on her leg. She felt like a turtle stuck on her back, and she saw their business the same way.

Betty sighed dramatically. "Are you kidding me? I can't believe *you're* really saying this. I don't even recognize you. Where's Unsinkable Molly—and what did you do with her?"

Molly had no answer for that—except to say that maybe Unsinkable Molly had not emerged from the car wreck. Her cell phone rang then, and she reached for it. "I'm sorry. It might be the girls. They just went food shopping. I'll only be on a second."

"Molly? Are you home or still in the hospital?"

It was Sam, and Molly was not up for speaking to him now. He had visited her in the hospital, but she hadn't been able to bring him up to speed on her business situation. He was probably calling about some problem at the new shop, and right now, it seemed to her that no work crews were needed there. He should just dismiss everyone and lock the door.

"I can't talk now, Sam. Betty's here," she said quickly, trying to cut the call short.

"Betty's there? Great. Put me on speaker. I have some news." Sam was talking so loudly—an unfortunate family trait—that Betty could hear him without the speaker on.

"What's up? What's going on?" Betty leaned forward in her chair. Surrendering, Molly pushed the speaker button on her phone and set it on the table between them. "Okay, Sam. We can both hear you."

She braced herself, hoping this wasn't another mold sighting or something worse. What did it matter now? That was going to be someone else's problem. Her beautiful Parisian café, her vision, her dream . . . She had failed so miserably reaching for that brass ring.

"That partial certificate you wanted, to open up just the counter area? I pushed it all the way to the top and spoke in front of the Newburyport Board of Trustees last night, and guess what? They voted and approved your request. I have the certificate right here in my hand. You could open right now if you wanted to."

Betty sat up and clapped her hands. "Sam, that was brilliant! I love you!"

"It was Molly's idea. She's the queen," he replied. "I was just the knight sent out to battle the dragon."

"Well, you definitely deserve a notch on your sword, Sir Morgan," Betty replied. "That's just the news we need right now. Don't you think, Molly?"

Molly nodded, trying to seem more pleased than she really felt. "Great job, Sam. I knew you could do it." She looked back at Betty. "I'm just wondering if that's really going to help us now. I think it's too little, too late."

"What did you say? I didn't hear that," Sam shouted from the phone.

Molly looked back at the phone and spoke to him directly. "Things have changed on this end since we talked about that partial-permit idea, Sam. I really don't think that's going to work out now."

"Hey, stop right there!" Betty sounded like an actor on a police drama, ordering a criminal to put down their weapon. "You're doing it again, Molly. I have some say in this," Betty reminded her. "Forget what she just said, Sam. We're going forward. We'll open the counter down there tomorrow. Bring the papers up to Cape Light. I'll meet you at the shop in an hour."

"Will do, Betty . . . Hey, glad you're back on the scene," he added.

"Thanks, Sam. I'm glad to be back." Betty smiled at Molly with satisfaction as she ended the call. "We *have to* open Willoughby's Too. I thought you of all people would get that. Here's our chance—a gift from the blue!"

"But how? Who's going to staff it? What are we going to sell? The entire crew is out at parties all week, or baking and cooking for the business in Cape Light. We can't even afford to hire staff for Newburyport, Betty. Even if we could find people on such short—"

"Done and *done*," Betty interrupted her. "Your girls have already offered to pitch in. Lauren called me last night. She said they want to do whatever they can to help us while they're home over the holidays."

"My girls?" Molly was more than surprised at that news. "They've never taken any interest in the business."

"Maybe they've grown up and can see that their mother needs their help right now. They can staff the new store. And I know Eddie can find a helper so we can bake enough extra stock. Hey, maybe Alain will let us use his oven for a few nights? Didn't you say he helped us when the oven broke last week?"

"He did." Molly wasn't sure this patched-together plan would work, but she didn't have the heart to voice any doubts. It seemed their roles had suddenly reversed. She was always the one with outlandish, long-shot solutions, and Betty the voice of logic and reason.

But she had forgotten that Betty had been the head cheerleader all through high school. It seemed the old training was coming back to her now. All she needed was a set of pom-poms . . .

"I'll go next door and ask him as soon as I get back to the shop." Betty made a reminder note on her phone, along with several others.

"Alain is a good egg. He might help us. Bring him a box of cream puffs. That's his weakness," Molly suggested, realizing that she couldn't stop Betty from this heroic plan. She understood that Betty had to try; she had to feel she had done something to try to save them.

Though Molly couldn't imagine it working. All of Betty's efforts would just push off the inevitable—which they would be forced to face after the holidays. But she didn't have the heart right now to object. It was Betty's turn to run the show. Molly knew she had to be grateful that Betty had forgiven her. Or was at least trying to.

The best thing I can do now is sit on the sidelines, coach when asked . . . and cheer like heck for any small victories.

MOLLY'S THREE OLDER GIRLS WENT UP TO NEWBURYPORT WITH BETTY that night and then left for the new shop very early Wednesday morning. Molly wasn't even awake to wish them well. She woke up to find the house empty, coffee mugs and cereal bowls scattered around the kitchen. She hobbled about, cleaning up. The boxes of Christmas ornaments had made it down to the family room. But her troop of elves had emergency business to deal with in setting up the new shop, and no time to decorate last night as they had planned.

Molly maneuvered around the boxes, a cane in her good hand. Aiming her bottom at the couch cushions, she came in for a soft landing.

She felt the silence in the house moving in on her and tried to shake off her sad feelings. There were several messages on her phone she needed to answer—her mother and sisters, checking on her. Besides Sam, she had five other siblings, living in all parts of the country now. She and Sam were the only ones still in Massachusetts, but her younger brother, Glen, was up in Vermont, the three of them the true sturdy New Englanders among the sibs.

It was nice of them to check on her, but Molly didn't feel like talking to anyone today. Out of range of Betty's determined attitude, she felt herself sinking back into a dismal swamp of self-approbation and feeling she had been knocked out flat—and this time, just couldn't get up again.

There would be no beautiful Christmas Eve party at her house this year. Jessica and Sam had offered to have the family over. Molly didn't even think she wanted to go. She had promised Amanda and Gabriel a celebration of their engagement that night, too. Now she would be lucky if she even managed to get a wreath up on the door. What a miserable holiday this was turning out to be.

A knocking on the front door roused her, but not enough for her to get up and see who was there. It was probably a deliveryman or someone coming around to read a meter, she reasoned. *Anyone who knows me would never stop by this early, especially without even calling.*

The knocking soon ceased. Molly sat back, feeling relieved.

But a few moments later, she heard someone knocking again, even more persistently, this time on the side door, near the kitchen. She stretched and peered to see who this annoying caller could be . . . and found Sam standing on the doorstep.

He caught sight of her and waved wildly. Molly sighed, but realized she couldn't hide from him. She levered herself up on the cane again and painfully made her way to the mudroom.

"Hey, Molly. How are you doing? Up and around already? That's a good sign," he greeted her cheerfully, enclosing her in a big, brotherly hug.

"Just barely. But I'm getting around on this cane a little better today. Want some coffee? I can work the coffeemaker if I lean against the counter."

Sam shook his head. "I'm good. Just on my way up to Newburyport. I thought you might like to come, see how everything is going. I just spoke to Betty. They opened the doors at seven this morning, and the customers were lining up."

Molly forced a smile. She knew that she should have been encouraged by the news, but she still doubted it would really help. "Sounds good. I hope they have enough on the shelves to sell." There were few things worse than a customer coming in and seeing all the shelves bare. It was disappointing and unappetizing. And it did not encourage repeat business.

"Betty says they're stocked, and I just got a call from the gas company. The new ovens are going to be connected in a few days."

"Thank you, Sam. Thanks for keeping the ball rolling. Though I'm really not sure any of this extra effort is going to make a difference."

"Hey, let's not even go there, Mol." Sam had obviously been hypnotized by Betty, too, just like her girls. "What happened to Winston Churchill?" he prodded her.

Molly shrugged. "Even Winston retired."

She actually wasn't sure if that was true. He was voted out of office eventually, she recalled. But then he was reelected.

"History was never my strong point. But I think it would do you a world of good to put on a parka and some shoes and come up to Newburyport with me. See what's going on with your own eyes. Maybe once you see the new shop actually open and doing good business, you'll feel a little more positive."

"Sam, I can't go with you. Look at me. I'm covered with bandages and I can hardly walk. I'll scare the customers away."

Sam laughed at her. "Now that you mention it, you might. Tell you what, you can just sit in the truck and we'll do a drive-by. You can wear big sunglasses or something, like a movie star."

The larger part of her still resisted, though some other part was tempted. "How am I going to get in the truck? I can't climb up there."

"I'll get you in there, don't worry." The tone of his promise worried her. "Stop arguing with me. You're going, even if I have to toss you into the flatbed and tie you down next to the Sheetrock."

Molly made a face at him, which soon melted into a reluctant smile. "I hate it when you get all big brother on me. It's so dumb."

"Whatever works," he replied, looking satisfied.

"Help me put that boot on." She grunted as she sat on the bench in the mudroom and pointed at the snow boot she needed. The other foot was covered by a large black fracture boot, and Molly hoped it didn't get too wet in the snow.

The truth was, she was very curious to see the new shop in action, and once she gave in to the idea, she was actually grateful to Sam for forcing her to go with him.

On the drive up to Newburyport, Molly told him about her heart-to-heart talks with Betty and how at first, Betty had been horribly angry with her, but how things seemed to be smoothing out. "Despite the odds—and honestly, Sam, they're overwhelming—Betty seems determined to see if we can stay in business."

"She does seem energized by the crisis," Sam agreed. "She has a lot of faith."

Molly glanced at him but didn't reply. She knew that Betty had a deep and abiding faith. And a lot of patience. More than she had, that was for sure. Was Sam trying to tell her she should be more like Betty and have more faith right now? Molly wouldn't doubt it, though she was glad he hadn't gone all preachy on her. That was the last thing she needed.

Molly felt a sense of excitement rising as Sam turned the truck onto the waterfront street where the new shop was located. He cruised down the street slowly and parked in a spot right in front of Willoughby's Too.

Despite the frigid weather, Molly rolled down the passenger-side window to get a good look. The awning was up and the gold-leaf letters were painted across the window. There was another, hand-lettered sign there, too, in big red letters that said OPEN FOR BUSINESS! COME ON IN!

Molly's jaw dropped as she tried to make sense of what she was seeing.

A line of people stood in front of the glass counter, stretched outside and then halfway down the block. It was beyond busy—it was a destination spot! Customers were emerging with coffee cups and white paper bags or big white pastry boxes. She could see her girls behind the counter, dressed in white aprons, and a few tables near the window, all the seats filled.

"What did I tell you? It's doing a bang-up business. Betty says she's going to double the baking order for tomorrow."

"Good plan," Molly murmured in amazement. "I think they'll need it." She turned to her brother. "This is not what I expected," she confessed. "I am so glad you brought me here—even if you practically did have to throw me in the truck. I do feel better. Seeing *is* believing."

Sam laughed and put the truck in gear to drive away. "Some people might say that," he replied. "But St. Augustine said, 'Faith is to believe what you do not see; the reward of this faith is to see what you believe.'"

Molly shook her head. "I'll try to remember that."

"You always knew that, Molly. You just forgot for a little while." Her brother glanced at her warmly. "I just brought you up here to remind you."

Chapter Thirteen

Vera left for her daughter's house in Connecticut around noon on the day before Christmas. Carrie and Noah helped her load all her bags and packages in her car.

"I'm sorry we won't be together for Christmas," Vera said as she hugged them both before she climbed in her car. "But we can exchange our gifts when I get back next week. It will make the holiday last a little longer. I think you'll like what I picked out for you, Noah," she added with a smile.

"I can't wait to see it. But I will," he said with resignation that made Vera and Carrie laugh.

"Have a great Christmas, Vera, and a safe trip," Carrie called to her as she started the car. They stood back from the sidewalk and waved as she drove away.

"What are we going to do now?" Noah asked as they walked inside again.

"We don't have that much time before we need to get ready for church. The service starts at five, and we're going to Reverend Ben's house tonight for dinner right after," she reminded him. "I have to go into town and get a little gift for Reverend Ben and his family. Want to help me pick something out?"

At first Noah didn't look very interested in shopping again but then, suddenly, his face lit up. "I know what we should get Reverend Ben—that birdhouse that looks like a little church. That would be a perfect present for him."

Carrie laughed at the idea. She had forgotten all about those silly birdhouses at Krueger's. Of course, Noah hadn't. "That's a very good idea. I think he'll love that. We'll look for something nice for Carolyn, too, and maybe get some chocolates and flowers."

"And maybe get a birdhouse for Jeff," Noah said, adding to their list. "Remember, I told you that he likes to watch birds?"

"Yes. I remember." It had only been two days since her lunch with Jeff, but she already missed him. It wasn't so much the amount of time that had passed but knowing that she had put their relationship on hold for an indefinite period of time, and there was little chance of hearing from him or seeing him. Would he wait for her to sort out her confused feelings? Did he really care that much about her and Noah?

Carrie's heart did a cartwheel at the notion that he truly did—while another part of her warned her to keep a safe distance so she wouldn't get hurt. She wished it wasn't so hard for her to just let go and open her heart. But she was scared. She couldn't help that.

"Can we get Jeff the birdhouse?" Noah's insistent question broke through her rambling thoughts. "He already gave me the snow saucer. It wouldn't be fair not to give him something for Christmas," he pointed out.

That meant seeing Jeff, a thought that made her heart beat faster. Carrie nodded. "All right. The birdhouse can be from you, okay?"

"Okay . . . And I want to get a chew toy for Elsie," he added.

"Of course. We can't forget Elsie." Though the only appropriately sized chew toy Carrie could imagine would be the size of a spare tire.

Noah ran to get his coat and gloves for their shopping trip without Carrie even having to ask him.

THOUGH CARRIE THOUGHT SHE HAD LEFT PLENTY OF TIME TO GET TO church that evening, the parking lot was already crowded when they pulled up. She found a spot and they quickly went inside. Carolyn Lewis waved to her as Carrie stood at the back of the sanctuary, looking for an empty seat. Carolyn gestured, indicating that she had saved a space for them with her family. Carrie prodded Noah forward. "Mrs. Lewis saved us a seat up front. Let's go up the side aisle."

"There are seats right here, Mom." Noah pointed to a space in the rear pew. "Let's sit here."

Carrie knew why he was so eager to claim that space. Just in case Jeff was looking for them. She had thought of that, too.

"Sorry, honey. It would be rude not to take the seats Mrs. Lewis saved. It was very thoughtful of her." She took his hand and led him away, hoping he didn't make an issue of this during the whole service.

Carolyn greeted them warmly and introduced Carrie to her daughter, Rachel, and her grandchildren. Carrie already knew that Rachel had lost her husband, Jack, a few years ago but was now engaged to be married again. Her fiancé, Ryan Cooper, stood next to her and shook hands with Carrie, too.

"My son, Mark, and his family are coming in from Oregon," Carolyn said happily. "But they won't arrive until tomorrow."

"Reverend Ben told me," Carrie replied. The reverend was greatly looking forward to a visit with his son. It sounded as if Mark didn't come east very often. "You're going to have plenty of company. Thank you so much for including us tonight."

"It's our pleasure, dear," Carolyn said warmly, in her slightly Southern accent. "Ben has been so happy to have you covering for Mrs. Honeyfield the last few weeks. He says he doesn't know what he would have done without you . . . and he's loved getting to know Noah, too."

Her words touched Carrie's heart. She loved her job at the church, too, and had grown quite attached to everyone there, even though it was temporary. But it had led her to this church and a congregation full of warm, friendly people, and for the first time in a long time, Carrie realized she had started to feel as if she and Noah were putting down real roots again. Maybe they didn't have a place of their own yet, but it did seem that they had found a real home here.

"There's Molly Harding and her family," Carolyn remarked, her bright gaze darting to the back of the sanctuary. "I'm so glad to see she made it to church tonight. She had quite an accident. Reverend Lewis and I saw her at the hospital over the weekend. She looks a lot better now," she added, sounding relieved.

Carrie glanced back and spotted Molly walking slowly, holding her husband's arm and using a cane, too. Practically everyone turned to greet her and extend good wishes, as if she were a celebrity. Three young women, one prettier than the next, preceded her; Molly's grown daughters. Her youngest daughter—Betty, who was in Noah's class—walked on the other side of her father, holding his hand.

Carrie was about to face front again when she spotted Jeff coming in. There were few seats to be found now, with many people standing. But he did find a spot in the very rear pew, the same place they sat with him last weekend.

Carrie tried to catch his eye, but he didn't see her. She finally turned and looked up at the altar, staring at the elaborate display of red and white poinsettias and flickering white candles, but hardly noticing the beautiful display. She was, to her surprise, blinking back tears. Had he seen her and pretended not to? Was he now having doubts about her? Or was he simply too hurt to look her way?

But she had asked him to do this, to give her some space and some time, she reminded herself. *He's only respecting your wishes.*

All she knew was that it felt very sad, and even wrong, to be at odds with Jeff like this, to feel so distant from him, on Christmas.

MOLLY FELT HER FACE GROW WARM WITH EMBARRASSMENT AND STIFF with a forced smile as she slowly hobbled up the side aisle to an empty pew. She was holding on to Matt's arm for support on one side and using her cane on the other. Everyone turned to greet her, even people she didn't know that well. She appreciated the good wishes but did wish she could sprout a pair of wings and fly up to her seat instead of moving at this torturous awkward crawl.

"Slow down. Where's the race?" Matt asked her quietly.

"I'm fine. We're holding up traffic," she replied. While she usually thrived on attention, tonight she wished she were invisible. Though she had always loved the Christmas Eve service, tonight she had only come to church because her family had forced her to. Matt had more or less insisted, saying if she didn't go, they wouldn't either. He knew how to get to her. She hated that.

She had told Matt that she didn't feel well enough yet to sit that long. But she was really just blue. He knew that, too. Even the visit to Willoughby's Too and Betty's positive reports on the new shop hadn't brightened her outlook. She was still waiting for the other shoe to fall. She would have to wait until after the holidays, it seemed.

"Molly, I was so sorry to hear about your accident." Jaqueline

Phillips from the Historical Society reached out from one of the pews and touched her arm. "How do you feel?"

"Coming along," Molly replied. "A little better every day."

"Oh, that's good news. Well, Merry Christmas. You look wonderful," she added.

Molly forced another smile, grateful now that her daughters had descended on her and whipped her into shape, dressing her in a fancy sweater and a long black skirt that mostly hid her cast, and even fixing her hair and choosing jewelry, as if she were their special life-sized doll.

"Thank you very much, Jaqueline. Merry Christmas," she replied. For some unaccountable reason, her sour feelings about losing the society's cocktail party had faded. Even that soirée wouldn't have saved Willoughby's. Right now it seemed nothing would. She wondered if anyone here knew about her business problems. She was sure that Betty and Sam were totally discreet, but it was a small town and word got around. No sense worrying about that now, she decided. Everyone would know soon enough.

She glanced around and caught sight of Betty and Nate, at the rear of the sanctuary. They looked very happy. Betty was positively beaming. Nate was dressed in a suit and tie. She noticed a cane, much like her own, dangling from the end of the aisle, but no wheelchair in sight. Molly's heart brightened with happiness, too.

"Look, Nate's in church—without his wheelchair," she said to Matt. "Betty told me he was improving, but I didn't realize he'd come this far. I should have called them."

"Yes, I'd heard he was coming along very well the last two weeks. It's wonderful news. But you've had your own recovery to worry about the last few days, Molly," he added kindly. "Let's try to say hello to them later, and wish them well."

"Absolutely," Molly agreed. No wonder Betty was betting on miracles for their business. She had just seen one on the home front. But Molly knew two in row was highly unlikely.

Maybe the business falling apart had served some higher purpose, she thought. If that's what it had taken to get Nate up and walking, it was worth the trade. The idea gave her some small comfort as she heard the organist strike the opening chords of the first hymn and the choir marched in, singing "O Come, All Ye Faithful."

Though the service was not long, Molly soon felt fidgety. She couldn't get up and down for the hymns and hated being seated while everyone else rose, towering around her. Her leg hurt and her wrist hurt a little, too, and she longed to be back in her pajamas, lying on the couch in the family room, watching *It's a Wonderful Life* for the umpteenth time this week. She would do that while the rest of her flock went to Sam and Jessica's for the family's annual Christmas Eve get-together, she promised herself. Church was one thing, but surely Matt and the girls would understand and not force her to go to a party and be social all night? Molly mulled over a strategy to convince them, wondering if she should start telling Matt now that she wasn't feeling well.

But Matt was paying close attention to the service, and she didn't want to distract him by acting like a baby. Even if she felt like one.

Reverend Ben was reading a Scripture passage, and Molly forced herself to focus.

"'Now there were in the same country shepherds living out in the fields, keeping watch over their flock by night. And behold, an angel of the Lord stood before them, and the glory of the Lord shone around them, and they were greatly afraid. Then the angel said to them, "Do not be afraid, for behold, I bring you good tidings of great joy which will be to all people. For there is born to you this day in the city of David a Savior, who is Christ the Lord. And this *will be* the sign to you: You will find a Babe wrapped in swaddling cloths, lying in a manger."'

"'And suddenly there was with the angel a multitude of the heavenly host praising God and saying: "Glory to God in the highest, And on earth peace, goodwill toward men!'"

"'So it was, when the angels had gone away from them into heaven, that the shepherds said to one another, "Let us now go to Bethlehem and see this thing that has come to pass, which the Lord has made known to us." And they came with haste and found Mary and Joseph, and the Babe lying in a manger. Now when they had seen *Him,* they made widely known the saying which was told them concerning this Child. And all those who heard *it* marveled at those things which were told them by the shepherds. But Mary kept all these things and pondered *them* in her heart. Then the shepherds returned, glorifying and praising God for all the things that they had heard and seen, as it was told them.'"

Reverend Ben closed his Bible and looked up at the congregation. "I hope everyone is ready. Because it's *finally* here. Isn't that what we say about Christmas? 'Get ready. Get ready.' And then, with vast relief for most of us, 'Thank heavens. We're finished. It's here.' Isn't that what the angels told the shepherds on the night Christ was born? 'The one you've heard about, been waiting for, the Messiah, the Savior, He's finally arrived. Go and see with your own eyes. It's finally happened. This is a moment to celebrate. The world will never be the same,'" he paraphrased.

"This Advent, I've been talking a lot in my sermons about seeing with new eyes, with a fresh perspective. Instead of through a lens of stale expectations. And as I read over this most familiar passage the other day, I suddenly realized something quite amazing." Reverend Ben paused and looked out at the congregation. "The way we think of Christmas is pretty much all wrong. The way most of us see it, experience it—myself included—is backward. We think of it mostly as if it were a square on a game board that we're struggling and strategizing to reach. Or for the more high-tech folks out there, the *final* level of a video game," he added, causing a small ripple of laughter in response.

"Christmas as a finite square, a place where we end our journey. Where we rest and enjoy ourselves. Where we give and receive gifts, tokens of affection and esteem. This finish line, where we share love and goodwill and fellowship with family and friends. Where many of us are also celebrating the birth of our Lord, Jesus Christ, as well. 'What's wrong with that?' you might ask."

Reverend Ben shook his head. "Nothing at all. As long as we are also mindful—as long as we also see—that within the conclusion to every story, in every pregnancy that results in a birth, in every prophecy fulfilled, there's a new beginning. An entirely *new* story.

"And when it comes to the well-known Christmas story, these familiar lines of Scripture I've just read are *only* the beginning. Christmas is only the beginning. Not a finish line. It's the start of a whole new world, taking the form of a tiny infant wrapped in rags. But much loved. Much glorified. And once you think of Christmas this way, how perfect that Christ would choose to enter this world as a tiny baby."

Reverend Ben paused for a long moment, then added, "Take this child into your hearts tonight, and let Him be the start of a fresh, new, beautiful story in your life."

He nodded and smiled, then stepped down from the lectern as the choir stood and sang the opening lyrics of "Joy to the World."

It was Molly's favorite carol, and she struggled to stand and sing along, leaning on Matt's arm to share his hymnal, though she knew most of the words by heart. Reverend Ben's sermon had surprised her. She had never thought of Christmas that way, as the start of something new. Especially the Christmas season at her shop. Christmas *was* a finish line to her. A square on the game board where you could finally just collapse.

But she liked his idea, this new slant. Every ending was the beginning of something new. It was true. She had seen that time and again in her own life, after her divorce from her first husband and so many times after. It was a hard lesson to learn, though. And it was even harder to have courage and hang on, waiting for the new story to start. But Reverend Ben's words gave her something to think about.

After the service, the aisles in the sanctuary were crowded as everyone tried to get out at the same time. "Why don't we wait a few minutes until it's a little easier for you?" Matt suggested.

Molly agreed. Her older girls took little Betty out with them and were going to warm up the car and pull it up to the church so Molly could get in more easily.

By the time she and Matt left, the sanctuary was practically empty. "We missed Betty and Nate," Molly said, feeling sad about that. Betty and Nate sometimes went to Nate's sister's house for Christmas Eve, though they were always invited to Molly and Matt's when they held their party. Not this year, of course. "Maybe they'll stop in at Sam's for a while," Molly said. "You can say hello for me."

"I can," Matt replied. "There's Reverend Ben," he added as they finally left the sanctuary.

Reverend Ben quickly walked over to greet them. "It's good to see you up and about, Molly," he said sincerely. "Where will you be tonight? Going to a party?"

Molly shook her head. "I don't think so. I'm not quite up to it," she explained. "Jessica and Sam are having the family this year. Matt and the girls will go. I'm just going to rest."

Reverend Ben nodded. "Could be for the best. Don't push yourself," he said kindly.

"We're taking very good care of her, Reverend Ben. Don't worry," Matt promised.

Once she and Matt were outside, alone, she said, "I really don't think I can make the party at Sam's tonight, honey. You go with the girls. You'll all enjoy it. Don't worry about me. I'm just going to relax and go to sleep early."

Matt nodded and took her arm. "That's all right, honey. We'll drop you off at home. Here's Lauren, with the car."

Molly felt relieved that he hadn't tried to persuade her. She let him help her to the curb and then into the front seat of their car.

There wasn't much conversation on the ride home. Molly hoped her youngest wouldn't make a fuss when she heard Mommy needed to stay home. But she was easily persuaded and cajoled into anything by her older sisters, and Molly was sure Jill and Lauren would work their special magic.

As they approached their house, Molly noticed a lot of cars on the street. "Someone must be having a big party. Maybe the Figarellos," she added, mentioning neighbors down the street. All the lights were on at their house. It did look lively.

"Could be," Matt murmured as Lauren pulled into the driveway. Everyone got out, and Matt came around to help her into the house.

"Just get me settled, and get all the presents in the car," Molly told him. "I don't want you to be late to Jess and Sam's."

"Don't worry. We'll be fine," Matt said.

The girls went around to the front door, but Matt took Molly through the side door in the garage. There were no steps, and it was much easier for her than going through the front.

With Matt at her side, they ambled along through the narrow hallway near the laundry room and pantry. She heard laughter in the kitchen and saw lights on. The girls were already in there, she thought, stealing a few cookies before dinner.

But when she walked into the kitchen she saw Betty, wearing an apron and putting a tray of canapés into the oven.

"Merry Christmas, Molly." Betty smiled and then leaned over and kissed her cheek.

"Betty . . . what are you doing here?" Molly heard her girls laughing at her, like a chorus of chirping birds.

She spun around and saw Jessica and Sam and their boys in the family room. And her mother in the dining room, setting the table, and her father, tending to the fire.

"What is going on here?" She turned to Matt. "How could we have Christmas Eve? It's supposed to be at Sam's house."

Matt smiled. "How could we not? We knew you wouldn't go, and we didn't want to drag you by your hair."

"What you have left of it, Mom," Lauren quipped.

"You little rat, don't you dare say that." Molly playfully swatted at her daughter with her cane. She looked back at Matt and at Betty, who had enlisted the help of the girls and had them busy at work, arranging trays of appetizers. Molly recognized many of them from their shop.

"You tricked me. All of you," she said, taking them in with a sweeping, condemning glance.

"Yes, we did," Betty said cheerfully. "You never suspected a thing, did you?"

"No . . . I didn't," Molly admitted.

Resolved not to pout, Molly threw herself into the party preparations as much as she could. Which was not much, since no one would let her close to the stove or counter where the work was being done.

She resigned herself to sitting on a stool in the family room at a safe but watchful distance. "Hey, what is that?" she asked Lauren as she shuttled out with a new tray of food.

"Chips, salsa, and guacamole," Lauren said, staring down at the food with a puzzled frown.

"I know what it is," Molly replied. "But you're not serving that at my party, okay? Save it for the dorm room."

Betty laughed and quickly intervened. "New rules, Molly. Anything red and green can and will be served tonight." She gave Lauren a gentle push and sent her on her way. "The Martha Stewart Police are giving you the night off. This is a potluck Christmas party, not your usual *Gourmet* magazine–worthy table."

Matt grinned at her. "If you think the salsa is bad, you'd better close your eyes when the girls bring out the nachos and mini–hot dogs wrapped in pastry."

Molly cringed. "Pigs in a blanket? Say it ain't so, Betty!"

Betty laughed. "It's so. And it's *les chiens chauds étouffé*, so that makes it okay. Very French, you know."

Before Molly could say more, the doorbell rang. She heard the familiar voices of Emily Warwick and her husband, Dan. And of Emily and Jessica's mother, Lillian.

"Is that Lillian coming in?" Betty said. "Wait until she sees this spread. There goes the Historical Society forever." But she was laughing, not dismayed one bit.

Molly laughed quietly, too. "What can you do? You can't please 'em all."

"Very true," a deeper voice replied.

Molly turned to see Nate. She wasn't sure he had even come tonight. But there he was, walking toward her, using his cane for balance, but otherwise standing with head high and shoulders back. And smiling very widely.

"Nate . . . oh, my gosh. I'm so happy to see you. I'm so glad you came to the party." Molly began to carefully slide off the stool, but Nate was soon beside her.

"You sit. It's fine." He gently hugged her as she sat back on the chair.

"No offense, but I'm finally glad to find someone in worse shape than I am," he joked.

Molly laughed. "I win that contest tonight," she assured him. "Betty told me that you were improving, but I had no idea that you had come along this quickly."

"I was stalled out for a little while," he admitted. "But my very amazing, angelic 24/7 nurse, cheerleader, and wife got me back on my feet again."

Betty looked up from the cheese platter she was working on and smiled at him. "That's not true. He did it all on his own. I didn't do much at all."

"You did a lot," he insisted, then looked back at Molly. "And I'm not exaggerating. Though I never said she could cook," he added with a mischievous grin.

Betty laughed at the barb. "That's more like it."

Nate walked over and kissed her cheek. He didn't need to tell her that he thought she was perfect anyway. Anyone could see that he did.

Amanda and Gabriel strolled into the family room, and Nate walked over to congratulate the couple on their engagement. Somehow, through the Christmas carols playing on the music system and the many conversations buzzing all around her, Molly heard a tiny bell on the stove ring.

Betty met her glance and grinned. "*Les chiens chauds sont finis!* Want to try one?" She held out the tray, and Molly poked at a tiny hot dog wrapped in pastry with a toothpick. They did look good.

She took a cautious bite and chewed. "Not a caviar crêpe," she announced, "but it's definitely *très bon*. Perfect choice of spicy mustard, too."

"Glad you approve. *Joyeux Noël*, Molly," Betty said, slinging her arm around Molly's shoulder for a hug.

"Merry Christmas, Betty. I'm so glad you're here. It wouldn't be Christmas without you. Not to me, anyway," she quietly confessed.

"I know, pal. I feel the very same." Betty nodded, her blue eyes looking a little misty.

They both turned at the sound of a sharp, scolding voice in the dining room. "Don't eat that, Ezra. It's far too spicy for you." It was Lillian, of course, sounding a shrill warning to her husband. "You'll be up all night and drive me crazy. Where did they find this food? In a gas station convenience store?"

"It just wouldn't be Christmas without Lillian either," Betty added quietly.

"I guess," Molly conceded, giggling a little.

"Matt said you were planning to stay home alone tonight. Is that true?" Betty asked.

"I was just going to sulk in my pj's and watch *It's a Wonderful Life*," she admitted.

"It *is* a wonderful life. Look around. You're living it," Betty replied.

Molly met her glance, but didn't answer. Mainly because she had no answer; Betty's words were so true. Christmas was a time for gratitude. And she did have so very much to be grateful for. For simply being alive after her accident. For her amazing family and friends, who seemed to love her, with all her imperfections and quirks. And especially for Betty.

Betty lifted a glass of eggnog to her. "I know we have a lot to figure out, come January," she said. "But there's nothing we can do about it now. Let's just relax and enjoy Christmas. There's so much to celebrate and be thankful for."

"Absolutely," Molly agreed, lifting her own glass in a toast. *Betty is right,* she thought. *Even if we decide to sell the business, my life will go on. My very wonderful life,* she amended. *And every ending is a new beginning. I have to remember that.*

Chapter Fourteen

Carrie got up very early on Christmas morning to make sure Noah's presents were all under the tree. She had hidden quite a few around the house, and she had to stuff his stockings with small toys and treats, too.

She had a special breakfast of French toast and hot chocolate underway by the time Noah woke up and came downstairs. Breakfast, however, was second on the agenda. First, she joined him in the living room to unwrap gifts.

Noah had bought her two presents. One was very practical, a new snow brush for the car, which she kept forgetting to buy for herself. The other, more of a luxury, was a necklace made from a thin, pretty ribbon with a clear, oval-shaped orb hanging from the center. When Carrie looked inside the pendant, she found a small blue angel floating there.

"Noah . . . where did you find this necklace? Who helped you shop?"

"Vera did. That day when she watched me after school."

Carrie thought back. She had not asked Vera for any help watching Noah after school, but one afternoon, Vera had been at the church for a meeting and had offered to take Noah home with her early, before Carrie finished work.

"We planned it," Noah confided. "We tricked you."

"I had no idea. You were both very good at keeping that secret."

Noah smiled. "Yup, we were."

"I think I'll wear this beautiful necklace today," she said, and put it on, even though she was still in her bathrobe and pajamas. She could see that Noah was pleased. And she really didn't mind the little angel at all. It certainly would make her think of her son every time she wore it.

When they went into the kitchen to eat breakfast, Carrie reminded Noah that they were going to church again. "We'll come right home after, and you can play with some of your new toys," she promised.

"All right. But what about Jeff's birdhouse? And Elsie's toy? You said we could drop them off," he reminded her.

Carrie sipped her coffee and didn't answer right away. "We'll see," she said. "You'd better get dressed."

"All right. I'll put their gifts in the car, just in case," he added.

Carrie nodded, hoping Noah's persistent, focused side lasted well into adulthood. It would serve him well in pursuing his goals—though it sometimes made it more difficult for her to parent him.

A short time later, they were headed to church. Noah was sitting in the backseat and, as promised, he had retrieved Jeff and Elsie's gifts from under the tree and placed them right next to him.

He was very quiet, watching out the window as they drove down Vera's street and then turned to the Beach Road. Suddenly he leaned forward and tapped Carrie on the shoulder. "Mom, we have to turn around. We have to go to Jeff's house."

Carrie caught his eye in the rearview mirror. He looked pale and worried. "Noah, what is it? What are you talking about? We're going to church now. We can go to Jeff's house later."

"No, Mom. We have to go now. We really have to go there. It's important." His tone was part pleading, part crying, part demanding.

Carrie felt a frightening chill. "Is Jeff in trouble? Is that what you think?"

"Yes, we have to help Jeff. Elsie is lost."

Carrie sighed. She felt confused and even a little annoyed. Was he making up some urgent story, just to see Jeff?

No, Noah wouldn't do that, she reasoned. It was the angel prompting him. She was almost sure of it.

She pulled over and turned to him. "Noah, did your angel tell you about Elsie?"

Noah nodded, his eyes filling with tears. "Yes . . . she's hurt. She needs our help."

Carrie stared at him a moment and didn't answer. He was so sincere, it was impossible to refuse him. Even though she didn't really believe it.

"All right . . . we'll go to Jeff's house. If you really want to," she said, pulling back on the road again.

Maybe this was it, the moment when Noah would see that he had been imagining these angel whispers. A broken stepladder was one thing. She had reasoned out several explanations for how Noah could have known that. But certainly this message about Elsie couldn't be true, could it?

They had been driving down the Beach Road toward the turn for Jeff's house for a few minutes. Noah had been completely silent. They were close but not there yet when Noah grabbed her shoulder again.

"Stop, Mom. Stop here," he said.

Carrie pulled the car to the side of the road. She turned slowly, ready to hear him admit that he had made up this entire story.

But when she looked back at him, Noah was unlocking his seat belt and had already opened the door.

"Noah? What are you doing? You can't get out of the car here," she said in alarm.

Noah ignored her. He slipped outside and ran straight into the woods. Carrie grabbed her keys and ran after him. Did he feel carsick or something? she wondered. Was that it?

No, not at all—he was running at top speed into the woods, not even following the path. Working his way through the slim bare trees, dried leaves and brush, all covered in a light layer of snow.

Carrie ran after him, calling his name. "Noah . . . stop! Noah, please . . . come back here . . . You can't just run off like that!"

She was glad she had worn jeans and snow boots today and hadn't dressed up for the service. But she was still no match for the fleet-footed seven-year-old, and could barely keep him in view.

Where were they? She had no idea. This was not the same stretch of woods where they had walked with Jeff on that wintry afternoon. If it was, she didn't recognize any landmarks.

She kept running, trying to keep Noah in view, sending up a silent prayer that she wouldn't lose him out here.

"Carrie? Wait!"

She spun around at the sound of Jeff's voice and saw him running toward her. His down vest hung open over his sweater, despite the cold, and his jeans were wet and smeared with mud stains. Carrie stood stone still at the sight of him.

"What are you doing here?" he asked breathlessly, finally close enough to talk to her.

"Noah made us come. He ran out of the car. Something about Elsie being lost?"

"She is lost. She got away from me this morning. I can't find her—"

She reached out and grabbed his hand. "He went this way. He's very fast. I don't want to lose him out here."

"Yes, of course. I think I see him," Jeff said, pulling her along now.

The woods soon thinned out and Carrie saw a meadow bordered by an old wooden fence covered in vines and brush, rotted out in most spots.

She saw Noah by the fence, kneeling beside Elsie, who stood with her hindquarters in the air and her head down near the ground. Carrie could hear her whimpering and Noah's soothing tones as he gently petted her.

"Elsie's head is caught in the fence," Jeff said, running ahead of her. "That's why I didn't hear her barking."

Carrie could see that now, too, and ran to catch up with him.

"She's stuck, Jeff," Noah called. "I can't get her loose."

"Don't worry, I'll get her out." Jeff concentrated on the dog, who now wagged her tail and whined with relief, making small yipping sounds when she could.

Carrie walked up behind Noah and rested her hands on his shoulders. He had been right all along. She could hardly believe it and had no idea what to say about his angel messages now.

Jeff quickly pulled off the board that held Elsie's head in place. "There you go, sweetheart," he crooned to her.

She quickly jumped up to lick his face, and then turned to Noah, nearly knocking him down. Jeff caught her collar and quickly grabbed her trailing leash, then pulled her down to a sitting position so he could examine her head and ears.

"You silly girl, you scared the dickens out of me," he told the dog, laughing and almost crying, too.

"Yes . . . you silly dickens," Noah echoed, crouching down on the other side of Elsie.

"Not too bad, just a scratch or two on her ears," Jeff said finally, standing up.

Noah leaned over and hugged her. "You just need a Band-Aid, Elsie."

Jeff rested one hand on Noah's shoulder. "Thank you for finding her, Noah. She was trying to catch a rabbit and got away from me. I couldn't keep up with her. I'm very, very grateful."

"You don't have to thank me," Noah replied. "My angel told me where to look. But you can thank Mom for driving me here," he added.

Carrie smiled at her son. "I shouldn't be thanked either. I argued with you," she admitted. "The truth is . . . I'm just amazed that what you said came true, Noah."

"Now do you believe me?" Noah asked her.

He meant did she believe what he said about Theo. He waited for her answer, an intent expression on his small, upturned face. She could sense Jeff listening for her answer, too. She leaned over and hugged Noah very tight.

"I don't know, honey," she said as they walked to their car. "I do know that the power of love can work miracles. Maybe you knew Elsie needed help because you love her so much."

"Of course that's why. That's how Theo works. Didn't you know that, Mom?"

"No, honey. I didn't." Carrie smiled at him. "But that does make sense."

Carrie opened her car door. Jeff got in the front seat beside her, and Elsie jumped in the back with Noah. Noah quickly moved the two presents and held them carefully on his lap, far away from Elsie's big, muddy paws.

"So what are you doing today?" Jeff asked Carrie.

"We were on our way to church this morning. But the service is just about over now," she replied, glancing at the dashboard clock.

"It is getting late. My company will be here soon. I didn't even start dinner yet." He glanced over at her. "My invitation is still open. But it's okay if you—"

"We'd be happy to join you," she said simply. "We can help you get ready. Right, Noah?"

"Absolutely," Noah agreed. He patted the two gifts on his lap, looking very pleased, but not surprised, at the way the day was turning out.

Once inside the house, it was all hands on deck, getting ready for Jeff's visitors—his sister, Diana, and her family, who lived in Burlington, Vermont.

Noah was put in charge of setting the table while Carrie helped Jeff in the kitchen. He had planned a simple meal and gave Carrie the job of cleaning some potatoes while he seasoned a large roast. There were also string beans, mushrooms, and a salad. Carrie was impressed with his skills in the kitchen.

"Oh, blast. I forgot dessert," he said suddenly as he closed the door on the roast and set a timer. "I meant to go out this morning, though I doubt I could have found anyplace open on Christmas Day."

"Let's see. What do you have on hand? Maybe I can make something," Carrie suggested. She opened a cupboard that held sacks of flour, sugar, and spices. "I can make an apple thing with crumbs on top if I can use that bowl of apples in the dining room."

"Sounds perfect. I'll peel them for you," he offered.

"Deal," Carrie said quickly. "I love to bake, but peeling apples has never been my favorite job."

The counter was soon set up for baking, and Jeff stood beside her, quickly peeling the apples while she put together the rest of the recipe, which she luckily knew by heart.

They didn't talk much, working in easy harmony. They didn't need to talk, Carrie realized. There was a peaceful, tender connection between them—something Carrie had never felt before, not even with her ex-husband in their best moments. This was all new for her, yet she was slowly but surely learning to trust it. Even to embrace it as her own.

Everything was ready by the time Jeff's family arrived. Bright, crackling flames in the big stone fireplace and the sweet, buttery smell of the apple-crumb dessert greeted the guests with Christmas warmth and cheer.

Jeff quickly introduced everyone. "This is my friend, Carrie, and her son, Noah," he said. "Carrie, this is my sister, Diana, and her husband, Tom."

Carrie shook hands all around. Diana seemed surprised but happy to see her brother had other guests for the day. Jeff had a niece and nephew, Maddie and Oliver. Maddie was nine and Oliver, six; Noah seemed to fit right in, Carrie noticed. The three disappeared almost immediately, happily seeking out the toy collection in Jeff's office.

The day passed quickly. Diana was an editor on a small, local newspaper, and she and Carrie talked about their favorite books almost the entire afternoon. They had very similar tastes in reading, and a similar sense of humor, too.

Elsie's escape made an entertaining story at the dinner table, though Jeff never mentioned the angelic intervention.

"I worry about you and that crazy dog," Diana said. "At least you've found someone who will rescue both of you," she added, glancing at Carrie with a smile.

Carrie didn't answer. She felt herself blush a bit and glanced over at Jeff. If anything, Carrie felt that Jeff had rescued her and Noah. It seemed funny that his sister saw their relationship in just the opposite way.

Jeff warmed Carrie's apple-crumb dish and served it with vanilla ice cream. He set the plate on the table, looking very proud. "I forgot to get dessert, but Carrie made this from scratch."

"You peeled the apples," she reminded him.

"Me? I'm just a kitchen swabbie. She didn't even use a recipe," he told the others proudly.

"Looks delicious. You make a good team. Don't they?" Diana glanced at her husband, who also looked amused at the exchange.

"If that tastes as good as it looks, all is well," Tom replied. "I'll have a big serving."

While the adults were content to linger over the sweets and coffee, the children quickly ran over to the Christmas tree.

"Uncle Jeff, can we open the presents now?" Maddie stood near the tree, shaking a box and listening.

"What gifts? Gosh . . . I almost forgot! Thanks for reminding me, guys." Jeff made a face that was almost convincing, and the adults laughed while the kids groaned a bit. "Only kidding. Time to get on with the main event. Everyone in the living room," Jeff announced. "Maddie, since you've probably memorized all the tags by now, you may as well give everything out."

Maddie looked pleased to be in charge and took the job very seriously. She called out the names while Oliver and Noah ran about, giving out the boxes. That is, until their own names were announced. Then they sat on the sidelines, quickly tearing open their packages.

Carrie watched Noah open a gift from Jeff. A pile of books, all children's classics, in beautiful, hardcover editions—*Mr. Popper's Penguins*, *Charlotte's Web*, *Charlie and the Chocolate Factory*, Madeleine L'Engle's *A Wrinkle in Time*, and even an edition of a Sherlock Holmes mystery.

"Mom, look at all these books Jeff gave me. Aren't they great?"

"Oh, yes. They are, indeed. You have a whole library there, Noah."

Before Carrie had to prompt him to remember his manners, he ran over to Jeff and gave him a huge hug. "Thank you, Jeff."

"I'm so glad you like them. I picked out a lot of my own favorites. If you already have some, you can exchange them. I don't mind."

"I haven't read any of these yet. Wait . . . I have something for you." He ran over to the tree and looked around for the gift they got for Jeff. Noah had wrapped it himself, so it wasn't hard to find.

He grabbed the oddly shaped package and ran back. Jeff's family had been busily opening—and delighting in—their own gifts, but now stopped to see what Jeff was unwrapping.

"Let's see . . . What in the world could this be?" Jeff smiled widely at Noah as he tore off the ribbon and paper. "Wow. Would you look at that, everybody?" Jeff held up the birdhouse as if it were the greatest treasure in the world. "Isn't that amazing?"

"It's a birdhouse," Noah shouted, totally delighted by Jeff's reaction.

"Of course it's a birdhouse." Jeff laughed. "But it's the greatest one I've ever seen. It looks like a little schoolhouse."

"That's because you work in a school sometimes. And I know you like birds. Because you showed me that feeder near the window in your office."

"That's right. It was so thoughtful of you to remember that. I have a good feeder, but no birdhouse. This is perfect." Jeff reached out and touched Noah's shoulder. "You'll have to help me find a good place out in the backyard to put it, okay?"

Noah nodded happily. Carrie felt misty eyed to see how satisfied her son was at the simple pleasure of giving a gift to someone he cared about. If that's what happened to little boys who talked to angels . . . well, it certainly wasn't such a bad thing, she decided.

"To Carrie . . . from Jeff," Maddie announced, reading a label off a small square package.

Carrie was surprised Jeff had gotten her something, too, and felt badly there was nothing under the tree from her to him.

"Jeff, you shouldn't have," she said as Noah delivered her gift.

"It's just a small gift, nothing special. But I thought you might like it."

Any gift from Jeff would be special to her. Though she didn't feel comfortable confessing that to everyone in the room. She pulled off the paper to find two books.

The first was a biography of Henry David Thoreau. "Oh, this is great. Thanks so much." Jeff had remembered their brief conversation while walking in the snow about Thoreau and her favorite writers in college.

"I hope you don't have it already?" Jeff said as he watched her.

"No, I don't. But I was looking at it in the bookstore. It has a lot of letters and journal entries that haven't been published before. I can't wait to read it." She had looked at the book with longing, actually, deciding she would get it out of the library or wait for the paperback. The edition Jeff had given her was quite expensive.

She opened to the first page and saw that he'd written a small inscription.

> To Carrie—Wishing you great happiness on Christmas and always.
>
> There are many wise thoughts and much good advice in these pages. Here's one that caught my attention and, I hope, catches yours:
>
> "Never look back unless you are planning to go that way." —Henry David Thoreau
>
> With love, Jeff

Carrie looked up to find Jeff had been watching her read his note. "Very true," she said. "I'll keep that in mind."

She looked at the next book, running her hand over the smooth brown leather cover, and opened it to find the pages blank.

"That's a journal. For your own writing," he explained.

Carrie looked up at him and smiled. "If there is any," she said.

"I have a feeling you can think of something to put in there. Just . . . give it time," he added, sharing a secret smile with her.

She met his gaze and held it, smiling back. "More good advice. I will," she promised.

After the company left, Carrie helped Jeff clean up. Noah and Elsie were tired out from having so much fun all day and fell asleep in front of the fire together, with Noah's head pillowed on Elsie's back.

One of Noah's new books lay open on the carpet beside Elsie; *Mr. Popper's Penguins.* It looked like Noah had tried to start it but dozed off a few pages into the story.

Carrie walked over and picked it up, then set it on a nearby table. "Thanks for the wonderful gifts, Jeff. But I feel bad that I didn't get you anything."

"Don't be silly." Jeff touched her shoulder as he passed by, gathering hunks of wrapping paper and bows from the floor. "Having you and Noah here today, that's my gift. Just what I asked Santa for."

Carrie smiled back. Lucky for her, Santa's magic had been more powerful than her own silly inhibitions. *Very* lucky for her, she decided.

She followed Jeff into the kitchen, carrying a tray of cups and plates that needed to go into the dishwasher. "I was relieved when you didn't mention the angel to your sister," Carrie admitted, "when you were telling her about finding Elsie."

"That's all right. I didn't really want to get into it," he said in an offhand way. "I'm not sure what my sister and Tom think of angels. But that was the strangest thing today." He shook his head, fitting the last cup into the machine. He closed the door and turned to her. "What do you think now? I'm just curious. Has today changed your opinion any?"

Carrie didn't answer right away. She folded a dish towel and set it on a rack. "I can't deny what happened. But I can't say I'm convinced that what Noah believes is true. Maybe he's psychic. Or has very strong intuition," she added. "And maybe we'll just never know. But I can see now that Noah needs his angel. I was wrong to think I had to take that away from him. I was also wrong to . . . to doubt you, Jeff. I was just scared, I guess, of something I couldn't understand."

"That's all right. I don't blame you. I don't really know how I would have reacted if Noah was my child, and not my patient," he admitted. "I'm not a parent. Though I hope someday I will be. I do know that's a whole different ball game."

Carrie smiled at that observation. "Oh boy, is it ever. And I think you'll be a great parent someday. I'm totally sure of that."

They walked into the living room, drawn by the fire. Jeff put his arm around her shoulder and they stood back, gazing at Noah and Elsie, who was lightly snoring.

"Noah had a perfect Christmas," Carrie said quietly. "I did, too. I'm sorry I put you off when you first invited us. I'm sorry I've been so . . . cautious and confused. You've been very patient and understanding, Jeff. And I was wrong about needing a break or whatever silly thing I said." Carrie felt embarrassed now, mentioning it. "It's only been three days . . . and I missed you," she admitted.

Jeff moved closer to her and smiled softly. "It was a long three days," he whispered. "I missed you, too. I'm not really sure how it happened, but I'm just glad we're together for Christmas."

"Me, too." Carrie moved into his embrace for a long, deep kiss. She felt happier than she had ever been and made a heartfelt wish that this would be the first of many Christmases they would spend together.

CARRIE WAS DEEPLY ASLEEP, IN THE MIDDLE OF A DREAM, WHEN SHE felt someone shaking her shoulder. She woke up to find Noah next to her bed. There was daylight outside, but it was still very early, and a vacation day. Carrie had hoped to sleep in a bit.

Noah had other ideas. "It snowed, Mom! Look!" He ran to the window and pulled the curtains aside. Bright light assaulted her eyes. "There's a ton of snow out there."

Carrie sat up and stretched. Everything outside was white, and the glowing light reflected back into her bedroom. "Oh, dear. We really got hit, didn't we?" The forecast had said an inch or two. But it looked more like a foot at the very least.

"I can use my snow saucer," Noah said, running back to his room. "Can you take me sleigh riding?" he called to her. She heard drawers opening and slamming and knew he was already putting on his snow clothes.

"Yes, of course. Let's have some breakfast first."

Carrie went downstairs and made scrambled eggs and toast for both of them and a big pot of coffee for herself.

"Can we call Jeff? He said to call if there was a lot of snow and I was going to use the saucer. He said he wanted to come."

Jeff had told Noah that last night, right before they left and just as the snow had started.

"Yes, we'll call him. I think he wants to try that saucer out, too."

"I hope he brings Elsie. She loves the snow. It was funny how I found her yesterday," Noah added.

"It was funny." More than funny, Carrie still thought. It was positively . . . eerie. But she sensed Noah wanted to talk more about this. She focused on him and just listened.

"I had a long talk with Theo last night. He told me that he would always be watching over us, but he has to move on. Another kid needs him more. Now that you and I are okay here and things are going good, Theo says we really don't need him anymore."

Carrie was very surprised by the news—and touched that the angel had included her among his charges. Or did Noah just add that? No, she decided, Noah was too honest for that. The angel was there to guide and help both of them, she realized now, though only Noah was loving and trusting enough to see and hear him.

"Does that mean you won't be able to see Theo or talk to him anymore?" she asked.

"I can talk to him any time I want. He'll always hear me and be right here if I need him. But I don't want to bother him if he's working," Noah explained.

"I see. I guess he's very busy."

"Yeah, he's busy. His job isn't easy, Mom," Noah said very seriously, "taking care of people night and day."

"That's not an easy job. And he's very good at it," she added. "I hope you won't be lonely. Theo was . . . well, good company for you," she admitted finally.

"I know. I'll miss him," Noah replied honestly. "But I have a lot of new friends—Henry, and Max, too."

Just as Reverend Ben had predicted, Noah and the infamous Max had become pals after all. Carrie would have to tell the reverend that.

"And Jeff," Noah added. "He's your friend, too, right?"

"Yes, Jeff's my friend. A very good friend," she added. "And I think I'm going to try that saucer thing, too, if you'll give me a turn. Maybe I should buy one for Jeff, so he has his own. You gave him the birdhouse, but I never gave him anything for Christmas."

A short time later, they met Jeff and Elsie on the village green. Jeff told them where the best hill for sleigh riding was, and it was crowded with kids when they got there.

Jeff was very pleased and surprised by Carrie's gift. She had stopped at the hardware store and picked up a snow saucer for him. While she held Elsie, he raced Noah to the bottom of the hill.

Carrie watched them, enjoying the sight of all the children in their colorful jackets and bright sleds on the pure white hill, dotted by tall pine trees. The fresh layer of snow made the whole world look clean and new, she thought, recalling Reverend Ben's sermon on Christmas Eve. *In every ending there is a beginning.*

If you let the new story begin, she realized. *Not if you hang on fast to the old ending, looking backward instead of forward.*

Though it had been over two years since her divorce, Carrie felt as if she had finally just found her fresh new start. Her new beginning. And a new story that was ever so much better than she had ever dreamed of.

Noah soon found his friends from school, Henry and some other boys, and dashed off to be with them. Carrie had a chance to tell Jeff the big news—that Noah's angel had moved on. She waited, curious to hear what he thought.

"It sounds as if Noah feels good about it and isn't worried about the angel leaving him. So, I guess he's ready to let go."

"The angel has a new job. Another kid needs his help, Noah said. Noah seems to understand that. He said he would miss Theo, but he has a lot of new friends now. Including you."

"He's right," Jeff said quietly, "maybe in more ways than one. I'm not saying Theo brought us together, because I doubt you'll believe that. But, however it happened, I feel like it was more than luck. It's a special blessing, a gift," he said in a quiet, serious tone. "Noah's angel may have to move on. But I never will."

Carrie put her arms around him, feeling that way, too. And unshakably certain it was true.

MOLLY HAD NOT BEEN TO THE NEW SHOP SINCE THE DRIVE-BY WITH Sam. But right after the holidays, on the first Monday in January, Betty picked her up, and they visited together.

"I'm glad you didn't come inside when we first landed," Betty admitted as she held the door open for Molly to amble through. "Sam and his crew did so much work since then. I can hardly believe the difference."

Molly stepped inside the shop and gazed around. Her heart was beating wildly. She felt almost light-headed as she took it all in, and knew her reaction had nothing at all to do with her injuries.

The antique-style chandeliers she had ordered were not in place yet, and the banquettes against the walls were not completely finished. But from the pressed brass ceiling to the vintage floor tile, the rest was very much as she had pictured it, complete with marble-top bistro tables, bistro-style chairs, soft lighting, and a classic look to the takeout counter, where trays and trays of pastries, cakes, tarts, and breads were beautifully displayed. There was even a colorful bouquet of flowers in a brass pot, set up next to the antique register—snapdragons, calla lilies, blousy-headed peonies—just as she had imagined in happy daydreams.

"It's crowded in here. A good sign, considering everyone is starting a diet this week," Betty remarked.

Molly laughed, but didn't reply, her attention drawn by two workmen who were hanging the big gilt mirrors along the back wall of the shop. Molly watched as the first mirror went into place. Perfect, she thought.

"It's really beautiful," she said with a sigh, turning in a full circle to soak up the atmosphere again. "It's just what I pictured. I feel as if I've stepped into a bakery café in Paris, so elegant and classy."

"—and sassy," Betty added. "Just like you. I almost sent those mirrors back when I saw the price tag." Betty rolled her eyes. "But I know it's worth the investment to create a certain atmosphere, a place that's a cut above a run-of-the-mill bakeshop. I was wrong about that little spot on the side street. It would have been all right, but nothing like this. This is going to be a destination," she predicted.

"That's good of you to say, Betty." Molly felt gratified and grateful for Betty's honesty. "You didn't have to, all things considered."

"Yeah, I know. But right is right," Betty replied. "All things considered. You sit, I'll get some coffees. We need to talk business."

Molly found a table near the window and watched Betty at the counter. The staff seemed quite competent, giving polite and fast service, moving the line along. Betty had given Molly good reports about the new baker and kitchen staff she had hired. Molly was going to meet them later.

Her three older daughters had left on Saturday. The house seemed empty without them, but Molly knew she would soon be busy and distracted with work again. And the wedding preparations would be front and center very soon. She was still very grateful for the way the girls had jumped in and worked here when it had all seemed so futile, even desperate, to Molly.

But I was wrong. She was happy to admit it. The new shop was doing well and already turning a profit. And their party business over the holidays had actually been better than Molly had expected. While their business still had some rough sledding to get through, it seemed apparent now that they would survive. Even thrive, once Willoughby's Too got some momentum.

Betty returned to the table with two coffees and two croissants. "I shouldn't be eating this. But I couldn't resist."

"We have to test the quality, Betty," Molly reminded her in a serious tone. "I haven't tasted anything made by the new baker yet."

"What do you think?" Betty asked, watching Molly take a bite.

Molly nodded, savoring the flavor and examining the flaky layers and texture. "So far, so good. I may have to test some of her other pastries, too."

"It's a tough job, but someone has to do it," Betty teased her. "Our finances are going on a diet at least," she added, taking out a thick folder with budgets and schedules for the new year that she had drawn up. "We're going to get lean and mean. And I'm going to be the personal trainer, cracking the whip. I've been looking things over, and we can save a lot of money without cutting our quality."

"As long as we keep baking with real butter and genuine vanilla extract, I'm fine with whatever you say."

"We need to start paying down our debts. But we may be able to get by without applying for another loan, after all."

Molly wanted to be optimistic but couldn't see how they could survive without some big infusion of cash, despite the many efficiencies Betty proposed. She looked at her partner skeptically.

"You're the numbers wiz. Are you really sure?"

"We needed either a new loan or to book a big-ticket event, right? Guess who called the shop this morning, right before I came to pick you up? Alicia Fillmore. She said that she loved the proposal you put together for the donor cocktail party—"

"Loved it so much we didn't get the job," Molly cut in.

Betty smiled and kept going. "She's giving her husband a huge surprise party for his fiftieth, and she wants us to plan the whole thing. From our trademark caviar crêpes to your seven-tier orchid-trimmed chocolate cake."

Molly's eyes widened. That *was* a big-ticket event. "How many guests?"

"Just their closest friends and family. Around two hundred?"

"That's twice the size of the cocktail party we lost."

Betty grinned with satisfaction. "She didn't like the caterer they chose at all. Would never go back," she told me. "This one is all ours. She's not talking to anyone else. And no committee," she added.

Molly blinked. Just the bolt out of the blue she had prayed for. Coming when she least expected it.

"That is great news, Betty." Molly took a deep breath; she could hardly believe it. They would survive. And thrive. "You've done a brilliant job, fixing our finances and pulling this place together," she said sincerely. "There's just one thing I'd change."

Betty looked alarmed. "I emptied every box and carton . . . and you bought a lot of stuff for this place, Molly."

Molly laughed at her. "The only thing I think we should change is the sign. It should say, 'Willoughby & Bowman's.' Even though it will cost a little extra to fix it, I think it's important, going forward. Don't you?"

"Now that you mention it, I guess I do." Betty looked very touched and very pleased by the suggestion.

Molly raised her coffee cup, and Betty did, too. "Here's to Willoughby & Bowman's," Molly said in a serious tone that was rare for her. "And to new beginnings, a new start for our business, and friendship, too."

Betty laughed and squeezed Molly's hand. "Partner, I'll definitely toast to that!"